The River Bend Chronicles

Old
Debts

The River Bend Chronicles

Old
Debts

Renee Kumor

ABSOLUTELY AMA⚡ING eBOOKS

ABSOLUTELY AMAZING eBOOKS

Books in
The River Bend Chronicles:

Small Town Secrets

Taking a Chance

'Tis the Season

An Act of Charity

Someone Cares

Forever, Sonny

Season of Revenge

Who Am I?

Old Debts

The River Bend Chronicles

Old Debts

Chapter One

She turned the paring knife in her hand. Studied it from all sides. Held the point in the light to check for scratches or … or something. Something to give her a clue as to why she found the knife in the drawer with her flatware. It should have been in the pretty wooden holder with the other knives sitting on the kitchen counter. Piper gave her that set years ago. Four small knives, each with a different colored handle, each designed for a specific task. They had laughed — the green knife to dice peppers, the red to slice tomatoes …

She rubbed her forehead. Why was it in the drawer? Was she really losing her mind? Her eyes skittered to the blanket on the kitchen table. Why had she found this blanket in the barn? Why had she carried it out to the barn? Why? Why were so many things misplaced, or lost or …? She gave herself a sad smile in the kitchen window. The darkness made her reflection look eerie and detached. A wrinkled brow. An old lady frown.

And the sounds. She thought she heard things in the middle of the night. Shuffling. Movement. Someone walking overhead? Someone climbing the stairs? There was always a feeling of movement overhead — especially at night.

And sometimes the movement sounded like whispers — like someone playing a radio real low.

She climbed the stairs to bed, taking each step slowly as

she listened. Washing up she glanced around the bathroom. Was a towel missing? Had the toothpaste been moved? She looked in the bathroom mirror and scowled at the old lady looking back.

Was she getting too old to take care of herself, she wondered? As she settled into bed, something startled her – a soft thud. Glenda Llewellyn stared at her bedroom ceiling in the dark. And she waited. No other sound came. She yawned and told herself to get to sleep, she had a lot to do in the morning. Tomorrow she would climb to the attic and see what was making those noises. Probably something fell, maybe something up there toppled over.

And tomorrow she should call Piper and tell her about the strange noises and losing things and ... she just hoped she remembered ...

~ ~ ~

He bumped into an old trunk as he navigated the attic in the dark and froze as he listened for any sound in the house beneath him. He waited. His heart seemed to stop. Nothing. The old woman must already be asleep. It had been almost a week since he moved into this hiding place and three full days since he had ventured out around the property.

Did they know where he was? Had he covered his tracks completely? He had to think.

Once he knew he couldn't trust the women in the office, he had slowly amassed his evidence and, he hoped, without arousing suspicion, slipped away. Now he had to find a more permanent escape – and find help.

Joseph Baikar slowly settled onto the old cot in the attic

and stretched out to think about his options. He had no doubt he was working for a non-profit that had ties to illegal activities. Sadly, he now understood why he had been recruited for the job as office manager of Personal Financial Management in River Bend. He was the squeaky clean front. He had been recruited, not because of the work he had done in Kentucky helping people reorganize their personal finances and lift themselves out of debt, but because he looked good on paper and wouldn't raise any eyebrows.

He thought about the job he left behind, and the people, and especially the good and meaningful work. Now, here in River Bend, he was hiding from his employer, trying to figure a way out of this dilemma, and hopefully stay alive in the process.

Joseph had no delusions about the evil he had uncovered.

Chapter Two

"**W**hat a beautiful morning!" declared Lynn Powers. "You haven't even looked outside." Her husband, Dusty Reid, kissed her one more time as he enjoyed the feel of their naked bodies together under the sheets this early August morning. He kissed her again before letting her get out of bed to start the day.

Washing and dressing, they ran through their day's activities. "Remember that dinner tonight. Is your summer blazer clean?" Lynn bit her lip trying not to laugh as Dusty described his hostility toward wearing ties, tuxes or anything else somewhat formal. Lynn was the executive director of River Bend Philanthropies, a community fundraising and nonprofit granting organization. Tonight she and the Philanthropies board members were hosting a summer reception for a select group of donors.

"You look so handsome when you're all dressed up. All the other women in the room envy me." Lynn patted Dusty's behind as she walked to the closet to find something to wear this morning. "What will your day be like?" she called from the walk-in closet.

"We've got a missing man." Dusty dried his face, working the shaving cream out of his ear. "That's why I got in so late last night. We're looking for some guy who worked at a place called Personal Financial Management." He shrugged into a shirt. "This guy's not been seen for almost a week and his family called in a missing person report."

Dusty was the chief detective of the James County/River Bend Joint Investigations Unit.

"PFM asked about our grant procedures." Lynn stood in front of the dresser mirror trying to organize her hair. It was out of control in the August humidity.

"They're a nonprofit? PFM does social work?" Dusty stuffed his feet into shoes as he gave her another quick kiss on the back of her head.

Lynn moved away because she thought the kiss might turn into a tumble as Dusty lost the battle with his shoes. "Yes, they do. They work with people who need help with their finances. They help people get their credit rating in order and work on reducing their debt."

"That's a business, not a nonprofit." Shoes on, pants zipped, he was ready for the day.

"Dusty, let's just say I know the place. So who's missing?"

"The office manager."

"Joseph?"

Dusty looked at her, almost surprised. Since the beginning of their married life he had learned that she had random facts floating around in her head, often proving of interest in investigations, and a random array of acquaintances, all of whom seemed to get robbed or murdered. "How well do you know him? Like maybe do you know where he would hide?"

Lynn gasped, "He's really the missing person? What can you tell me? Should I ask around?"

No matter how often Dusty asked that she stay away from his investigations, nothing seemed to get through. He scowled. "I have a staff of professional investigators who will be doing the inquiries this morning." He kissed her cheek. "You stay out of it."

She gave him a nonchalant shrug. "I have enough of my own work to do today — the reception. Remember?" *Hmmph! So there!* But she kept that comment to herself.

They finished dressing and began their usual morning routine for breakfast. Dusty let the dog out, then made the coffee and Lynn brought out some hard boiled eggs and tomato juice, then let the dog back in. Chips, their dog who never missed a meal, trotted over to his dish to see what treats awaited him then reviewed the offerings at the breakfast table.

"Are we on a low carb diet again?" moaned Dusty. The dog ignored the people food this morning and ate from his dish.

"My skirt's a little tight this morning." Lynn wondered if it was from the 'Death by Chocolate' she had shared with Piper last evening.

"Why not just put on a different skirt?" Dusty ignored Lynn's breakfast offering and found a stale jelly donut to have with his coffee. "Your friend Joseph disappeared about a week ago. His sister called my office late yesterday because the family hasn't heard from him. He has no wife, lives alone. We checked his apartment. His vehicle is gone, and someone had searched the place. No sign of violence." He looked at Lynn and she caught the jelly dropping from his lip with her finger. "Any ideas?" He wanted her to stay away from his investigations, but he didn't feel guilty about mining her for information.

"None. I only know him through his office. A very quiet

man, about our age, always polite." Lynn shrugged at her breakfast and returned it to the refrigerator. Dusty laughed. She scowled and looked for a yogurt. Coming back to the table, she asked, "Did he steal anything, or threaten someone, or anything that might be criminal?"

"Why do you ask?" Dusty licked donut sugar from his fingers.

"A couple of ministers from the church association, you know that pastors' club, came by to ask about the agency. Some people were unhappy with the help they were receiving." Lynn spooned her yogurt thoughtfully. "They said that PFM was offering to loan money on houses when people needed large sums of cash for some emergency, explaining that it would save their credit rating. Then PFM offered horrible deals when structuring the loan repayment, but some of the clients had to accept."

"That doesn't sound like helping anyone manage debt." Dusty frowned. "Is it like those TV ads prompting reverse mortgages?"

"That's not the same thing," explained Lynn. "Those deals are for older people, not young families, or ..." she shrugged. "I really don't know much. Joseph was very quiet." She sipped her coffee. "The ministers agree with you. They didn't think anyone was being helped. In any case PFM allows people to stay in their homes as long as they make payments on the loan. Many of these people will never live long enough to repay the loan."

"Are you suggesting some sort of real estate scam?"

Lynn shrugged. "I'm just telling you what I heard. I was going to ask Robert O'Hara about it at our board meeting next Thursday."

He smiled. "Maybe you can find out some background information and other stuff that would be helpful."

"I thought I was to let your professional investigators handle this," she countered.

"You weren't going to listen and you were going to ask around anyway." He could read her like a book. His phone rang.

"See you later." He kissed her and walked out the door already talking on his phone.

Lynn had returned to River Bend almost three years ago as a young widow, deciding that her hometown was the best place to raise her son and build a new life. She was hired as the executive director of the River Bend Philanthropies and for the past year and a half had been Dusty's wife. Lynn had gotten involved with a number of his cases, all by accident, as she always told anyone who asked. But she enjoyed the adventure.

So many changes had happened since her return to River Bend. Her son, Jason, had finished high school and would be moving on to college in another week to begin his freshman year. As she thought of her son, he walked into the kitchen. Jason had gotten up early to run with some of the young detectives, hastily returning home to shower and get to his job at Umberto's bakery.

"How was your run?" his mother asked.

"Those guys just wanted to brag about their babies," he complained. "Buck said his baby cried half the night and Danny said his baby screamed. They bragged like they were trying to win a prize." Jason shook his head in disbelief. "Is it good for a baby to cry all night?"

His mother laughed. "I think they just want to talk

about their babies. Eventually they'll sleep through the night and then the dads will brag about that."

"That's what Mars said," replied Jason. "He told them to get over it." Jason was thoughtful for a moment. "I think he'd like a baby, too."

"Mars?" asked Lynn. Jason nodded. "I think you're right. He wants to be married just like his friends. How about some breakfast? I'm afraid we don't have much to eat," Lynn apologized as he took orange juice from the refrigerator and drank from the carton.

"Mom," Jason replied in his almost adult superior voice, "I work at a bakery." He raced up to shower and Lynn left for work thinking about crying babies and her missing friend, Joseph.

~ ~ ~

By chance Personal Financial Management demanded Lynn's attention at the office early this morning. The first call was from an investigator in a neighboring state. "Ma'am, we're looking into activities of this group. Some folks in our town have had some bad experiences."

"Such as?" asked Lynn.

"I'm not at liberty to say," came the professional voice, "but, if you have heard of similar concerns, I'd like to send someone to talk with you."

Lynn was surprised at the offer. She knew how tight law enforcement budgets were. This would be an overnight trip. Something was up. Hmmm. "I'll let you know if I hear any rumors," she responded in her professional voice and they disconnected amicably.

This was followed, almost immediately, by a call from Adam Gates of the United Charities office. "Lynn, I've gotten a weird call from someone about that new agency in town, Personal Financial Management. They're not one of the agencies we fund, so I knew nothing. Is something going on?"

"Like what?" asked the detective's wife.

"I'm asking you," replied Adam, "you're the one with the network. Everyone spills their guts to you."

"Thank you for the compliment, I think," said Lynn as she laughed. "The office manager has been reported missing. Dusty's working on it. That's all I know. Someone just called me from another state asking questions that I couldn't answer."

Adam sighed into the phone. "Wow. You always have the lowdown. Let me know when you learn anything more." He hung up, but those two conversations left Lynn thinking about the missing office manager.

They had met several months ago when Joseph moved into his new position. He had come from a similar financial service program in Kentucky and was delighted to be in River Bend. As he said when they first met, "I'm looking forward to starting my life here."

"Are you bringing a family with you?" Lynn asked.

"I'm alone. My mother moved to Colorado to live with my sister and I'm all I've got." He was a slender, dark haired man with dark eyes that always offered a shy smile.

Lynn wondered if he had begun to build a new life. She hadn't heard any rumors about him dating anyone. And her network for gossip was really great, almost as good as her network for fundraising. For a few minutes she ran through a mental list of available women and tried to find a match for Joseph. She frowned – nothing. He was too quiet. She found she really didn't know much about him. Maybe he wanted to disappear, she thought. A quiet man, deep secrets, looking for family. Hmmm. But the Philanthropies was paying her to raise money, not solve Joseph's personal problems. She got to work.

By mid-morning Lynn decided she needed a break. It had been a hectic few hours, getting all the Philanthropies' scholarship awards sent to respective colleges, dealing with the paper work and, always, phone calls. She made a cup of tea and sat in the conference room stretching her legs under the table. Staring out the window she saw a woman help a little girl out of a car seat and take her hand as they dashed to the pediatrician's office in the building on the far side of the office park. "Babies," she murmured aloud. Memories flashed by as she recalled images of Jason all those years ago. Then she recalled her discussion with her son this morning. He thought Mars wanted a baby. She thought so, too.

The young detective, Mars Healey, had seen three of his good friends marry within the last months. And parenting was a hot topic. Buck Rawlings was happily married to Penny who had been very pregnant at their wedding. Their daughter, Olivia, had arrived on schedule, at their two-month anniversary. Lynn smiled at the idea of her friend, Nathan Taft, Buck's uncle and now a great-uncle, in a role he enjoyed from morning till night. She was certain he loved every moment of his new and expanded uncle-hood.

Another friend who married was H. Lawrence Grayson, a pompous, but skilled, local attorney. He had married Michelle Seymour just days before Buck's baby arrived. Buck bragged that baby Olivia was considerate because she knew he and Penny wanted to attend the wedding of their good friends. Lynn decided that left Mars the last eligible bachelor in River Bend, at least the last rich one.

And then the other baby. Danny Valeri, Mars' partner in the James County/River Bend Joint Investigations Unit, had presented his family with the first baby of the next generation of the long time Italian-American family of River Bend. Danny's child, a son, delighted four generations of the Valeri family. Lynn recalled the celebration for the baby's Baptism as music and singing filled the air while friends and relatives drank wine and toasted the young family.

Then three weeks ago Teniquia LaMont, the young woman detective in the unit, married her boyfriend, Lonzo, in a small, but joyous, celebration at the black church in South End. Mars was now the only detective not married.

Marriage and babies seemed to elude Mars. Raised by battling, disinterested parents, Mars made his way into adulthood, mentored by Bergy, the former sheriff and his family. Mars' parents had opted for divorce and lives that didn't include a youngster. He finally found his love in the form of Nancy Rawlings, Buck's younger sister. But Nancy had moved to Australia and seemed to have settled there. Lynn shivered, and surprised by her involuntary response, tried to explore the feeling. Nancy and Mars — they didn't match. She was certain Nancy was not as interested in marriage as Mars. Lynn thought over her friendship with Nancy. It was cool, but cordial. So why did she think Nancy was not the girl for Mars? She explored the idea for a moment and couldn't answer her own question. It was just a feeling, a feeling that Mars was going to be hurt.

A phone rang and Lynn shook her head to come out of her morning reverie. Her tea was cold. She nuked it and returned to her desk. The phone call was from Tim Powers, her brother-in-law, the only remaining family connection with her late husband, except for her father-in-law who lived in a nursing home in River Bend, in the dementia unit.

"Hi, Lynn," Tim shouted across the miles, "I'm hitching a ride with a student pilot and will be there Friday." He was career Navy currently assigned in Norfolk.

"Great," she returned his enthusiasm. "One of us will be at the airport." As she hung up the phone she thought, there was another man like Mars, looking for family, for a life with a loving wife. Tim had been in a relationship for five years that had ended badly. He was still feeling the effects.

Last May in town for Jason's high school graduation, Tim had asked if he could move his father, an Alzheimer's patient, to a care facility in River Bend. Tim's Navy life made it a challenge to care for his father. Lynn had been happy to agree telling him that it meant she and Jason would see more of him. So for the last few months Tim had been popping in and out of River Bend for brief, but enjoyable visits. Lynn smiled to herself as she thought about how easily Tim fit in to the household in The Heights – he, Dusty and Jason sitting around the breakfast table in torn T-shirts and sweat pants, talking summer sports. She smiled again – family. As she thought of family her phone rang.

"Lynn, can you help Mom?" asked Piper Zubov in a panicked rush of words as she connected with her best friend.

"Sure, where is she?" Lynn had promised Dusty to look into PFM, but Piper needed help.

"She's home and she sounds a little confused." Piper was principal at a local elementary school and tied up with a week of pre-opening activities. There was always so much to do at the beginning of the new school year, and the students weren't even on campus yet.

"Tell her I'm on my way." Lynn grabbed her purse and ran from the office.

Chapter Three

Joseph was glad the curtains on the attic window were so thin. He could watch the activity around the yard and barn without moving the fabric too much. He was certain the old woman would never notice, but he was being cautious.

There she was again, walking into the barn. Had he left any signs of his activity there? He hoped not. He'd lost track of a blanket, but he hoped it wasn't in the barn. She came out of the barn with a basket and walked out of his view toward her garden.

A car drove into the yard and his nerves tightened. But then he saw Lynn Powers climb out and call for Mrs. Llewellyn. He was so relieved to see that the car was friendly that he leaned into the curtain for just a second then pulled back, hoping she hadn't seen any movement in the small window.

Joseph sighed to himself as he stepped back from the attic window. He had liked Lynn from the moment he met her. At a different time and circumstance he would have enjoyed working with her on community projects. She got it. She understood nonprofits and the synergy of groups working together – creating solutions so much bigger than anyone could accomplish alone. He sighed again.

He thought he had heard her husband was in law enforcement. Another reason he should have gotten to know her better. Her husband might have helped. Or maybe not. What evidence did he really have?

In addition to his computer snooping and just things he had heard around the office and from clients, he didn't have much. He glanced at the papers balanced on an old table in his attic hideaway. He had been quietly collecting information for weeks. The information was interesting, but there were holes. And there was that funny feeling at the back of his neck. But how did you tell that to a detective?

Joseph thought about his meeting with that computer woman, Janet. He knew she was brilliant, no matter how vague she was. Sitting with her one afternoon, he had asked her to look at his computer because he told her it was slow. She had gotten into it and started talking about firewalls and stripping data and alternate paths and monitoring. It didn't make specific sense, but it suggested to him that someone was watching his work and sniffing, yes sniffing, through his files. That's when he quit doing anything but the most basic work related tasks on the office computer. All other cyber work he did at home on his personal computer. Just thinking about lack of privacy made him shiver.

The two women in the office did preliminary intake for clients and managed the interface with the main office. Personal Financial Management was a three state operation. And that was another mystery to him. The women in the office seemed to have access to data from all the other offices and his computer seemed to be restricted to local clients. As the manager of the office he had the responsibility to advise a potential client that their financial situation might be helped through services of PFM. Those clients with credit problems or other issues needing a quick infusion of cash or long-term credit restructuring and management were helped to organize their credit card debt and to develop a personal budget based on real income. Sometimes it just took a suggestion of a new way to manage assets or income. That was the part of the job he liked.

Take the Llewellyns for instance. He was able to show them that they had assets in land that could be managed in a few ways to get them through this tough period. He also suggested that they ask family, especially that rich son-in-law, to help them out. Mr. Llewellyn had gotten angry at that suggestion saying something about Piper and Will having kids to raise. Joseph didn't know what they finally decided, but the good part of the whole discussion was that he had found this great place to hide – as the first phase of his escape from his job – from all the things that gave him a funny feeling. He looked around the attic. It got a little stuffy in the afternoon, but he always managed. It was the next phase of his plan that was murky.

~ ~ ~

When Lynn arrived out at the Llewellyn farm she couldn't locate Glenda, Piper's mother. A quick search of the house found no one. Lynn ran to the barn, nothing. She decided to explore some of the nearby fields. Glenda was active and could have taken a walk while she was waiting.

Piper had been concerned about her parents recently. Her father had knee replacement surgery a week ago and was recovering slowly while receiving rehabilitation services at a local nursing care center. Glenda had insisted on staying alone out at the farm to make certain all of her vegetables were picked and preserved, as she had done every summer for the past fifty years.

And there she was — carrying a basket of tomatoes up to the house.

"Glenda," Lynn called, "I'm here to help. Piper couldn't get away."

"Away from what, dear?" Glenda looked vague and a little disheveled as she walked past Lynn and continued up to the house.

Lynn reached for her cell to call Piper as she followed Glenda. "Why am I here?" she asked as Piper answered the call.

"I don't know. She called me." Piper spoke to someone in her office and then returned to Lynn. "Sorry, I wanted to clear my office before I talk with you."

"What's going on?" Lynn had known Piper since first grade. This was strange behavior.

"Mom has been acting differently since Dad had his surgery. Doesn't she remember calling me?" Piper was trying to control the strain Lynn could hear in her voice.

"I found her out in her garden picking tomatoes." This conversation, coupled with Glenda's strange attitude, began to worry Lynn. "What do you want me to do while I'm here?"

"I honestly don't know," sighed Piper. "Bring her back to town. Tell her she's coming to dinner. In fact, pack up a few of her things. Then call when you're at my house."

"I've got it under control." Lynn walked up the path to the house as Glenda disappeared inside.

When Lynn entered she noticed the disarray in the kitchen. It was unusual to find Glenda's kitchen with spills on the floor and open food containers on the counter. Lynn walked through the house looking for the woman and found her staring out a window in her dining room. "Glenda, let's get some things for an overnight with Piper."

"With who, dear?" The older woman smiled sweetly, "I'm sorry, I wasn't listening." She returned to staring out the window.

Lynn felt a tingle in her spine at the response and said, "You watch the birds while I clean up."

"Certainly, dear." Glenda sat at the dining table and folded her hands. Lynn went into the kitchen and gave the room a quick cleaning, putting the basket of fresh tomatoes in her car. Then she ran upstairs and packed a bag. Coming back into the kitchen, she found the house keys where they had hung for decades. Lynn placed the overnight bag in her car then did a circuit of the house to lock windows and doors.

"Glenda, let's go for a drive."

"What a fine idea! I love to go for drives in the country." The older woman stood, ran her hands through her hair and walked out the kitchen door. Lynn locked the house, did one last scan of the property and joined Glenda in the car.

~ ~ ~

Joseph stood at the attic window and watched Lynn and Mrs. Llewellyn drive away. He moved the drapery to get a better look, to make certain they left the farm. He sighed again. It was time to hide these papers and maybe take a walk, get some fresh air and stretch his legs. Lynn had put an overnight bag in the car. No one was coming back here for a day or two. It was time to get moving. He'd try to be gone by then. He let out a deep breath.

How did he get here, he asked himself? Trying to stay alive was the answer. Someone had searched his apartment while he was at the office. Once he realized the implications, he quickly disappeared. He felt fortunate to have seen this farm just days before his world began to disintegrate. All his experience in working through legitimate nonprofits to help people organize their finances, pay their debts and get on the road to financial solvency, and he missed this scam. He was angry with himself. He never suspected that the great job he had been recruited for was just a cover for a broader loansharking and gambling operation. He was the window dressing. He was to keep it all looking legal. Even the office staff was in on the scam — people who were hired by the main office. Main office hires, he snorted to himself, was a euphemism for criminals — people who shoplifted, ran illegal betting operations and had been arrested for various white-collar crimes against former employers. In short, the offices in a tri-state area hired people skilled in cheating.

He wasn't certain what made him do an Internet search on the newest hire. She had just looked 'off.' But he was able to learn her correct social security number and was able to do a background check. Fortunately he had done it on his home computer. To his surprise she turned out to be recently released from prison for embezzling from her employer. He tried to check the human resource information for the agency, but didn't have password access.

That Janet woman who was so ditsy came from the local IT consultant's office to help him access computer records and he was able to check references which all turned out to be false. He thought about telling someone, but at the same time he received that strange letter written by the former sheriff alleging misconduct in the PFM office.

It was a very strange letter, saying things about the

agency's methods in strong-arming clients who had not paid on loans. What loans? The agency helped direct elderly clients to reverse mortgage providers, helped young families manage their credit card debit. They didn't loan money! So he began some more snooping. With more IT help from that woman, he learned that many people who were in need of ready cash were offered loans by a subsidiary of the PFM nonprofit. The subsidiary, here he shivered, was a loansharking operation that was taking over properties from unsuspecting victims, many of whom had family members in nursing homes or were very ill themselves. Or the clients seemed to owe money for gambling debt or for purchases of illegal things like drugs or weapons. What a mess!

So now he was hiding because someone had searched his home and the letter from the old sheriff was missing from his desk and that IT Janet woman had called him to say that she had "seen" someone searching his computer files when she was doing work on his latest request.

That was when he knew he had to disappear and plan his next move. The Llewellyn farm was a perfect spot. With her husband in rehab for that knee, the old woman was all alone. She'd never notice his presence.

Chapter Four

As Lynn and Glenda settled in the car preparing to leave the farm, two men watched from a copse of trees on the other side of the road. "Looks like we might have some time to check this place out without interruption," the first man said.

"Yeah. I'm getting tired of this burg, Al," replied the curly haired man. "We been in this town for a week. The boss had a good idea about checking out some office appointments. Good thing that manager kept such good notes on his calendar. This farm never got on the client lists. I wonder why?"

"Because he was setting it up as his hideout," concluded Al. The two men watched the house. This was the second day of stakeout. They hadn't spotted their prey, but this farm seemed to have more possibilities than the other locations they had watched for the last week.

"Need a drink?"

Al accepted the small flask. After a good swallow, he asked, "This why they call you Scotch?"

Taking another swallow himself, Scotch answered, "My grandfather came from Glasgow."

"Where's that?" asked Al as he accepted the flask again.

"Scotland, you know — the Loch Ness monster and heather on the hills and all that shit."

"Good thing they didn't call you Heather." Al laughed

as he crouched back into the trees, adjusting his binoculars to watch the house. A few minutes later, they noticed a flutter in the attic curtains. "Did you see that?" asked Al.

"Yeah." Scotch lowered his binoculars and rubbed his eyes.

About fifteen minutes later a man walked carefully from the house to the barn. He carried some folders and large envelopes. "Looks like our missing records," offered Scotch. The two men proceeded cautiously across the quiet country road and ran along side the barn toward the back, a place not visible from the road. Slowly opening the door they watched as the man placed the files in an old barrel and covered it with a dirty burlap sack and some hand tools.

"Need help?" Al asked as he and Scotch sauntered into the barn.

"Who are you?" challenged Joseph.

"We got some mutual friends," replied Al, "and our friends are worried about you."

Joseph spun and made a mad dash for the door he had just entered. For a man of his size, Scotch was quick, in five steps he reached his prey, locking an arm around his neck. With a nod from Al, Scotch gave a quick and deadly twist. Joseph fell to the floor.

~ ~ ~

While Piper waited for Lynn to call, she checked in with Dr. Rita Rutledge, the family's physician. "Rita, what do I do? This is not like anything I've experienced before." Piper wasn't used to needing assistance, especially with her parents — the people she had always thought of as strong, independent and ageless.

"Let her stay with you for a few days. Take her to visit your father. Let me know what you observe. This has happened too quickly." Dr. Rita didn't want to be pessimistic, but she was concerned about Glenda, too.

After the phone conversation, Piper decided to walk through her domain, as her husband called the elementary school, and assure her staff that this would be another successful year. Piper loved her career, her staff and her pupils. Last year she had turned down a promotion to the board of education administrative offices, knowing that leaving daily contact with her kids would be unbearable. Spending a few more years in her domain was the icing on a rosy professional future.

But Piper hadn't foreseen all of these issues popping up regarding her parents' health. As an only child she felt a responsibility to respond to their needs, and she worried about how much longer they should stay out on the farm alone. Although her father hired help and restricted his farming to growing a few vegetables and some orchard fruits for a local cider operation, he was beginning to look his age. This accident with the tractor had forced him to reevaluate the farm operations for next year.

What to do about aging parents? Piper had watched many of her friends and colleagues wrestle with the problem. Lynn had been consumed with her own father's care three years ago when she resettled in River Bend. Her father, Jim Hoefler, had been undergoing chemotherapy and looked to all his friends as though he would lose the fight. But Jim was back to his old self and back at his law practice. He had even remarried four months ago. Old age wasn't Jim's enemy!

No matter how other parents were handling aging, Piper sighed, she had two parents who were both suddenly challenged by declining health. So she was back where she started. What should she do?

Her phone rang. "We're here," Lynn announced.

~ ~ ~

Arriving at Piper's house, Lynn stopped the car and looked at Glenda. Tears were streaming down the woman's face. She looked at Lynn then began to sob in great heaves and gasps.

Lynn took her hand. "Glenda, I'll help you, just tell me what to do."

"I'm losing my mind." Glenda cried and pulled a large white hanky from her pocket. "I think I put things someplace and they move. I think I have food in the house and it's gone. I hear walking and noises and no one's there." She released her burden like a flood as she continued with her errors and lapses. "I don't remember bringing that blanket into the barn. I have no idea how I ever carried that water into the loft." Something nagged on the edge of Lynn's mind. Something that hinted ... Glenda spoke again and Lynn's thought escaped. "I feel as though someone is watching everything I do and following me everywhere. You know, just out of sight." A wisp of a thought distracted Lynn as Glenda completed her memory. "My mother used to say "helpful fairies" – my fairies feel evil." She turned to Lynn, "Don't you see, I'm crazy."

Lynn was processing what she was hearing with what she had recently heard from Dusty. If someone were trying to hide or to disappear, wouldn't the barn of a woman living alone be a great spot? Wouldn't that person need food and water and blankets? Would Dusty say she was just imagining things?

"Glenda, let's get into the house. Piper will be here soon." Lynn ran around to the passenger side of the car and helped the older woman. "We'll take care of you. You're the only mom Piper and I have." She hugged Glenda, the lady who had come into her life the day she met Piper back in kindergarten.

Piper pulled up to the curb as the ladies were walking onto the porch. "Mom, I'm here." Glenda began to sob. Piper ran up the steps and they embraced.

"Now that you're here," said Lynn, "I have an errand." Piper, who had been anticipating Lynn's support through this challenge with Glenda, looked at her in surprise.

"I have to see Dusty. I'll be right back." Lynn ran to her car and was gone.

As she drove toward Dusty's office, she called him on the phone. When he picked up, she babbled, "The Llewellyn farm, missing stuff."

She had caught Dusty on his way to lunch. "Lynn, calm down. I can't understand you. Meet me in the parking lot at Uncle Chicken," he said, "I'll get you something."

As Dusty located an empty concrete table on the edge of Uncle Chicken's parking lot, Lynn screeched around the corner and came to a stop near his SUV. Running to the table, she gasped, "Glenda Llewellyn thinks she's crazy." Her husband looked at her. "She thinks she's done things and can't remember." Dusty continued to stare at her as she stood before him waving her arms to punctuate her rant. "If you wanted to hide out, wouldn't the Llewellyn's barn be a great spot?"

"Just because someone hid out in our barn last year?"

"No." Lynn would have stomped her foot in protest but she was settled on the bench unwrapping the Uncle Chicken white meat and jalapeno special. After savoring the aroma, she said, "I just brought Glenda to Piper's house. She complained that she's losing her mind because she –" Lynn opened her eyes wide, indicating she would soon say something profound, but first she took a bite of the chicken wrap. Dusty sat there staring at the salad he had purchased for her, waiting for her earth rattling revelation, while she chewed his lunch. Swallow. "– she didn't remember leaving that blanket in the barn, nor carrying water up to the loft." Lynn raised her eyebrows higher as an exclamation point to her evidence.

Dusty gave this information some thought. "Did she say when these lapses began?"

"No."

"Did she say she had seen strangers around the farm?" He watched his lunch disappear.

"No, but she did say she heard noises and heard walking." Lynn slurped up Dusty's chocolate slushy and sampled the onion rings. When he tried to get his share she passed him her diet drink.

"If I say I'll go check it out, can I finish my own lunch?" He pushed the salad aside.

"Can I come?" she asked. When Dusty tried to protest, she said, "I practically grew up on that farm. I know my way around." Dusty had to admit that she had a point. She also had the rest of his onion rings.

Then he remembered. "Hey, what happened to that diet you started this morning?"

Dusty and Lynn arrived at the Llewellyn farm as a cloud passed in front of the sun. The forbidding omen caused Lynn to shiver. Dusty stopped the SUV halfway between the house and barn and asked, "Does this look the way you left it this morning?" She nodded. "Did you check the house and barn?"

"I looked for Glenda around the property. I glanced in the barn and didn't hear or see anything unusual. Then I stuck my head in the house. Finally, I walked out toward her garden." Lynn pointed to the row of tomato stakes that they could see beyond the barn. "That's where I found her. She had a basket of fresh tomatoes."

"Then what?"

"I helped her carry the tomatoes into the house. She was behaving, I don't know, like she was hypnotized or in a trance. I called Piper and she told me to pack Glenda up and bring her to town. That's what I did and I checked and locked the house before we left." Lynn tried to recall all the details. "Glenda acted so strange that I made certain all doors and windows were locked before we drove away. I even made sure I locked her car and Bri's truck." She nodded toward the vehicles under a metal canopy.

"Did you check the barn before you left?"

"No. I didn't have any reason to; I'd looked inside when I arrived."

Dusty opened his door. "Why don't you stay here?" It was a plea not an order. Lynn ignored him and soon stood by his side. They both walked toward the barn. Dusty stopped and listened. "Do they have live stock?" Lynn shook her head. She heard the fluttering sound from the barn. Looking up she saw several birds fly out of the loft opening.

Dusty un-holstered his weapon and handed Lynn his phone. He indicated that she should walk behind him as they proceeded toward the barn doors, which were slightly ajar. Inside, the barn was like any other barn in the area – stalls, equipment, barrels and sacks. Some things were arranged as if stored, others were thrown around as though they would be used as soon as the farmer returned. To the left against a supporting pole, Brice Llewellyn had attached a winch threaded in series to a pair of pulleys. It was evident that the apparatus was used to lift items to the loft or lower them as needed. It wasn't clear whether the body at the end of the pulley rope had been intended to be raised or lowered. What was clear was that the body was suspended from a noose.

Chapter Five

"Hit one, and tell the dispatcher we need a crime scene team and backup." Dusty nodded at the phone in her hand. "And stay close." As they moved through the barn, Dusty listened to Lynn talk with the dispatcher.

"She wants to know a code to make certain this isn't a hoax."

"Good for her." Dusty let go of Lynn's hand and took the phone. After a whispered conversation, he handed the phone back to Lynn.

"That's OK," Lynn whispered to the dispatcher as the woman apologized for following protocol. There was a pause. Then Lynn began to whisper again, responding to the dispatcher's request to describe the scene. As Lynn spoke softly into the phone she and Dusty walked around the hard packed dirt floor of the barn, looking into corners and under sacks.

"I hear the sirens. They're in the yard," Lynn told the dispatcher. There was a conversation distracting the dispatcher. "What?" Lynn was startled and Dusty turned to look at her. "She says we have a flat tire."

Dusty took the phone. "Tell the backup team that we're coming out the barn door closest to the car." Dusty turned to Lynn. "Stay behind me." Dusty moved quickly to the door, shouted, heard the officer respond then opened the door walking out while keeping Lynn behind him. The officers were crouched behind their car with weapons in their hands.

As Dusty appeared they stood but kept their weapons at the ready. "I'll stay here. You two look behind the barn," he directed the backup team. The ambulance and other support crews were just entering the property.

As the staff arrived, Lynn pulled on Dusty's arm, "I know the man." Her eyes moved toward the barn. "It's Joseph, the missing man you were talking about this morning." Dusty weighed the information and looked around the property, as Lynn added, "I have a key to the house."

Dusty took her hand and walked with her toward Martin Healey, Mars to his friends, the first unit member to arrive. "I want you to walk through the house with Lynn," Dusty told the young detective. "She has a key and can tell you what's out of order." Dusty gave Lynn's hand to Mars.

Lynn pulled her hand away. "The key is in my purse in the car."

Dusty nodded and walked to the SUV and waited for her to search her purse as he looked at the rear tire.

"Someone shot it out," said Dusty as his stomach flopped. "He must have a silencer on his gun. A pro?"

Mars stood beside him. "Chief, someone who didn't want to be followed was here when you arrived." Dusty nodded in agreement with the young man's conclusion.

Lynn held up the key and followed Mars to the house. As she inserted the key the door eased open. "I locked this when I left with Glenda," whispered Lynn. Mars turned to her before they entered. "I know," she said, "stay close and don't touch anything." He smiled at her.

Tiptoeing into the empty house behind Mars, Lynn gasped as she grabbed his arm. "Look at the mess on the floor. I swept the kitchen before we left." Mars nodded and stepped around the debris – dried leaves and dirt that might have fallen from the shoes and trousers of an intruder. Walking from room to room on the first floor, Lynn again commented, "I made certain that door was locked." She nodded toward the front door, slightly ajar, that opened to the front porch and yard that faced the quiet country road running through the farmlands.

Mars nodded. "Let's finish our survey before we let the techs in." They climbed the stairs to the second floor and found the attic door open. The detective looked at Lynn,

She shook her head. "That door was closed when I came up to pack some things for Glenda."

He told Lynn to stay at the bottom of the stairs as he proceeded up to investigate. After a look through the attic space, he called, "Lynn, could you come up here?"

She moved up the stairs trying not to touch the handrail. As her head poked through the floor, Mars asked, "Have you ever been up here?"

"Not for years." She soon stood in the center of the attic. "Nothing seems changed." Lynn surveyed the area. The trunks and old furniture appeared to be the same things she and Piper had played with years ago.

"Did someone ever live up here?" Mars' voice came from behind the chimney.

"No one ever stayed up here." Lynn thought he was being silly until she joined him and stood looking at a makeshift bed, some clothing and a small lamp and radio.

"Let's look over the bedrooms and then get out and let the lab unit do their thing. I wonder if the dead man was staying here," offered the detective.

"He's the man that you've been looking for." Lynn shrugged. "It makes sense to have picked a place with a woman living alone. No wonder Glenda told me she was hearing noises and misplacing items."

"You mean the dead guy in the barn?"

"Yes, he's Joseph Baikar from Personal Financial Management. I told Dusty." Lynn stopped. "I'm sorry you haven't had a chance to be briefed."

"I like getting my information directly from the source." He smiled at her.

They climbed down from the attic and Mars said, "Stay here while I check out the bedrooms." She nodded and leaned against the bathroom doorjamb.

As Mars moved through the three bedrooms, opening closet doors and checking behind draperies, Lynn stared at the bathroom. Something wasn't right. She studied the fixtures, twisted to see behind the door. "Mars," she called, "I want you to give me your opinion."

He poked his head out of a room and raised an eyebrow. She tilted her head toward the commode. "The seat is up, like a man just used it. But, if Joseph were living here trying to stay off Glenda's radar, he would keep the seat down. Do you think someone else used it after Glenda and I drove off?"

"Hmm," Mars considered her observation. "That's an interesting observation. If someone were out in a field watching the place, they may have preferred to use indoor facilities. We'll point all these things out to the techs for a closer look." Moving down from the upper floors they met Dusty in the kitchen.

"Someone's been living in the attic," reported Mars. Lynn shuddered at the thought of Glenda alone and vulnerable on the farm.

The rest of the unit arrived and huddled under a tree with Dusty. Lynn marveled again at the way the three young officers respected Dusty and enjoyed the camaraderie of their small close-knit group. Mars was a former Marine with exceptional physical skills and a degree in forensic accounting. Younger and smaller than Mars was Danny Valeri, the new dad in the unit. He was part of the long time Italian-American community in River Bend. The last member of the team, Teniquia LaMont, the recent bride, was a twenty-something African American woman with an investigative ability that could only be defined as ESP. The young woman brought a mirth to the squad to balance the serious side of the men.

Lynn listened as Dusty assigned tasks. "Danny, get to that office where our victim worked. Take some patrolmen with you. Interview the staff and send them home. Put our lock on the place. Tee, get to the vic's apartment to see if anything has changed there since our first visit, and get warrants started to look over information at that office. Mars, you handle this place. Lynn and I are going to talk with Glenda Llewellyn. Let's try to meet back at the office at five."

Dusty looked at his car with its flat tire and said, "Mars, I need your keys."

Once he and Lynn were on their way back to town, Dusty said, "Call Will. He needs to be with Piper when we talk about this." She nodded and dialed her brother.

~ ~ ~

"Good thing I was looking out that attic window," said Al as he stopped to watch the activity in the farmyard from their old spot across the road.

"Did you find anything else in the attic?" asked Scotch.

"Nope," confirmed Al, "I think we got it all from the barn. Good thinking to shoot out that tire." When they scrambled from the Llewellyn house Scotch had detoured to disable Dusty's SUV as Al made certain no one was watching.

"Now what?" Scotch asked as they moved quickly to their car that was hidden in some trees at the edge of a cornfield about a quarter of a mile from the farm.

"We get our asses outa here," said Al as he started the engine and moved in a direction away from River Bend and the dead man.

Stopping at a diner in one of the small farm communities, they rapidly scanned the papers they had taken from the barn. "This looks like our stuff," said Scotch. "Can we go home now?"

"I'll check with the boss." After some conversation on his cell phone, Al reported, "He says for us to get settled in one of those motels at the airport."

"You mean we gotta hang around here some more?" groused Scotch as he slipped his flask back into his pocket after stirring a few drops into his diner coffee.

Chapter Six

Will Zubov, Lynn's half-brother, had the good sense to marry Lynn's best friend, Piper, about three years ago, turning Lynn's best friend into her sister-in-law. Both women thought it was a very efficient arrangement. Will thought it was the best way to live. He was the result of a brief affair between his mother and Lynn's father. Jim finally told Lynn about her half-brother during his illness. Since that time, with Jim's two children, joined by Piper's three teenaged sons, Lynn's son and her new husband, along with Marianna, Jim's new wife, life moved at a hectic pace through the usual family events, holidays, school activities, birthdays, anniversaries, but always seemed to include a few dead bodies.

When Dusty pulled the car up in front of Piper's, Will was standing on the porch waiting. He ran down to the sidewalk. "What's this about a body?" he demanded.

"You didn't tell Piper did you?" asked Lynn.

"Tell her what? You didn't tell me anything." He scowled at both Dusty and Lynn.

"Calm down," whispered Dusty, "we found a dead man at the farm."

"What? Why?" Will sputtered with questions. "Calm down?"

"Just be strong and silent and listen," said Dusty, "you'll hear everything."

They walked into the house. "Will?" Piper was puzzled

to see her husband walk in followed by Lynn and Dusty. "What's wrong? Dad?"

"No, babe," said Will, "Dusty wanted me here about ..." He shrugged.

"Where's your mother?" asked the detective.

"I'm here," Glenda called from the dining room. She was sitting at the table with a cup of tea. Her hand rested gently on the head of Piper's dog, a big, blond setter resting its snout on Glenda's lap.

"There's been an incident at the farm," said Dusty, "and I want to ask you some questions."

"I got here as quickly as I could," announced Dr. Rita as she barged into the house.

"Who called you?" snarled Dusty. He hated doing interviews in a crowd.

"I ... well ... you don't need to know," she snapped back at the detective as she went over to check on Glenda. "Let's sit in the living room. It's more comfortable," the doctor directed her patient.

Once Glenda was settled on the couch with Piper on one side and Dusty on the other, the detective began again, "There's been an incident at the farm."

"Yes, dear, you told me," replied Glenda.

Dusty shuffled some papers on his lap and showed her a photo. Glenda said, "I know that man."

The detective had a file photo of the murder victim. "Why was he living in your attic?"

"My attic?" Glenda rubbed her eyes and looked perplexed. Nothing seemed to make sense. Life had been very confusing since her husband entered the hospital. The noises, the missing blankets and vanishing food. "My attic?"

she repeated.

Dusty took her hand. Piper placed a reassuring arm around her shoulders. "We found this man in your barn, dead," explained the detective.

Glenda gasped and searched the faces of everyone in the room for an explanation. Will was pacing and Lynn was sitting on the edge of a chair while Dr. Rita stood quietly against a wall watching her patient. "Bri invited him out to the house to talk about borrowing against the farm."

"You need money?" Will demanded as he stopped pacing and stood in front of his mother-in-law.

"We didn't want to …" she stopped.

"Ask me? I'm your son!" By the decibel level of his voice everyone within two blocks of the house knew he was concerned.

Before this little family drama got teary, Dusty reclaimed the interrogation. "You two sort this out later. I've got a dead body." Everyone scowled at him, reminding him that family was their priority. He relented. "Just let me finish, please."

Glenda clasped Dusty's hand in both of hers. "I'm not crazy?"

"It looks as though this fellow, or someone, was living in your attic," the detective explained. "I'll tell you more when my team analyzes the evidence they collect. But tell me how the man might have gotten in."

Glenda thought for a moment. "He was very kind and very concerned about Bri's surgery, asking me if I would be staying at the farm alone." Her eyes grew wide. "He was planning to move in!"

"I'm the detective, I'll collect the evidence," cautioned

Dusty, "just tell me about his visit."

She continued her narration. "He looked at the house and went all over, including the attic. We showed him everything he asked to see. Then he asked about Bri's surgery, you know, the dates and was I staying at the hospital until he came out of surgery." She stared at the ceiling as though she were trying to retrieve a thought. "He wanted to see the guest bathroom and my pantry." She nodded her head slowly as she had a thought. "Do you think he wanted my canned okra? It got a first place at the county fair last year"

Dusty scowled at her. "Just give me those dates again – when he visited and Bri's hospital stay. And what kind of car did he drive?" Dusty balanced his notebook on his knee.

"It was a dark blue truck – one of those small ones, not the kind farmers around here use."

Dusty, the farmer, nodded. He knew what a farm truck looked like. "Over the last week, did you see his truck parked near your place?"

"I did. I mean I saw one like it. It was sometimes parked at that little church on Nettle Road over the last few days. It's unusual for anyone to be there during the week in daytime. It's a small congregation." With each question Glenda seemed to be morphing back into her old self – competent farm wife and retired schoolteacher. Her features relaxed and she was even smiling, eager to answer Dusty's questions.

They all thought about the location of the church and the Llewellyn farm. "He walked through the old corn field," said Will. "We've been getting it ready for our snowmobile race at Christmas." He grinned at Dusty, reminding him about last year's race and the inconclusive results. During the Christmas holidays Will and Dusty had raced through an obstacle course designed by the kids. All of Dusty's brothers and the young detectives of the unit had shown up at the farm – spectators for the big race.

"Are you going to add more ramps?" asked Lynn.

"How about a gauntlet of corn stalks?" suggested Piper. Will opened his mouth to respond, but one look from Dusty and he closed it.

"This is an investigation," the detective reminded everyone, again. He turned back to Glenda. "Did the victim give a clue that he was looking for a place to hide?"

"Why would he tell her if he planned to use her house?" asked Dr. Rita.

Dusty frowned at the doctor and reframed his question. "Can you tell me about his attitude that day – nervous, happy?"

"Businesslike. He took notes and asked questions that seemed related to our case." Glenda hugged Piper. "And I'm not crazy or demented ... or ... or something? I really did hear noises?"

Dusty nodded. "He was hiding in your attic and probably stole food and things when you were at the hospital. Somehow the murderer found him." Everyone shivered.

"Are you finished with your questions?" Will asked Dusty. The detective gave a resigned shrug, rising from his seat beside Glenda. "Good, because I have some questions." Will stared at his mother-in-law. "Why didn't you ask me for help?" He knelt beside her and took her hands.

"We didn't want to be a burden," she admitted. "Bri is very proud. He, we weren't prepared for this accident to happen. When we realized that we would lose two crop seasons with the surgeries and recovery, we didn't know how we would survive with just my teacher's pension." She shrugged and seemed to become very small. "We decided to see if we could use the value of the farm to help tide us over."

"We'll give you whatever you need," said Will as Glenda brushed tears from her eyes. Piper and Lynn both tried to hug her.

"I still have a dead body," Dusty complained as he stood in the center of the room. "I still may need information from you."

"Oh, bosh," said Glenda, "you and Lynn will solve this case without my help."

"Yeah," said Will as he led Glenda, Piper and Dr. Rita into the kitchen. Dusty swore and Lynn laughed.

"Don't worry. I'll help you," offered Lynn.

"No, you won't," he scowled. "You stay out of this." He looked up as he heard laughter from the kitchen. "She can't go home," he shouted. Will and the ladies came back into the living room. "You stay here until I tell you it's okay to go home," Dusty told Glenda. "That means no visits to pick up a few things. You need something one of my detectives will pick it up."

"Don't worry she's not going anywhere," said Piper, "until you and Lynn solve the murder." Dusty swore again.

"I agree," said Dr. Rita who had been observing her patient throughout the discussion. "She needs rest and some TLC."

Lynn had been quiet for most of the interrogation, but

she turned to Dusty. "There's something going on at that agency. I've heard rumors and was called by someone from another state early this morning who wanted information about the group."

Dusty looked at his wife, then tracked his eyes around the room, noticing all the curious listeners waiting for Lynn's comments. He pulled her to her feet. "It's getting late. We should get home and let the dog out."

Chapter Seven

Clickety-click came the sounds from Janet Bergman's laptop keyboard. She was perched on a chair in her father's room at the nursing home. Clickety-click. She watched intently as he grunted while he used stiff fingers to form letters with his rusty American Sign Language skills. Since his stroke his speech had become nonexistent. Fortunately he had taught Janet to sign when she was a child and he was falling back on this method for communication. He was rusty, she was rusty, the process was slow.

Janet squinted at his fingers. She nodded, typed, and said, "I think I got it. Listen to this. *"Dear Sir, This is a follow-up letter to the one I sent three weeks ago. I respectfully request a response to my inquiry about the questionable practices of your organization or I will do all in my power to bring about an investigation into your activities."*

Bergy, her father and retired sheriff, nodded. She continued, "I'm surprised you didn't hear from Joseph. I did some work for him." She squinted at her father's hands. "He's very nice. But they have a computer system that shuttles information someplace. He asked a question similar to yours. He thought someone was taking information and approaching his clients." Bergy worked his hands again. Janet nodded. "He had heard from some people that they were approached by someone that was referred by Personal Financial Management." Janet nodded again at her father's signing. "Joseph said people were offered loans at high rates. He had no knowledge about this and told me that going through the computer might help him see how the information was getting out and who this other group was."

Bergy signed. She nodded and replied, "If it makes you feel more comfortable about this, go ahead and talk with Dusty. You always said the more eyes the more you see."

Bergy motioned to her and she closed her computer and moved closer. He kissed her hand. "I'll be careful. Joseph doesn't know that I helped you write that first letter. I don't think he knows my name." Bergy signed again. She kissed his forehead. "Love you, too. I've got to get back to work." He smiled at her.

~ ~ ~

"Dusty, that inquiry this morning was from a sheriff in another state." Lynn was breathless as she tried to give Dusty all her information at one time. "I'll give you his name. Personal Financial Management has offices in several nearby states. And the caller suggested things weren't on the up and up in his community."

They slowly walked up the porch steps and opened their kitchen door. The dog nosed out into the afternoon air, yipped a joyous sound and raced into the yard. Dusty brought out two beers and sat beside Lynn on the porch settee. They were silent for a time, listening to the dog enjoy himself. Finally Chips returned to the porch and sprawled at their feet.

"Tell me what you know," said Dusty.

She took another sip of her beer. "I haven't heard much

from people here. I told you about the call I got from the pastors' group. And Adam from United Charities had some questions. Clients get the basic financial counseling, credit consolidation, and help with developing a personal budget. If they qualify they are sent to various other agencies for help or assistance, rent money, medication money, even reverse mortgages. But Personal Financial Management doesn't give out money, only planning assistance for personal finances."

"What else are people concerned about?" asked the detective.

"I'll ask around." She sipped her beer.

"Another body?" asked Jason, Lynn's son, as he climbed the porch steps, icing and cake crumbs stuck to his clothing. He always smelled like sugar when he came home from his bakery job.

"How did you hear?" asked Lynn. Dusty scowled at the lack of security and the entertainment dead bodies seemed to bring to the house.

"I stopped at Piper's to check on her order for her party Saturday. They were all talking about it." Jason grinned, waiting to be brought into the loop, hoping Dusty's information would be more current than the info floating around Piper's place.

"This is an investigation," growled Dusty.

"Yes, dear, and we can't keep secrets." Lynn patted his arm. Then she proceeded to tell her son all she knew. "Dusty and I found a man hanged out at the Llewellyn farm this afternoon. He had been hiding in Glenda's attic."

"Cool."

Dusty said, "Listen, pal, Glenda might have been in real

danger. I don't want you to make light of this."

Jason nodded. "But, can I tell the guys?"

"I think they know as much as you," said Lynn, certain Piper's sons already knew about their grandmother and the body.

Not discouraged, Jason asked, "What's for dinner?" as he pulled off his sweet smelling shirt. Then he stopped. "I delivered those cookies to the country club for your party," and dashed into the house to shower.

"The donor appreciation dinner!" screeched Lynn, "I'm late." Fifteen minutes later she was driving out of the yard to get to a Philanthropies' function. Dusty settled back on the porch grateful that a dead body had saved him from an evening playing dress up. Then he jolted to his feet. He had told his team that they would wrap up the day's findings at five. He checked his watch. He was ten minutes late.

~ ~ ~

Dusty stopped outside the office and slowed his pace. He didn't want the unit to see him rushing in as though he were late and knew it. "What have we got?" he asked as he tossed a file on his desk.

"How's Mrs. Llewellyn?" asked Teniquia.

"She's fine," replied Dusty. "Once she realized she wasn't crazy, that the victim had been hiding out at the farm, she perked up. What have you found out?"

Dusty looked at Danny who straightened up in his seat and reported. "We talked with the two ladies at the office. They said they know nothing and said they didn't know this Joseph very well." Danny chewed on his lip. "It was real strange. You know how people like to talk and think we'll give them information in return? These ladies wanted no part of any interview and barely admitted this guy worked there."

"Can we look at the office computers and files?"

"Tee says she'll get the warrant. These ladies demanded one. I put our locks on the office and I disconnected the computers from the Internet so no one could do things tonight," said Danny.

"We were too late to get a warrant this afternoon," replied Teniquia. "I'll get it first thing in the morning. I have a team going over the vic's apartment. Someone had been there. We could tell the first time we looked, before his body turned up. It wasn't tossed, but very professionally done. I've got some people out talking with the neighbors."

Mars cleared his throat. "The crime techs are combing the farm, too. It'll be slow because half the team is working the vic's apartment. The ME called to confirm that Joseph was dead before the rope was put around his neck. He'll give us a full report in a few days."

"Let's save the rest for tomorrow," Dusty told his staff. He yawned, then remembered he wasn't getting any dinner since Lynn was at her donor party. "Go home. We'll meet back here in the morning and wait for Tee to get the warrant."

As his staff filed out of the office Dusty called Jason, "Want to meet me at Pedro's?" Jason cheered into the phone. The boy had probably been staring into the empty refrigerator, thought Dusty.

~ ~ ~

Cory Estridge's phone rang as he unsnapped the young woman's bra. He knew the ring. It was his unofficial, very lucrative client. He smacked the girl's behind and told her to

51

watch the TV for a few minutes then he slipped into the bathroom.

"Yeah."

"Estridge, I got a little problem," Rupert Rothman's voice rasped into Cory's ear. On paper Rothman was the national executive director of Personal Financial Management, Cory knew better and worked hard for the money he was paid, secretly, to keep Rothman and his schemes afloat. "My guys helped a fellow move to the next life today. They're pros, it was clean, but I'm worried that the locals may want to search my offices. They were at the office earlier and the girls wouldn't let them touch anything. So the cops said they would get warrants in the morning."

Cory leaned against the sink. "Why will they want to search your offices?"

"The fellow worked for me."

"Where are you?"

"I'm in some burg called River Bend."

Cory almost laughed. Three years ago he had been engaged to Nancy Rawlings, the young woman currently Mars Healey's love interest. Good old Mars, the detective, would be hip deep in this murder investigation, he was certain. Rothman's people were good. Mars would chase his tail on this one. But Cory was delighted to add more bumps in the investigation. "I have a friend, a lawyer in the next county. He's clever and hungry. He can represent you before the judge on this warrant. Tell him you want him to challenge any warrant because the cops haven't shown that the death is related to your office or the victim's employment with you."

"That's it?"

"Hey, you're an innocent man protecting client

confidentiality and your employee may have had some sordid secret life. It doesn't affect your office." Cory turned around to study himself in the mirror. "Just have my guy call the judge early in the morning. You want to be there before the cops."

"Okay, gimme the guy's name."

Cory reeled off the information, and added, "I'm going to be out of the country for a few weeks. But call anyway, if you need something. I should get all calls. If you're worried, send an email and I'll call you."

"Where you going?"

"Australia."

"That's pretty far out of the country."

"Yeah, my father-in-law's trying to keep me away from my wife. He suspects I'm not the nice guy he thought." Cory wondered if he should have married Nancy Rawlings. His current wife was a nag, always running to her father with her suspicions about Cory's extra-marital life.

"Just stay outta trouble until I get through this," Rothman directed his attorney.

"One last piece of advice," said Cory, "I know some of the cops in River Bend. Stay away from a guy named Mars."

"That his first name or last?"☐

"First, and he's mean. Don't let him find out I work for you." Cory ended the call and went to find the young woman he had just met at the hotel bar.

~ ~ ~

Dusty watched Lynn come into the room as he sat up in bed reading. It had been a late night for her. He had taken Jason out for dinner and had been home in time to watch part of a baseball game. Putting aside his book, he sat and listened to the sounds of his wife preparing for bed. Water splashing, things spraying. He caught a soft scent wafting from the bathroom. Clothing rustling, more water sounds. He knew she was scouring make-up from her face. It would be shiny and pink when she finished. He smiled to himself and enjoyed the wait.

Finally Lynn crawled into bed, more like flopped, too tired to even turn back the sheet. "Ugh!" she moaned, "those people are crazy. They all wanted to talk about the murder and was I going to help you solve this case."

Dusty was alert. "Why were you talking about this case?"

"I wasn't, everyone else was." She struggled with the sheet. Dusty helped her get untangled and relaxed under the covers. He turned out his bedside lamp and slid down beside her.

From the dark Lynn said, "Everyone thought this was a game. I guess because it was someone nobody knew."

He felt her shrug under the covers. "I wish you'd let me and my staff do the investigating. I only say this because this is an ugly murder. We're not dealing with a local hood. If his employer is part of this murder and has offices in a tri-state area, they operate at a more sophisticated level than you and our local non-profits."

"I'll just ask around tomorrow. No one will suspect I'm collecting information for an investigation." She kissed his cheek and he pulled her closer, enjoying the fresh soapy smell of her scrubbed face and the soft feel of her nightgown and the scent of her hair.

"You really tired?" he asked in her ear.

She snuggled closer and met his lips with hers.

Chapter Eight

Teniquia was furious. She stood before the judge requesting a routine warrant to search the workplace of a murder victim. And someone objected!

"Ms. LaMont," explained the judge, "I had a call early this morning from Mr. Rothman's attorney. I invited him to argue his point for consideration."

"Your honor, I represent Rupert Rothman, executive director of Personal Financial Management," the attorney introduced himself for the record and signaled for his client to stand. "We object to this warrant for my client's offices in River Bend. I don't think the investigators have shown sufficient evidence that Mr. Baikar's murder is an established fact nor that his death is related to our offices. We have confidential information about our clients on our computers and in our files."

Teniquia looked at the judge, puzzled. He shrugged and looked at her expectantly.

"Your honor," offered Teniquia, "a preliminary report from the medical examiner concludes that the victim was dead before the rope was placed around his neck. We have sufficient information to determine that this is murder."

The attorney said, "That's a tragedy, however, I challenge the investigators to show that it is related to our office." Mr. Rothman looked at Teniquia with a steady gaze.

"Come back with evidence that you need information from those offices, detective," said the judge. "Next."

Rothman and his attorney moved out of the courtroom quickly. Teniquia followed. When she called to the attorney, he stopped and waited.

"May I have a word with your client, sir?"

"Officer," he said, "you heard the judge. My client and I are not to be a part of your investigation unless you have proof that Mr. Baikar died because of his job. Please do not bother us or I'll file charges against you and your department."

Teniquia stood in the hall and watched the men stride triumphantly away as her blood boiled. She paged the unit.

~ ~ ~

The community college ran a nonprofit business center in conjunction with its small commercial business center. As the college president told everyone, "The books have to balance, and the IRS wants good records. The only difference is this profit thing."

"You helping Dusty?" asked Lev Nikolinski, manager of the community college nonprofit and small business center, as he offered Lynn a chair.

"No, I'm just ..." Lynn flapped her hand.

"You're helping Dusty." It was a statement this time. "So I'll tell you, those guys never came to our nonprofit roundtable meetings. They never joined any workshops that United Charities put on about administrative issues. They never, ever, talked with the agencies who served the same population, you know, services for older people, some single moms trying to learn about finances – the groups of people we all work with to help them learn to organize their lives better."

"What about Joseph?" she asked sitting forward and

placing her elbows on his desk.

"They really find him hanging from a beam in Bri's barn?" Lev was interested in the investigation.

Lynn scowled at him. "Did you ever talk to him?"

"Once or twice. He was very polite. Several attendees at the roundtable thought he had information that could benefit their clients. He just said he wasn't a presenter."

"Did he seem nervous or anything?" asked Lynn.

"He was polite and a gentleman. He said he'd contact his main office and ask for someone to talk at our next roundtable meeting." Lev shrugged. "I never got it on our agenda."

~ ~ ~

"What do you mean, no warrant?" Dusty was furious. It had been a long time since a judge denied any of his investigation requests.

Teniquia frowned, blaming herself for this failure. "I presented our case to the judge, but this Rothman fellow's attorney argued that we didn't demonstrate any clear evidence that this man's death was related to his job. Then he argued that it was all to keep his clients' information confidential." She shrugged. "The judge said he was correct and we should come back when we had more to support our request."

Dusty spun around and pointed to Danny. "Find out everything you can about this guy, Baikar. Talk with his neighbors and his family." He paced the office then stopped at Mars' desk. "You stay on those crime techs and see if you can't find his truck. Glenda thought she saw it at that church on Nettle Road."

I'm sorry, Chief," said Teniquia as she hung her head.

"Just stay in the rest of the day and get this case organized. Get the information up to date and look for holes where we should be going for more information. The guys will keep sending anything they learn back to you."

He paced the office for a few minutes then added, "Tee, I also want you to check out that Rothman fellow and ask Lynn about some out of town investigator. Tomorrow, we'll see where we stand." They all nodded.

~ ~ ~

"Audrey, I saw you myself, having lunch with Joseph Baikar," Lynn challenged the director of Exceptional Children, an agency working with mental health issues for children and developmentally delayed adults. Lynn always enjoyed seeing Audrey Decker who was the most stylish executive director in town. Whenever they met Lynn always felt as though she were wearing hand-me-downs from a third world country. How could someone just add a scarf and look so elegant? It was not one of Lynn's talents.

"I thought he might have ideas to help the parents of some of the clients at our group homes," explained Audrey. "Help from state and federal funding streams is inconsistent and uneven for my clients, so their families always need assistance. I thought Joseph might have long-term asset management ideas."

"What did you learn?"

Audrey thought a moment. "I thought he really wanted to help, but something was holding him back. He finally suggested that I contact an agency in Kentucky that he had worked with in his previous job."

"Did you?"

"Yes. And they have been marvelous." She sniffed back

a tear. "I'm sorry I won't be able to thank him for the connection." Audrey doodled on some papers. "You know, my clients could use that kind of financial planning help. They don't overspend, but their families need advice on setting up trusts and long-term care planning." She shrugged.

"Maybe you'll learn those things from Joseph's friends," suggested Lynn, "and maybe you'll learn something about him."

"He just said this job was different than he had anticipated. He was sorry that he didn't mesh easily with the other agencies in town." Audrey sipped her tea. "I think he wanted to get to know us, but his office didn't work like that."

"He *was* quiet, wasn't he," said Lynn, "I can't imagine anyone being angry with him." Another source with no real information, she thought.

"So what do *you* know?" asked Audrey. "We all want a fair exchange of information."

"I don't know anything," admitted Lynn, "Dusty's unit just began investigating and he doesn't tell me much because he says I blab."

"I hope so," said Audrey, "we're all counting on getting the lowdown from you."

Lynn frowned. She was disappointed with her interviews. No one had any information to share. The PFM staff had kept to themselves. Two interviews and she already knew she was giving out more information than she collected. She'd have to rethink her interrogation methods.

~ ~ ~

Rothman decided to spend the morning at the River

Bend PFM offices to make certain the police stayed away. Walking through the doors he nodded to the two women who worked for the enterprise. They had each been on the verge of arrest until he stepped into their lives. They both had a flair for scamming, and he had schooled them to be better and given them jobs. All his offices were staffed mostly by similar folk. The office manager was usually some dumb guy. Rothman liked to think of his office managers as firewalls. They were impenetrable because they knew nothing – until Baikar!

"No police can search our offices," he announced as he strolled toward a desk. "They may come here to ask you questions. Keep it simple – nobody knows nothing."

The women nodded.

"What can you tell me about this guy?" he asked the women.

They looked at one another and the older woman spoke. "He was quiet, but he was starting to get curious. He had a computer person come in here because he thought there was something wrong with his computer."

"What did he find?" □

"She. The computer person was a woman. She complained about a lot of firewalls and I don't know what else. She was real frustrated with your system."

"That's what I pay for." Rothman thumped his fingers on the desktop as he listened.

"She wanted to look at our computers, but we said the company had a policy that only our regional IT touched our equipment."

"Good thinking."

The woman Rothman always thought of as a retired

roller derby player spoke next. "We went through his desk and found a few things. Here's an interesting letter we found before he disappeared."

Rothman took the letter and scanned it. "Did he do anything about this?"

"Not that we know. But it's only dated two weeks ago and he was missing right after that."

"Do you think he contacted this guy?" The women both shrugged. "I'll take care of it. Anyone asks, send them to me." He folded the letter and stuffed it into an inside pocket.

With that information Rothman sat at Joseph's desk and did a quick search of the drawers and files. Then he contacted his computer people and asked them to search through Joseph's computer for any telltale signs of hacking.

He was told that someone tried to get in one day and the techs kept that person out. But, he was cautioned, that person was sharp. The hacker had almost maneuvered around the barriers.

Rothman thought about that. He decided he wanted to know who the IT person was. He checked an address book and studied a calendar. He also looked through the business cards Joseph had alphabetized in his center desk drawer. One card, River Bend Computer Solutions, caught his eye. He accessed the Internet and explored the River Bend Computer website. And there she was, Janet Bergman, the only woman working for the outfit. Something sounded familiar. The letter that the girls had found was signed by a Charles Bergman. Maybe they were working together. Maybe that's why she was hacking into the computers. Maybe they had to be investigated. He made a few notes, put the business card in his pocket with the letter, left some instructions for the staff and was gone.

~ ~ ~

After questioning some other nonprofit directors, Lynn returned to her office. She looked at her calendar and was puzzled by the name in her appointment book. Martha Snyder. "Nelda," she called to her assistant, "Who is this person Martha coming at two?"

"She said it was about a scholarship," replied Nelda, "she's coming with her daughter."

"It's August," moaned Lynn, "we gave out all our scholarships for this year and we don't open the application process for next year until January." She flopped into her chair and wondered how she could say 'no' without causing too much disappointment.

Granting college scholarships to local kids was one of the greatest programs the Philanthropies supported. All the board members volunteered to review applicants. Local donors loved to help local kids. This year they had managed to give almost a hundred thousand dollars in aid to local kids. Not big bucks, but amounts that would help with books and finish off some tuition payments. Her file was full of 'thank you' notes from the kids. And she always encouraged them to reapply for a second and third year.

With Piper's help and a lot of support from the community college guidance office, the Philanthropies had even sponsored a college financial aid workshop for parents and kids, offering all sorts of information helpful to the students' families regarding tuition matters. She rested her head on her hands as she stared out the window. So what did good old Martha want? Because all Lynn could offer was disappointment.

Nelda finally signaled that the two o'clock appointment had arrived. Lynn stepped into the reception area prepared to meet a stranger. "Shelby," she smiled a greeting, "what are you doing here?"

Shelby Bowman was a recent scholarship recipient. The young woman smiled at Lynn's enthusiastic welcome. "I brought my mother to meet you. We have some … er … questions."

Lynn now understood the name on her appointment calendar. She turned to the woman with Shelby. "You must be Ms. Snyder."

Martha Snyder was a thin woman who looked as though she worked long, hard hours. Her hands were red and dry and her hair was a lifeless brown. "Yes, ma'am. I came here with my daughter. We have to give that there scholarship back."

Lynn looked at Shelby as the young woman tried to contain her tears. "Let's go into my office." She led her visitors toward the back of the Philanthropies' suite and offered them each a chair at her small worktable. "Can I get you something to drink?" Both women shook their heads. Lynn sat at the table with them. "I didn't recognize your name, Ms. Snyder. I didn't expect to see Shelby today."

"She got her daddy's name," explained the woman, "Snyder is my second husband. And he don't want to pay for her college."

Shelby shuddered as she tried to control another sob. "He says he doesn't owe someone else's bastard anything." A tear tracked down her cheek. Lynn handed her a box of tissues.

She recalled Shelby's application. The teen was a very

gifted student with an outstanding GPA, obvious need and marvelous recommendations from her teachers. The youngster had indicated an interest in criminal justice studies with the idea of law school somewhere in her future.

"So we have to return the money," said Martha, "because she can't go nowhere to school."

"Have you given some thought to student loans or -,"

"We, me and Shelby, went to that Personal Finance Management place to see if we could borrow on something or learn to budget what we had and do it better," explained Martha. "But we didn't have anything that wasn't my husband's, too, and he wouldn't let us borrow."

"They did say they would loan us money," said Shelby, "but they charged such high interest rates and had very strange payment schedules that I told Mama we couldn't take the loan. It wasn't smart and I didn't think it could be legal."

"What do you mean?" asked Lynn hearing something that fit into Dusty's investigation.

"They wanted a payment every week. And the interest rate was very high." The young woman wiped her eyes with the tissue.

"Who spoke with you?"

"We talked to that Mr. Baikar. But I saw he's dead." Shelby looked at her mother. The older woman nodded and Shelby continued. "We talked with him in June right after school was out and I got all the financial information from college. When we realized he couldn't help us, we left his office. A few days later someone called us. It was a woman. She had all our information from Mr. Baikar and said she was a colleague and if she came to our house she would explain how she could help."

Her mother interrupted, "She said we couldn't tell Mr. Baikar because she was with another branch of the company and her work was confidential."

"She came and gave us the information and said we had to answer her right then," said Shelby. "Mama and I didn't like moving so fast. We like to study and think things over."

Lynn nodded and patted Shelby's hand as it rested on the table. "Can you describe the woman?"

"She was the blonde woman who was working in the office the day we talked with Mr. Baikar. I don't recall her name."

"It was Ms. Jones," offered Shelby.

I'll bet, thought Lynn. Aloud she said, "I think you were wise to avoid the financial pitfall of a loan such as you describe. But, I also think you have an option that you haven't explored."

Both women looked at her with restrained hope.

"Our community college." Lynn's answer didn't get the response she expected. She thought she better explain further. "Our community college has a college transfer program that allows you to earn college credit while staying here and paying community college tuition. You can take your first two years of college and stay at home. That allows you to work and save for future tuition."

Neither woman said anything, so Lynn asked, "Don't you want to attend the community college?"

"We still don't have any money," said Martha.

"Yes, you do." Lynn was emphatic. "You have the scholarship. In fact, I think it's enough to pay for almost your full tuition for one year. You'll have to pay the rest and pay for your books."

"The scholarship can pay for the community college?" Shelby's face was aglow.

"Of course." Lynn was catching her excitement. "You can enroll and give them your scholarship letter. Why don't you let me call the guidance office and we'll set up an appointment for you?"

Martha was now crying. Shelby threw an arm around her shoulder. "See, Mama, we just had to ask. I don't need to look to your husband for help."

The two women whispered with one another as Lynn made a phone call. "You can go right from here to the campus, the guidance counselor is waiting for you. I'll email your scholarship approval letter to him and it will be there when you arrive."

Both women were smiling. They stood and embraced Lynn. "Come back and tell me how it all works out," she instructed as she led them out of the office. After she watched them drive away she did a small dance around the office. It was always a great day when she had the answers. Then she stopped – answers. She better call Dusty and tell him what she just learned about Joseph and his company.

Chapter Nine

"**D**ad," whispered Piper, "are you awake?"

"It's about time you got here," the old man snarled from his bed, propped up on pillows and staring at a muted TV.

"Why?" she asked, "do you need something?"

"No, I've been waiting all day to hear about your mother and that body." Bri Llewellyn struggled to sit up straighter.

"How ..."

"I'm not dead or deaf," he reminded her, "I've just had knee surgery, and I've been asked by every person in this place for the real scoop and I don't know a thing. My family keeps me in the dark." He was winding up for a long harangue.

Piper said, "I'll tell you everything. We weren't here earlier because we didn't want to upset you."

"Upset me?" If he could move easily he would have jumped out of bed. "My wife living with a dead man."

"He was alive while he lived at the house," explained Piper, "he was dead in the barn." Bri was apoplectic. Piper placed her hand on his shoulder as she stood next to his bed. "Let me tell you the story." He scowled and she began.

"Since your surgery and rehab, Mother has been alone at the farm."

"I told her to stay in town with you." Bri smoldered in his bed.

"She is now." Piper gave him a kiss on the cheek. "Let

me finish. She thought she was going crazy because food was disappearing and things were moving to different places and she heard footsteps and noises. Lynn went to the farm yesterday to bring her to my house. At the same time Lynn knew that Dusty was looking for a missing man, so when she heard Mother talk about noises and things, she wondered if a person could be hiding at the farm." Piper kissed her father's forehead then sat in a nearby chair.

"I can't believe, as old as you are, you girls still get into trouble," groused Bri. As youngsters Piper and Lynn had caused their parents a fair amount of grief. These days their sons enjoyed the stories.

"We never murdered anyone," protested Piper.

"It was probably only a matter of time," countered Bri. But he squirmed in his bed and waited for the rest of the story.

Piper knew she had his attention. "Lynn convinced Dusty to go out to the farm and look around. They found a body hanging in the barn. It looked like suicide."

"Looked like?" This was the best entertainment Bri had enjoyed since he entered this dismal place.

"Dusty says there were no fingerprints, and that suggested the man was hanged by someone else. I guess he couldn't wipe his fingerprints off things after he died." Piper thought about that a minute then shook her head to clear it and continue her story. "But the other thing was, while Dusty and Lynn were in the barn looking at the body, someone shot his tire."

"That wasn't the dead man." Bri liked this detective stuff. He knew a thing or two about what a dead man could do.

Piper sighed. Her father was enjoying this too much. "Dusty's staff searched the house and farm. They figured out that the dead man had been sleeping in the attic. But they haven't found much to identify the murderer."

"Who was this dead man?"

"Joseph Baikar. Mother says he's the man that you talked with about borrowing against the farm." Piper looked at her father and raised an eyebrow – the same look her students knew meant trouble. "Why didn't you ask for our help?" Now she had tears in her eyes. "Your own daughter. You didn't think I would help you?"

Bri hung his head. "We can take care of ourselves," he mumbled.

"Really?" Piper's tone of voice challenged that idea. Bri couldn't look at her.

He sighed. "I put your mother in real danger because of my pride," he finally said in a low, sad voice. "It's no fun to get old. I used to be able to do so many things. I barely survived the workload for last season. I was thinking it was time to do something."

"Why didn't you talk with me and Will?" she asked, caught between anger and affection for her father. "We could have helped you find a solution. We wouldn't tell you it was our way or the highway."

"I know," said Bri, "I just never knew how to start the conversation."

She took his hand. "Why don't we start it now?" Piper watched her father pull himself together and sit erect in his bed. She saw the tough, independent man climb back into his skin.

Bri snorted. "I got ideas. I could rent my fields and I

could rent the farm. But I don't know what Glenda wants to do. And I sure as hell don't want to move in with your family and become a lump in front of the TV. And I don't want you to put us in some old folks home. And I still want to drive and go to breakfast at Joanie's Diner and meet the guys at the Feed and Seed," he looked longingly out the window, "and all the other things I do."

Piper smiled to herself; her dad was back. "We have plenty of space at our house for Mother to stay until you're back on your feet. In the meantime, you think about what we could do, together, to make your plans work." She stood and kissed his forehead. He grabbed her hand.

"You're a good daughter."

"I know." She grinned at him.

He pointed to the door as if to dismiss her then grinned back at the best project he ever had a part in – the cute little imp.

~ ~ ~

Another busy day wound down as Lynn and Dusty got ready for bed. They had come up to the room together to sit for a few minutes on the sun porch attached to the bedroom to listen to the crickets and watch the fireflies. "Did you collect fireflies on the farm?" Lynn asked as she snuggled against her husband.

"Hell, yes," grumbled Dusty, "and my brothers used to try to get me to eat them."

Lynn laughed. "Did you?"

"Hell, yes." He rested his head on her shoulder. "They didn't taste as good as you." He kissed her neck, massaged parts of her body and, in general, made her anticipate a lot more action. "I need to do something that's not related to a murder," he mumbled between kisses.

Lynn pulled away and scowled at him. "I'm a diversion? Why? Because I taste better than a bug?"

Dusty flopped onto the settee as she stood. He was going to have to warm her up all over again with some of his charming pre-love-making banter. He scrambled to his feet and wrapped his arms around her. Take two, he thought.

He rubbed her back and nibbled at her ear. "You smell good, too."

Lynn jerked away. "I forgot to tell you about one of my scholarship students. I planned to call you this afternoon but got too busy." She leaned against the windowsill and related the story of Shelby Bowman and PFM. "So all the stories about creepy loans must be true."

Dusty flopped back to the settee. "How did this murder get back to our bedroom?"

"I just remembered about the scholarship." She hung her head, showing contrition for dampening his firefly attempts at romance. "I had so much to do because Tim arrives tomorrow." She blushed as an apology. "I forgot to tell you. Tim's coming this weekend. Jason will pick him up at the airport." Lynn pulled him to his feet. "Let's go to bed and talk about something else besides murder."

Chapter Ten

The nursing home sounds filtered all around them as Janet Bergman and her father carried on their discussion. "Dad," Janet said, "I got that second letter out." She looked around. "I'm glad we were able to get you this private room."

Old Sheriff Bergman signed, letting his fingers dance across the bed sheets. When he finished he scowled at his daughter. "I know," she nodded, "it's too bad we didn't stay in practice. Spelling each word takes time." Janet's parents taught her to sign as a child. It was a game they all played. Janet was very bright and finding new intellectual challenges for a seven year old was difficult for two parents surprised by her IQ.

She nodded again. "You asked for a lot in that first letter. I'm surprised they ignored you." Bergy frowned then rolled his eyes.

"Have you heard about his murder?" she asked. Bergy nodded and gave her a look she knew meant *quit treating me like I'm sick.*

"But you are sick," she argued. Another frown. She conceded, "I'll see what I can find out."

Bergy made a fist as he tried to control his anger and frustration. Forty years in law enforcement and he never had to rely on anyone to do his investigations. And he never brought his family into any cases. But what was he to do? Tied to this bed, unable to speak and the only one who understood him was Janet, his smart as a whip scientist daughter who had no skills in criminal investigation.

But Janet always seemed to know what he was thinking. "It'll be OK, Dad." She patted his arm. "You'll have your voice back in a few weeks and Dusty will have solved the crime."

Bergy signed, she answered, "All I know is what I read in the paper. I know you don't think it's suicide, but you taught Dusty to keep his information to himself."

Bergy frowned and Janet laughed. "I accessed the PFM computer system a few times from my office. I can probably still get in. I'll do some exploring and see if I can learn anything."

With another flurry of signing, Bergy displayed his concern.

"All right, I won't do anything," said Janet, calming her father. "I'll wait for you to speak with Dusty."

~ ~ ~

Lynn was seated in her office talking with her sister-in-law, Salley Connelly, the wife of Dusty's brother, Carl. They were talking about Personal Financial Management. "It's all over town, Lynn," laughed Salley, "we know you're working with Dusty on this case, vacuuming information out of us nonprofits." Salley was the executive directive of the local domestic violence shelter program.

"I was subtle," pouted Lynn.

"Like a rock through a glass window," countered Salley. "But, to answer your question, I was trying to get Joseph to set up a presentation for my clients on how to manage what few resources they have. His agency has these little packets of checkbook samples and household budgets to handout.

We have a group that meets in the evenings working their way through the information. They just need some leadership."

"You should ask Piper and her investment club to help out," suggested Lynn. "They know a lot and might be less scary than a man doing a presentation to victims of domestic violence." Salley nodded at the suggestion as a man tapped on the office door. Lynn sprang to her feet and hugged him. "How did you get by my receptionist?" she asked.

He smiled sheepishly. "She remembered me from my last visit and just let me through your defense perimeter." Tall, dark haired and brown eyed, the shy naval officer blushed at Lynn's enthusiasm.

"You remember Tim Powers, my late husband's brother?" Lynn asked Salley. "He's in town for one of his visits." In May Tim had asked Lynn and Dusty if he could transfer Jackson Powers, his father, to River Bend. Navy assignments were keeping Tim from being a frequent visitor to the nursing home. Moving the elderly man to River Bend placed him near Lynn and his grandson. Lynn and Dusty were happy to help lighten Tim's burden as Jackson's only remaining son and a career naval officer.

Salley shook his hand. "I remember you from Jason's graduation. At first I thought you were someone here about that body." Lynn tried to quiet Salley, who ignored her. "We all want to know about the case and Dusty won't share any information."

"Body?" Tim was interested.

"It's nothing," said Lynn, "just one of Dusty's cases."

"Lynn found the body," detailed Salley, "and she's

trying to get information from everyone."

"Body?" Tim was really curious.

Salley sat back in her chair. "I want to see if you give more information to your brother-in-law than you give to your sister-in-law." She folded her arms across her chest and waited.

"Sounds good to me," said the brother-in-law. He settled in a nearby chair.

Lynn frowned at both of them as she brought Tim up to date. "We found the office manager of a local nonprofit hanging in the barn at the Llewellyn's farm."

"A colleague?" asked Tim.

"Sort of," admitted Lynn.

"Are Glenda and Bri all right?" asked Tim.

"They're fine. Bri's in rehab after his knee surgery and Glenda's staying with Piper."

"So, who did it?" asked Tim.

"That's what I want to know, too," seconded Salley.

"This is the beginning of the investigation," said Lynn as she rolled her eyes at both of them. "I dare you to ask Dusty that question." They all knew that Dusty never speculated, always reminding those who asked that guessing before all the evidence was in was a futile exercise.

"This will be a great visit," grinned Tim.

~ ~ ~

Dusty walked into his office after a tense meeting with the group of elected officials who were his unofficial advisory board and his very official bosses. He bumped into Jason rooted to the office floor. "Hey, Dusty," greeted the youngster, "I brought the biscotti you wanted."

"Thanks," muttered the detective as Jason stood nailed

to a spot while he studied the timeline board. "Don't you have a job? That information is not for discussion." Dusty glowered and Jason ran out of the office.

"It's not Wednesday," said Danny, "why the biscotti?" Everyone in River Bend knew that Dusty haunted the bakery on biscotti Wednesday to eat the broken pieces of Umberto's famous cookie. All pieces not acceptable for sale were usually claimed by the detective.

Dusty glared at Danny. Then he did a three-sixty so Mars and Teniquia could read his mood.

"The advisory board out-did themselves today," concluded Teniquia. Dusty ate biscotti.

"We've got feelers out, we're waiting for the tech information, some of it is promised Tuesday," outlined Mars. "We're ready as soon as something pops." Dusty ate more biscotti.

Finally, he gulped some coffee. "We're done for today. I'll be *on call* this weekend."

"It's Piper's party," Teniquia reminded him.

"I know, and she has chores for all of us," grumbled Dusty, "so I want *on call*. That way I can leave." The unit nodded. Piper's annual party took up everyone's time. No one understood how that had happened, but they all knew what they had to do, or else. No one crossed the tiny principal.

~ ~ ~

After leaving the Llewellyn farm, Al and Scotch did as they were instructed and stayed out of sight at one of the hotels near the Shaw County airport. Rupert Rothman, the executive director of Personal Financial Management and their boss, met with them late Friday afternoon. Looking over the papers the two men had retrieved from the barn, Rupert said, "This is what he took? I don't know how he figured this out. I hired him because he looked dumb." He studied his men. "You did the right thing." He shook his head. "It's been awhile since we had to off somebody."

"I ain't lost my touch," bragged Scotch, "besides I gotta stay in practice."

Al stood. "You got anything else?"

"Those nerds that watch our computers say someone has been nosing around."

"At the office?"

"No, in that cyberspace," explained Rothman. "Seems someone, probably our dead friend, must have let a hacker use his computer to get our business information. The girls kept her away from the other computers. They know no one touches our computers."

"So we go after some computer guy?"

"It's a woman."

"A computer woman?" Scotch shook his head at the mystery of it all.

"We go after her?" asked Al, "or can we leave for home?"

"Not today. Just stay here. I want to see how this all plays out. The local police came to the office to ask questions. I met them in court yesterday and convinced the judge to deny a warrant to search the office," explained Rothman.

"Are those office women going to talk?" asked Al.

"No," replied Rupert, "they're my people. Did you learn anything else at the farm?"

Al shook his head. "That Joseph fellow never said a word. He just tried to run. We did search the house.

Nothing there."

"One of the office girls found a letter on his desk," said Rupert as he pulled the letter from his jacket. "It was sent several weeks ago, talking about," he scanned the letter in his hand, "complaints from clients, unsavory methods. The guy who wrote this wanted to meet with the board of directors."

"What's his name?"

"Charles Bergman." Rothman slapped the letter against his hand. "Let's find out who this guy is." He pulled out his phone and worked the screen, then squinted at the results. "Can you read this fucking print?" He handed the phone to Al.

The man scanned the screen. "Shit. He's the retired sheriff of James County."

"And our computer hacker is a Bergman, too." Rupert looked at his men. "Stay put. I gotta think about this. You'll hear from me."

~ ~ ~

Since Tim was in town, Lynn prepared a dinner meal that they would eat under the trees in the yard beside the kitchen porch. Her father, Jim, and his wife, Marianna, joined them for dinner.

"There's talk all over town about that body," said Jim, his hazel eyes laughing. Dusty glared at him. "Do you want to tell us anything?" asked Dusty's father-in-law.

"Give him another beer and he'll break down," proposed Marianna. She was a retired actress who had come to River Bend last year and fell under Jim's spell, or as she liked to say, she found someone older than she was who still liked to kiss. "After all, Lynn's been talking to people all over town."

"You have?" roared an angry Dusty.

"Not all over," explained Lynn, "just a few agency directors."

Dusty reconsidered his anger because collecting information was more important. "Did you learn anything?"

Marianna laughed. "See, Tim, he runs hot and cold. As long as he thinks she can help we'll get some gossip."

"It's not gossip," growled Dusty. Marianna kissed his cheek as she placed the potato salad on the table.

"I've never been here to solve a case before," Tim pleaded, "Can't you show me how you work?"

"You were here in May when that woman attacked Lynn," Dusty countered.

"But I got here late. The case was almost all solved." Tim grinned at his brother-in-law. "This one's fresh." On one of his earlier visits he had been present as Teniquia tackled a suspect in Lynn's back yard. But, in Tim's opinion, that wasn't the same as being present at the beginning – when the body was almost still warm.

"Watch it, Uncle Tim," said Jason, "Dusty says we're insensitive when we get curious." The youngster piled food on his plate. "I keep saying it's not Mom's fault she's so good at finding bodies."

"More bodies?" asked Piper as she, Will and the boys trotted into the yard, trailed by their dog.

"Who asked you here?" groused Dusty.

Piper looked at Tim. "I keep telling Lynn he doesn't like us."

"I think it's just you he doesn't like," replied Will. "I'm his best pal." Then he looked at Tim. "Unless you're trying to come between us."

Tim laughed. He loved every visit to River Bend. "If you're his best friend, does he tell you all the clues about his cases?"

Now Will laughed. "Dusty's so tight with information, they have to pull it out with pliers."

Dusty had enough. "This body is only three days old. No one saw anything. He never talked to anyone. The ladies in his office know nothing. His apartment is clean although someone searched it. And Glenda is feeling great."

"You bet I am," called Glenda as she walked out of the house carrying more food. She kissed Tim on the cheek and sat beside him. "Do you want to hear my role in this drama?"

"Sure," said the eager visitor.

And Glenda entertained the family with all she knew while Dusty had a few more beers and felt sorry for himself.

When she was finished, Tim cleared his throat. "This may be a dumb question, but why didn't you just get a reverse mortgage? I've seen them advertised on TV. Or just a plan equity loan?"

Glenda patted Tim's cheek. "You're the first one to ask. And I'm sorry to have to answer you so publicly, but it's time everyone knows."

"Knows what?" Piper demanded.

"We don't own the farm or the house in town," said Glenda.

"What?" screeched Piper, "You're already in debt. How long have you been in financial trouble?"

"It's not like that." Glenda tried to calm Piper. "You own the properties."

"Me?"

"When you were born my mother was dead and my father was sickly. He owned the property. I thought I would inherit. But when he died, you were about eighteen months, and we learned that he left it all to you."

"Why?"

Glenda shrugged. "I think he wanted to keep the farm going and give you a legacy. He used to play with you every day." Glenda hugged Piper. "It all worked out. Bri was delighted to farm and we moved into the city house for the school year so I could teach and you could attend River Bend Elementary. All those years, I've just signed your name and we got along fine until we needed money." She put her head on Piper's shoulder.

"That's why you wouldn't take any money for the house when I moved back to town," said Piper.

"We would have given you the house, if it was ours," said Glenda. "Since it was already yours, we just didn't have to do any paperwork." She smiled at her cleverness.

"So what does this mean?" asked Piper.

"It means we've got to start paying the property taxes on the farm," groused Will.

Chapter Eleven

Saturday morning Tim Powers walked down the hall of the long-term care nursing facility to visit his father. Since his transfer to River Bend, with frequent visits by Lynn, Dad Powers seemed to have a little of his old self back. Tim knew that he shouldn't get too hopeful. A dementia diagnosis is final. Still, it was great to see a slight gleam in his dad's eyes.

As Tim turned a corner he bumped into a woman. "Excuse me," he said as he steadied her by placing his hand on her arm. Then he held it a little longer. "Don't I know you?" he asked. The young woman was slender with short dark hair, dressed in a polo shirt and khaki slacks. She was tucked in and belted, leaving the impression of someone buttoned up and very reserved.

She looked at him. "Lynn Powers' relative?" She squinted even though she hadn't worn her glasses since her Lasik surgery last year.

"You or me?" asked Tim.

"You." The head of short hair shook. "I'm sorry I always get distracted after a visit with my father. I'm Janet Bergman, a friend of Lynn's. I was one of the waitresses at the kids' graduation party." Tim pulled her to one side of the hallway to allow several wheelchaired patients to pass. "I remember now," Janet continued, "Lynn told me that her father-in-law is here."

"Yes, ma'am" replied Tim, always polite and reserved in

his military way. "She and Dusty agreed to this move because I was having difficulty managing Dad's care because of all the travel required for my job."

"If you like, I can visit him, too. I'm here every day to see Dad." Janet hung her head.

Tim studied this woman. She appeared to be a little younger than he was, but even more shy and retiring. "Don't you already have too many responsibilities? Children, family, job?"

"I work and visit Dad. I live with my mother." Janet shrugged, "Adding a visit to your father will liven things up." As she spoke Tim could see a loneliness and heavy melancholy in her face.

"Is your father in Dad's unit?" asked Tim.

"No, he's recovering from a stroke," she said. "He seems very alert but he can't talk yet and that makes him restless."

"How does he communicate?"

"When I was little he taught me the signing alphabet as a way to keep me from fidgeting when we attended functions." Janet wiggled her fingers in a signed greeting.

"Functions?"

"He was the sheriff here and was always attending dinners and other things. Mom and I went along for moral support."

"Wow! Was it like living with Dusty?" Tim's crime solving enthusiasm showed. "He always has a case."

"If you mean, did he always do background checks on my dates and investigate those he didn't trust?"

"Oh." Tim blew out his breath. "I guess that could cramp your social life."

"That's why I told you it's me and my folks. No one in

River Bend has a background that can survive one of Dad's inquisitions." Janet hung her head. "What did your dad do?"

Tim slipped his finger under her chin and lifted her head up to look into her lonely eyes. "He was an accountant for a small manufacturing company until they shipped the plant to India. Then he got a job as the CFO for our local school board. No politics. He just did his job. Come on, I'll introduce you." Tim said this as he placed his hand on her back and guided her in the direction of the lockdown wing. "Then I'll take you for coffee as a 'thank you.'"

Their visit was brief. Jackson Powers had fallen asleep, giving Tim the opportunity to point out some of the photos and mementos used to decorate his side of the room. As they left the lockdown, Tim confessed, "I can only get you a coffee out of the vending machine. You see, I walked here from Lynn's."

Janet thought over his offer. She hadn't given a man any notice since the hurtful episode last Christmas. She blew out her breath. "I can drive you to a coffee shop near Lynn's if you're buying. Then I guess you could walk home."

"I'm not being a nuisance, am I?"

"I've got time." Janet led him out to her car.

~ ~ ~

Lynn was working in her garden on a beautiful August morning. This evening everyone would be involved with Piper's party, so she was taking some time to herself. Tim was visiting his father and Dusty was helping at the farm. She was already planning the flowers for next year and was giving some thought to tomatoes and some squash when a man walked out of the tree line at the far edge of her property. He stopped and waved. She squinted at the figure then waved in return. The man started to jog in her direction.

"Gary," Lynn greeted her old friend. "I'm sorry about your mother. I didn't realize that she was ill."

"Thanks for coming to the service last week," he replied. "She had health problems but never told us. We were all surprised." He ran his fingers through his hair. "She kept telling me and my sisters that she was in great shape. When we asked if she wanted to move closer to one of us, she always said she wasn't ready yet." He frowned at his shoes. "I'll always wonder if we could have done more. Been more insistent."

"She was living the life she wanted," said Lynn. She was reminded that dealing with aging parents seemed to be on everyone's agenda these days. "I saw her frequently out in her old dinghy fishing. She and Dusty's mother always visited. She wasn't lying to you, she was doing well. Tell your sisters that she lived as she wanted to live and none of you should feel any guilt."

He gave her a soft smile. "She was the perfect mom. She even died without causing us trouble. My summers are free. I didn't even have to take off workdays. My sisters said the same thing. Everyone had returned home from summer vacations and we're waiting for school to start."

"What do you do that you have free summers?"

"I teach high school math and science in Charlotte."

Lynn laughed. "You almost blew up the chemistry lab when we were in high school."

"I've learned a few things since then."

"Still not married?" She leaned her rake against a tree and urged him to join her on a garden bench.

Gary shrugged. "I never seem to connect with anyone. And don't you make any suggestions. My sisters both have women they want me to meet."

Lynn laughed again. "What are you doing with the house?"

"We thought we should rent it for a year at least. That would give us time to settle her affairs and decide if one of us wants it for a summer home."

"That's right, those cabins," she nodded toward the tree line, "were all summer homes for families who liked our cooler summers." The cabins were six small homes down the hillside from Lynn's property. They had been summer cabins eighty years ago for families who wanted to escape the summer heat in the lowlands by coming to the higher elevations in towns such as River Bend.

"That's why I hiked up here to see you. I'm the one my sisters thought should deal with everything. I have to get back and get ready for school to start. So if you know anyone who needs a rental, refer them to me. In fact, if you find someone soon, I'll reduce the rent and they can help clean out Mom's things. We all took what we wanted."

"What about a property management company?"□

"No, that's too complex with contracts and all. I want to keep this informal. I don't think we'll go much more than a year. We'll probably sell it after that."

"I'll ask around."

He gave her a quick peck on the cheek and disappeared back into the trees.

~ ~ ~

"I don't want to spend the rest of the weekend in this dump," complained Scotch. "Maybe we can run over to that

Indian reservation and do some gambling." He was pacing around the motel room he was sharing with Al.

Al sighed. He didn't want to spend the weekend here either. There was this gal at one of the other offices. "We stay here until we hear from the boss." As if to grant his wish the phone rang.

"Meet me at the office in Mocksville," came the boss's voice. "We got a client problem you can solve with a quick visit."

Al grunted and hung up the phone. He made certain not to grin. That was the office he wanted to visit. The gal he wanted to, well he knew what he wanted and she knew what he wanted, no one else needed to know. He sent a short text message and turned to Scotch. "You got what you wanted. The boss needs us to talk to someone in Mocksville."

~ ~ ~

Sitting quietly at a table by the window in the coffee shop, Tim and Janet sipped their drinks and stared at life on the street. Finally, Tim asked, "What sort of work do you do?"

"I have a small online marketing site that helps local artists sell their work." Janet looked at him with a frown. "I also help Kevin. He has an IT firm and has many of the local small businesses as his clients. I write code, debug, personalize software for his clients. That sort of thing. And when they need me, I teach at the community college." She stared down at her coffee.

Tim was at a loss. He had expected a similar question about his work. But Janet seemed uninterested in him. He tried another conversational gambit. "How long has your father been in the nursing facility?"

"Three weeks." Janet looked at Tim. Her response was wistful and heavy-hearted. She explained. "He's been very influential in my life. I feel helpless and indecisive now that he's ill." She stared at Tim as she voiced this secret for the first time, surprising herself with her candor. "He always told me what was best, intervened in my relationships to offer opinions and sometimes helpful suggestions."

"He loves you," offered Tim.

"I hope so, because if he was just doing it so that I wouldn't cause him any embarrassment, that would mean he never really cared about me, only about his reputation." As she looked at Tim a tear appeared on her lash. "I'm sorry. I don't usually talk like this. I'm your usual computer geek, no emotion or people sense." They both stared out the window.

Tim said, "Had your father been ill before this episode?"

"He's been having health problems for several years. That's why I've stayed in River Bend. It all came to a climax with the stroke. I can't shake the feeling that my behavior last December brought on his stroke."

"Ah," breathed Tim as Janet's attitude began to make sense. "He's recovering then?"

"Not as quickly as he would like." Janet wiped her eyes. "He's an independent man and is frustrated at his helplessness. I'm frustrated because I'm being asked to make decisions and I'm not prepared. We never talked about these life choices. I never thought he'd ever be ill. Who thinks about these things with a strong father? Who suddenly knows how to cope with a frightened mother? I don't know anything. I'm a failure." Tim reached for her hand across the table. They were silent again.

"Parents are a challenge," Tim whispered, "I've felt like a failure having to turn to Lynn. She's my brother's widow, but has a new husband and here I am bringing her worries from her old life."

"If he could only speak," sighed Janet as though she hadn't heard Tim, "then Mom and I wouldn't be always arguing about these decisions. She doesn't trust my recommendations. Dad's eyes just jump from her to me and I can see his frustration." She twisted her cup on the napkin. "Signing is so slow and he gets so tired. If he could only speak ... ."

Under the circumstances, Tim began to think having Janet visit his father would be a hardship on her. "You're kind to say you'll look in on Dad, but you don't have to." He sort of half smiled. "Besides Lynn visits." By the look on Janet's face he sensed he had said something wrong. "I mean, you're welcome but I don't want my dad to monopolize your time." He had no idea what more to say.

"See," she snapped, "you're like my parents, thinking I can't make good decisions. I can figure things out."

Tim's eyes bulged open in surprise. "I didn't mean anything like that." He tried not to escalate her tension with attitude of his own.

"I'm sorry." She stood. "Thank you for the coffee." She ran for the door. Tim sat in the shop watching her car leave the curb and hoped she would be less confrontational when she visited his father.

~ ~ ~

"Lynn," Tim greeted his sister-in-law as he walked into the kitchen in The Heights, "I saw Dad. He looks good. I even thought he knew me for a minute." Lynn was touched by his optimism.

"I get to visit him at least four times a week. Several of my friends check in on him, irregularly." She handed him a beer and he settled at the table. Lynn liked having Tim pass through River Bend on a regular basis. He seemed to find a weekend every six weeks or so. But he was hinting at a sea assignment within the next several months. "Do you have plans this evening?" she asked. "We're going to Piper and Will's anniversary party. We'd love to have you join us." Since their marriage in August several years ago, Piper and Will had held an end-of-summer-beginning-of-the-school-year anniversary party for all of their friends.

"I only brought one other shirt." Tim looked down at the tired golf shirt he was wearing.

"You'll be fine. We're talking about a party that Dusty and Will are attending." She rolled her eyes. "They live by a dress code that's hard to insult." They both laughed as Dusty came through the door. Jason came in right behind him.

"I delivered a cake for Piper's party today. How many people is she expecting?" Jason found drinks in the refrigerator.

"Probably everyone she and Will know," offered Dusty as he accepted a beer from Jason.

"What about this dead body?" Tim asked Dusty.

"Don't worry about him," the detective replied, "my staff is working on it."

"How can they work on it?" Tim challenged, "Lynn says your whole unit will be at Piper's tonight."

"They worked this morning," replied Dusty. He scowled at his adopted brother-in-law. "You think this is like TV, all solved in forty-five minutes?"

Tim shook his head. "No, I'm just surprised at murder in River Bend."

"I thought Lynn told you about all her bodies," said Dusty.

"I know. She told me. Jason told me. Will told me." Tim shrugged. "I can't believe you let her find them."

"I don't *let* her find them. They find her." Dusty scowled at the younger man.

"How can they? They're dead," replied Tim. Dusty swore. Tim laughed. He enjoyed these visits. Dusty laughed. He enjoyed the visits, too.

"We're to be there at six to help set up," said Lynn as she interrupted the body talk, "Dusty, you're bartending and Jason's helping park cars." She looked at Tim. "You can help Dusty bartend. No one will notice your shirt." Lynn settled everything. The men moved out to clean up for the party.

~ ~ ~

Piper's party was unstoppable. On Wednesday a dead body was found at her parents' farm. By Saturday all seemed forgotten, because, as Piper told everyone, "It wasn't anyone we knew." Besides, as Piper thought to herself, it had proved to be the explanation for her mother's confusion.

So this evening friends and relatives gathered to celebrate Will and Piper's anniversary, the start of the school year, seeing the kids off to college, and, best of all, Glenda's good health. It was hard to be brought down by a dead body.

Everyone that Will and Piper knew came to the party.

Fortunately, the high school parking lot across the street had space for everyone. Piper's sons and Jason spent most of the evening directing traffic and having their own party out in the street with their friends.

When Tim arrived he shared a few words with Jason and his friends before joining Dusty at the bar on the back patio. The kids were really wound up. Most of them would be off to college before the end of the month. The gang all greeted "Uncle Tim" as he enjoyed the role of community uncle. He looked around; his gang of nieces and nephews seemed to grow with each visit. He shook hands and cuffed the guys while making certain he gave Patti Ann a hug and kiss on the cheek. She was the only consistent girl member in the gang and seemed to be able to keep the boys in line with just a look from those blue eyes of hers.

At the bar, Dusty kept hoping that his phone would call him to some emergency because he was exhausted trying to keep everyone in drinks.

Danny and Bertram Luft were providing the music, with a little help from Johnny, a young friend of Jason's who had become Danny's student. Tim leaned over to Dusty and asked, "Where do these musicians come from?"

"The one guitarist, Danny, is one of my detectives. I thought he only played cello." Dusty watched Danny play a guitar and wondered if he had his cello in the car. "The keyboard guy runs the Hunger Alliance." Dusty waved to Bertram who flashed one of his dazzling smiles. "And that young kid, Johnny, playing the other guitar, is a friend of Jason's. There's a long story there. Ask Jason about him." Dusty smiled at Johnny as he remembered how Johnny and another of Jason's friends helped the unit save Jason and clear up a mystery last summer.

The two men poured and refilled drinks and dragged out more bags of ice as the evening edged toward morning. Will checked with them often to assess their supplies and send one of the boys for more of everything. Tim had a sense of food someplace, but he never saw any nor did he have the opportunity to eat. "Dusty, I'm starved. Aren't you?"

"Go and fix us a plate. There're probably mountains of food in the dining room. Or look in the kitchen. There's probably more there." Dusty and Tim were tending bar on the patio in the back yard. Eager for food, Tim slipped into the kitchen and grabbed the first plate he found and began piling on food.

"Hi," he said as he came face to face with Janet. "Are you working this evening, too?" She looked at him with a glassy gaze. There were spots of cocktail sauce on her khaki slacks and her polo shirt was hanging out of her waistband.

"You don't want me to visit your father," she slurred. Swaying into his arms, Janet continued, "You're just like my father, always telling me what to do." Other guests were looking at the couple in front of the shrimp, angry that the food was blocked.

"Let's go outside," suggested Tim as he set his plate aside, "I'm tending bar."

"You're the help?" Janet was clinging to him because she was having trouble walking. Tim brought her to the bar and sat her on a bench against the back of the beer keg.

"Stay there," he ordered. "I'll get us some food." He motioned to Dusty and ran back to get his dish.

"She a friend of yours?" asked Dusty as Tim returned.

"Don't you know her?"

"Yes, I know her. I didn't know *you* knew her." Dusty raised an interested eyebrow.

"I met her at the nursing home today. She visits Dad when she visits her own father." Both men turned to look at the drunken woman. "Maybe I should take her home?" Tim asked. Dusty nodded.

Tim spoke very distinctly to the unfocused woman. "Janet, give me your car keys and I'll take you home." She stood and was fumbling through her pants pockets when Jason came to the bar for a soft drink. All three men watched as she moved from pocket to pocket, having forgotten what she was seeking. "Let me help you," offered Tim. He looked her over and determined that there was something in her back pocket. He reached behind her to pull out what he hoped were keys when Janet responded to his touch by flinging her arms around his neck and passionately kissing him.

Dusty turned to Jason, "Not one word to your mother." Then he gave the young man a look that made Jason run from the patio and back to parking cars. Dusty watched as Janet kissed and groped Tim. Finally he pushed them to the side yard away from the patio lights, as he said to Tim, "Get her home."

"But I don't know where she lives," he gasped through her kisses and feverish groping. Dusty grabbed a drink napkin and quickly sketched a map.

"Here's where she lives, and I added my cell number." Dusty rubbed his jaw. "Get her home in one piece."

"What kind of guy do you think I am?" Tim challenged the detective.

Dusty frowned. "I know. But she's never like this. Really quiet and reserved, kind of a nerd." He was trying to talk with Tim but Janet kept attacking, so Dusty finally just waved them away.

Chapter Twelve

The usual Sunday dinner prepared by Flora Reid at the Reid farm, for her five sons, spouses and grandchildren, was in overdrive. There was a lot of talk about Piper's party. Since Lynn had married Dusty, the Reid clan had become part of the extended family at The Heights, and by extension, part of Piper and Will's extended family.

"The food ..."

"... more than last year."

"The crowd ..."

"... bigger than last year."

"And you'll never guess who I saw ...."

"I know. I couldn't believe my eyes."

Carl, the third oldest of the five brothers, banged on the table for attention. "I have an announcement," he shouted as everyone made a comment.

"What can you say that would interest us?" was a question that came from down the table.

"Who cares what you have to say?" Another comment on Carl's importance.

"You guys having another baby?" shouted one brother. Carl's wife threw a napkin at him.

"She's finally leaving you?" asked another. Carl scowled.

His wife, Salley, took control of the conversation. "My husband," the brothers all hissed and booed, Salley ignored them, "My husband has been awarded the *Respecting History Cup* by the state Home Builders Association."

Cheers and applause. "It's for his work on Palmer Mansion. They're coming to town to make a video and they'll show it at the dinner and on the public TV channel all over the state." Whistles and more cheers.

When the noise died down Salley added, "And that's why he needs a hair cut." She looked at her husband and he knew there would be no discussion.

"That's marvelous," said Lynn as she tousled Carl's long hair. "You'll look even handsomer." Salley gave her sister-in-law a grateful look. "But when does this all happen?"

"A week from Monday, they're coming to town to make the video," said Carl. "The big dinner is in Raleigh in September. You can all come with us. I get a free table for my guests." Everyone agreed that was a great idea. The discussion turned to everyone's calendar.

"I want to be there," announced Flora, matriarch of the Reid clan.

"The girls can't come. They have schedule conflicts with things at school," Salley explained about her daughters. "But Way can join us because the dinner is at the convention center near campus." Way was their son enrolled for his sophomore year at the state university.

"How many seats at this table of yours?" asked one of the brothers.

"I don't know." Carl shrugged. "Just let me know how many seats I need."

~ ~ ~

"I DO NOT SNORE," Piper challenged her husband as they barged into Lynn's kitchen Sunday evening, followed by Tim loaded down with food, leftovers from Piper's party.

"I didn't say you snored," Will pleaded, "I said you

gnawed."

"Gnawed?" His wife did not appreciate this description, either.

"It's sort of cute," he said, "except when I'm really tired and you won't be quiet."

"Hmmph." She grabbed a part of the newspaper Dusty was reading then sat down beside the detective at the kitchen table. Will and Tim ran out to the porch to bring in more food.

"I'll ask you again," Dusty complained, "Don't you have a home? Because you're a pain in the ass when you come to mine." He tried to turn his back on Piper.

"This is Lynn's kitchen." Piper smoothed the paper on the table encroaching on Dusty's space.

Dusty made a big exaggerated motion of scanning the kitchen. "I don't see anyone here but me." Will came back in with mysterious foil wrapped packages.

"Hi, guys," Lynn greeted everyone as she walked into the kitchen.

Following Will into the house, Tim grinned at his sister-in-law and waved the food he carried. "We brought dinner." He loved his visits and was still laughing at the exchange between Piper and Dusty. "The boys are eating at Piper's with a dozen or so friends."

"We had a big meal at the farm," Lynn moaned as she rubbed her stomach. "You guys can help yourselves." She pulled out some dishes.

"I won't eat with them," scowled Piper as she gave Will and Dusty one of her evil principal looks. Then she smiled sweetly at Tim.

"What did you do now?" Lynn asked the husbands,

"Because I know Tim is innocent."

"I told her she's a pain in the ass," grumbled Dusty. "That's only because that was the nicest thing I could think of to say." Piper smacked his arm.

"Is that how you treat your students?" snarled Dusty. "No wonder you have such a bad reputation." Tim carried the food to the kitchen counter and Lynn helped him open the packages. Will added his packages. Lynn placed serving utensils in bowls and set them on the table. Will handed out flatware and dishes.

"I do not," screeched Piper. "They love me. You're the mean one." Then she turned to Lynn. "I told you he doesn't like me."

Lynn rolled her eyes at Piper's common complaint about Dusty. Then turned to Will. "What did *you* do to rile your wife?"

"I told her she gnaws in her sleep."

"You said I snored," countered Piper. She grabbed at a bowl of kale salad, piling it on her plate. Dusty scowled, but no one was certain if it was at the kale or at Piper.

"I told you it's more like a chirping," Will said defensively, "and usually cute."

"I don't make noises when I sleep." Piper made a definitive statement telling one and all that the discussion was closed. She and Dusty wrestled for the last of the corn pudding.

"Do you still make those noises?" Lynn asked her old friend.

"I don't make noises, besides Will said I sounded cute." Pout.

"I always thought you sounded like a chipmunk,"

offered Lynn to her old slumber party friend. "It was sort of cute, except when I was really tired and wanted to sleep."

"That's what I told her," said Will, grinning at finding an ally. He grabbed three sliders. Tim had taken them from the heavy insulated pouch and barely got them to the table.

Dusty looked Piper up and down. "You could always sleep on that dog bed in your laundry room. You're small enough." He turned to Will. "I bet that dog doesn't snore."

Piper whacked him on the back of the head.

Tim laughed some more and handed out beers. "I love you guys."

Chapter Thirteen

"What have we got?" asked Dusty as he walked into the office Monday morning and found his staff still discussing Piper's Saturday night party.

"That was some party," said Danny. "I never saw so many people who wanted to sing *My Way*. Did you hear the ob-gyn?" Mars and Teniquia laughed.

"And the food," offered Teniquia. "Even Lonzo couldn't eat another bite."

Mars nodded his head. "I drove a lot of drunk people home. I hope Piper finds someone else to do that next year. I never have time to talk to people and she had some cute new teachers there this year."

Dusty scowled at his staff. "The party's over."

"People wanted to sing that song, too," said Danny. The chief glared at him. Mars and Teniquia laughed.

"Do we have a plan for today?" Dusty asked.

"I'm spending the day completing background on our vic," said Teniquia. "He wasn't here long enough to build any friendships so I'm going to chat with his family and former employers. I'll be on this phone all day." She scowled at the instrument on her desk.

Dusty glared at Mars who said, "I'm spending the next three days doing safety presentations and trainings for the public schools." He blew out his breath. Dusty nodded. It was another task that had been given to his unit. At the beginning of each new school year Danny or Mars or

Teniquia presented trainings for teachers on various school lockdown and evacuation methods. It was a serious and useful training for which the Superintendent was always grateful. And for which everyone hoped there would never be a need. Later in the school year they would return to evaluate each school's safety and evacuation plan.

"I'll follow up on this Rothman character," said Danny. "And I told Mars I'd check with the crime techs for information."

Dusty frowned. The only other chore to be done at the office was paperwork. Every report seemed to be the unit's responsibility – the FBI wanted stats, the state wanted stats, FEMA wanted stats. Dusty swore and sat at his desk.

Members of the unit tried not to laugh.

~ ~ ~

Nathan Taft, Lynn's friend and a generous donor to the Philanthropies, walked into her office early Monday morning. "Have you heard the news about Carl and the Palmer Mansion?" he asked without his usual greeting.

"I have," replied Lynn. "Carl told everyone at our family dinner yesterday. All the brothers are interested in attending."

"That solves my problem." Nathan grinned in delight. "I've been asked to buy a table at the dinner since my house is featured in the video that will be shown. I didn't want to be sitting alone. It's a table of eight, so I can fill it with leftover Reids." He clapped his hands at his solution. Nathan, a successful businessman, enjoyed frequent visits to Lynn's office now that his nephew, Buck Rawlings, was taking on more responsibility at Taft Manufacturing. She delighted in his friendship and his charming shyness.

"That's great, because Carl was worried about accommodating the family. He asked Dusty to split the cost of an extra table to minimize the cost of the trip for some of his brothers." Lynn picked up her phone. "Let me text Salley. That will be one less worry for this event." Lynn tapped at her phone as Nathan waited.

Her phone rang. "Salley!" Lynn exclaimed in surprise. "Yes, he's right here." She turned to Nathan. "Salley's relieved and accepts your offer."

"We'll have a delightful weekend. I'll organize brunch for all of us on Sunday morning before we return home," said Nathan.

"How generous!" said Lynn as she smiled at her friend.

"Carl outdid himself on this project and once he knew Penny and Buck were moving in with a baby, he quickly redesigned their wing into a family suite that allows for a few more babies." Nathan rocked back and forth on the balls of his feet, excited about the thought of more babies at Palmer Mansion.

"I think Penny and Buck have to decide on more babies, not you and Carl." Lynn brought reality into Nathan's plans.

~ ~ ~

As Tim entered his father's nursing home room he heard a startled gasp. "What are you doing here?" demanded Janet, her face turning a deep red. "I thought you were only here on weekends."

"There's a storm over Norfolk and all flights are grounded. The student picking me up can't take off until we get the OK from the air station that the weather is clearing." Tim looked at the woman who had become very familiar with his body Saturday night. He was sorry that he hadn't been able to do the same with hers.

Janet sat at Jackson Powers' side, and held his hand. Tim was moved by her gentle affection for his father as she tried to regain her composure. She stopped, placed Mr. Powers' hand on the bed sheet, then self-consciously buttoned the top button of her polo shirt. "Did I, ah, did we?"

"You didn't," Tim said. "We didn't." He smiled to himself because he knew she was recalling snippets of Saturday night. She might still be suffering from a hangover. He couldn't help himself, he grinned at her.

She looked sharply at him. "Are you sure?" she demanded.

"I know what I did." Tim was distracted by his father who turned on his side asleep. Tim moved closer and whispered in her ear. "Do you want me to show you what you did?"

"No." She crossed her arms in front of herself and closed her lips in a determined frown.

"And you asked me if I had a place, so your father wouldn't find us." He moved closer still. "Then you asked me if I was kissing you only for your money." Janet gave him a look of panic.

"I didn't say that." She could hardly control the fury in her voice. She moved away from him and backed into a corner of the room, as though she were ready to defend herself.

By her response, Tim sensed the conversation had gone to a darker space, someplace Janet feared. He said softly, "Maybe I misunderstood." They stood in Mr. Powers' room without speaking. Finally, Tim said, "Thank you for your kindness to Dad. You'd have enjoyed knowing him in better times." They stood there longer.

"He does seem very kind, even in his condition. My father just fights everyone." She hung her head and Tim heard her sniff.

"Since I have this extra day, can I take you to dinner tonight?" he asked.

She looked at him then at his father. "Do I have to drive?" she asked.

"Maybe I can borrow Lynn's car. Can I call you later and settle on a time?" Tim asked.

As an answer she pulled a business card from her pocket. "Call the cell number." She sort of smiled as she left the room.

~ ~ ~

Lynn was disgusted with her investigation attempts trying to glean information about the dead man. All of the agencies she visited saw her coming a mile away. She didn't want to hear another comment about Mata Hari or Inspector Clouseau. Bringing her car to a stop, she sat and stared at the office for James County Council on Aging. This organization had just been awarded an administrative grant by the Philanthropies. The money was designed to help the board and staff reorganize after recent cuts to federal and state funding, while experiencing growth in the size and needs of the local aging population. The board would be revisiting its mission statement and strategic planning goals. Lynn hoped they would go into a virtual huddle and come out stronger. The community needed advocates for the elderly.

Walking into the office she was greeted by Vicki Gillespie, the executive director. "I was beginning to feel unwanted," she pouted. Vicki was in her early thirties, much younger than her clients, but she had the energy needed to be a great elder advocate.

"Why?" asked Lynn, knowing what was coming.

"I thought I wasn't important enough to get interviewed by the newest detective in town." She grinned at Lynn.

"What if I said I just came to take back the grant money?" Lynn was losing patience with sassy local nonprofit directors.

Vicki's face dropped. "Wait right here while I get the red carpet."

Lynn laughed. She was a victim of her own grapevine. Since taking the position at the River Bend Philanthropies, she had encouraged all agencies to stay in touch and improve communication with one another as a way to also encourage collaborations. Right now the grapevine was keeping up with her.

"You know the questions," she teased the young woman, "give me the answers and I'll be out of here."

"I think I have more to tell you than the others," Vicki said thoughtfully.

Lynn's detecting antennae vibrated.

"Come into my office where we can talk." Closing the door she said, "I saw you drive up and made us some fresh coffee." There were cups and cookies on a small worktable.

"You really must have something to say," Lynn observed.

She settled into a chair as Vicki began, "I've been concerned about that financial management outfit. I had an appointment to meet with Joseph tomorrow."

Lynn's eyes bugged out in surprise. "What were you

going to talk about?"

"Some of our clients have been advised by the outfit to get reverse mortgages or home equity loans. And for those it seems like the financial counseling worked. That's not the part I'm concerned about." She stirred her coffee. "Some of our clients have no homes. They rent or live with family and have very few assets. PFM seemed to find ways to help them."

"Joseph was doing this?" Lynn's fingers crept toward an oatmeal cookie.

"I don't think he knew what was happening," explained Vicki. "It seemed that if a person had no home, they were sent to another branch of PFM. That's where things get shadowy."

"Shadowy?" Lynn held her cookie in midair, concern at the corners of her eyes.

"And scary." Vicki sipped her coffee, then frowned into the cup. "Some of my clients were offered loans at outrageous interest rates. Many walked away because they understood the deal. But some were so desperate for money to help family or to pay other debts that they got pulled in."

"Why take on a bigger debt when you already have a big debt?" asked Lynn.

"I think those people are my clients who border on dementia. Sometimes they can think clearly and sometimes they are very confused. Whoever deals with them is very skilled in exploiting the confusion." Vicki hung her head.

"How do they keep up payments?"

"I think they sign over insurance policies or retirement accounts or even give family heirlooms. It seems these people take anything of value." Now she was crying.

"Are there any of your clients that you think would talk with Dusty?"

"I don't know if he would learn anything," she answered as she wiped her tears, "I can barely make sense out of their discussions."

"Maybe this incident will help your board work on developing a safety net for your clients," said Lynn. She always tried to find some positive aspect of any situation.

Vicki was pleased with the encouragement. "We've already started making some changes in the way we do business. We've just re-negotiated a contract with the Hunger Alliance for meal delivery."

"Will they continue to deliver meals to your clients?" asked Lynn. "I mean in many other communities that's a big job for the Council on Aging."

"It is," Vicki agreed, "but we've found so many other elder issues that need addressing that we're happy with this new arrangement. Bertram is so easy to work with. He purchases meals for so many people that our costs per client have gone down and we can feed more. That's the good thing to share with you today."

"What other services are you thinking of providing?"

"We're becoming elder advocates with a capital 'A.'" The young woman stepped over to her desk and collected some notes. "I've been organizing our information for our planning retreat in response to the Philanthropies grant." She shuffled the papers. "We want to work with people who have no family or whose family lives out of town. We want to help them with housing and care. We want to protect them from scams. Get into high quality case management for our folks." She hung her head. "This loan scam happened too fast for us to get organized. We also want to work with social services in identifying elder abuse."

"Abuse?" Lynn gasped.

"Some of our clients are victimized by relatives, usually by giving a power of attorney to someone who steals from them. Then, of course, there are those folks who are not fed much and probably nothing nutritious and do not receive medical treatment. Their caregivers," here she made finger quotes, "are trying to hasten death for some inheritance or are just using the client's income for their own use with nothing left for the aging relative."

Lynn patted the young woman's hand. "I see there's a lot more to growing old than I thought. Are your board members up to this challenge?"

"They are. Some of them have been doing a lot of Internet research. A few of them have visited agencies in other locations to learn what they can. And because of the grant we've contracted with a consultant who is coming to help us understand all these issues and plan the future of the agency. I think I'll have a lot of good things to tell you in a few months, but this PFM thing is something we missed." Vicki was silent a moment. "I think Joseph didn't know this was happening either until I asked him questions."

"Did he say anything to you?" asked Lynn.

"No, he just said he'd get me answers. That was why we were to meet tomorrow." Vicki wiped a tear from her eye. "I think that's why he's dead."

They both wondered if finding those answers had killed him.

Chapter Fourteen

Late afternoon and Teniquia was alone in the office. Her ear was numb. She had spent the day talking to people in four different states and had collected some surprising information. As Dusty walked into the office, she said, "This is a strange case, Chief."

He pulled up a chair beside her desk and waited.

She began, "I called his family. That was terrible. Evidently he called and checked in like clockwork, every Wednesday and Sunday. He'd missed three calls. That's why they reported him missing. They didn't have much to say about his private life. I think that's because he was a lonely man who had no friends yet in town. Then I started making calls to communities where this Personal Finance crowd has offices."

"You called the offices?"

"No, I called local nonprofits."

"Why?"

She shrugged. "That's a good question. At Piper's party I heard some of those executive directors talking about their contact with Joseph, and you told us that Lynn was approached by the local ministers. So contacting those nonprofits seemed like a good idea. And I remember that you told me to contact the investigator who called Lynn." She flipped through her file. "The nonprofit agency people out of town all say the same thing our people do. This PFM group doesn't talk to anyone. And the investigator, he's in

Tennessee. He says he started his investigation because of some people in his town complaining. But by the time I got to him, he had been silenced by his state's attorney general."

"Really?" Dusty was interested now. By this time the other members of the unit had settled at their desks listening to Teniquia's report.

"He said he couldn't get a straight answer and his boss didn't have the political will to buck the state guys. But he also said he didn't have a dead body like we have." She looked at Dusty. He took her challenge and dialed a number.

The staff listened as Dusty tried to talk with various state investigators. His last call went directly to the state Attorney General's criminal division. By the remarks they could hear, the unit members knew Dusty had hit a brick wall.

He slammed down the phone on his desk and swore in a low voice, the words coming in a tempo that followed the steady drumming of his fist on the arm of his chair. The members of the unit drew in their heads and sat quietly, waiting for the storm to pass. Finally he exploded in repeatable words. "I can't solve a murder in my jurisdiction because it might interfere with a case under investigation at the AG's office. Isn't that always the way – upcoming election and he wants to make a splash?"

Mars put down his pencil and said, "Chief, you've suspected that this is bigger than our murder because PFM has offices other places. Did the AG's office ask for our cooperation? Do they want any of our information?"

"They want everything we've got." Dusty was livid. "And they want us to stay a mile away."

"You want us to pack it all up, and me and Mars to take

it to them?" asked Danny with an innocent cock of his head.

Dusty swore again and they all laughed.

"Maybe we could just solve our murder and let them handle the tri-state investigation," suggested Teniquia.

"You know that crowd," blustered Dusty, "they want it all. Our dead body will disappear. Then next year someone will ask why we never closed the case." Now he was on a roll. "And we'll say the AG took it and the AG will say they never heard of a dead body, they were only going after white collar criminals. They don't do murder." The members of the unit snorted. Dusty paced the office for a few minutes to calm down.

Mars popped up out of his seat. "Penny Rawlings used to work at the AG's office. Maybe she has a friend who would tell us something."

"Don't forget to bring a baby present," Teniquia reminded him as he prepared to leave.

Mars rolled his eyes. "I already did that, but I've been promising Buck I'd visit."

"I hope he isn't offended that you're mixing business and pleasure."

"Find out what you can. We're taking Jason to college tomorrow," the chief announced. "While I'm gone get all these interviews done." He swore again, painting an unflattering image of those politicians who use crime to help their re-election. The unit tried not to laugh out loud.

~ ~ ~

As the family gathered in The Heights after work, Tim asked, "Lynn, may I borrow your car this evening?"

"Sure." Lynn was putting the final touches on her summer salad. Jason had come into the kitchen to inspect dinner. Dusty came in and went through the ritual of locking up his weapon and placing his phone on the charger. Lynn finally brought her attention back to Tim. "Got a date?"

"Yes." Everyone in the kitchen froze waiting for the rest of his answer. He swallowed then said, "I'm taking Janet Bergman out to dinner." Dusty gave a warning look to Jason, as Tim continued, "She visits Dad regularly so I thought I would thank her."

"What a great idea!" Lynn handed Jason dishes for the table. "She's had a rough year."

"With her father's illness?" Tim asked.

"No, some fellow she was getting serious about." Lynn stopped, thinking about her next words. "It was unpleasant, but it's too personal for me to tell you. She'll have to." It was settled – Tim had a car for his date.

~ ~ ~

Mars drove up to Palmer Mansion to interview Penny Rawlings. Buck drove onto the property right behind Mars. "Penny called me," announced Buck. Then he squinted at his old friend. "She said it was a business call."

"I didn't want her to bother you," said Mars.

"What business could you have with my wife and baby?" Buck didn't want the police dragging his little family into some sordid investigation.

"You can listen to it all," said Mars as he followed Buck into the house.

Penny and the baby were waiting in a small sitting room near the kitchen that the family had turned into a baby shrine. Mars smiled as he inspected the room – rocker, baby toys, baby supplies, baby bed – with late afternoon summer sunshine spilling over the place.

Mars greeted Penny and admired one-month old Olivia, but declined an offer to hold her. He took a chair as Buck pulled Penny and the baby to a small sofa where he could sit with his arm around both of them in case Mars went crazy. Buck stared at Mars, but was constantly distracted as he patted the baby bundle curled on Penny's shoulder or used his free hand to stroke Penny's arm or hold her hand. Mars enjoyed watching shy, quiet Buck in his new role as husband and dad.

"I just came to ask Penny if she could call some of her friends at the AG's office and see what's up?"

"See what's up?" Penny laughed. "You want me to mine them for information?"

"Sort of."

"Is this about that dead man in the barn?" Buck challenged his friend.

"Yes," sighed Mars, sensing that Buck didn't want Penny involved. "We've been called off the case because the AG is in the middle of an investigation, but we have a murder to solve." He shrugged.

Penny smiled at the detective. "As much as I'd like to help you," she said, "I still do work for the office and am under the same confidentiality restrictions as any employee."

Buck grinned.

~ ~ ~

When Tim arrived at Janet's place her mother answered the door. "Who are you?"

"I'm Tim Powers, Lynn Powers' brother-in-law. I came to take Janet to dinner."

"You look like you have more sense than that last fellow."

Janet's mother looked about seventy with frizzy white hair and a slight mustache on her upper lip. She was stocky, but compact, in a drill sergeant kind of way. Mrs. Bergman stood for no nonsense. "Come in. I'll get her."

Janet came into the living room followed by her mother. She greeted Tim, "I hope this is OK?" This evening she was wearing a variation on her khaki slacks and polo shirt by wearing khaki slacks and a somewhat dressy cotton shell with matching cardigan. Her mother stood close, listening to the discussion and studying Tim, trying to divine his intentions. The tension between the women steadily increased as they all stood in the room.

"You look fine," offered Tim. "Are you ready?"

"How late are you going to be?" asked her mother. "Where are you taking her?"

Tim asked his own question. "Do you have any suggestions for our dinner?" The woman shook her head and withdrew to sit on the sofa, picking up the TV remote as though she would be planted there until Janet returned. Through this exchange Janet stood at the door looking humiliated and angry.

"We won't be late. I have to fly out in the morning." With that Tim placed his hand at the small of Janet's back and guided her out of the house.

Once in the car, Tim asked, "Where would you like to go?"

"As far away from here as possible." Janet sank into the seat and shuddered.

"I don't live here, so you'll have to direct me." He gave her a sidelong look. "And I do have to leave in the morning, so we can't go too far." He gave her a soft understanding smile.

She straightened in her seat and said, "I'd enjoy a drive-thru-burger that we could eat in the park." Tim nodded and drove the car out of the neighborhood.

Chapter Fifteen

Declining dinner at Palmer Mansion, Mars stopped at Pedro's Casa for dinner in the courtyard, a perfect place to watch the summer evening traffic drifting through downtown. Staking out a table against the wall he caught sight of Michelle, the new wife of his old friend, H. Lawrence Grayson. Mars sighed. It had been a busy few months. Buck marrying Penny followed shortly by Michelle marrying H. Lawrence, then Teniquia marrying Lonzo. All of this followed by Danny's baby and Buck's baby. Mars was the last single guy standing.

Keeping an eye on Michelle, he watched her wander into the outdoor dining area. He waved and whistled. She nodded and made her way to his table. "I'm looking for Herbie," she said, calling her husband by his nickname. "He said to meet him here with a margarita in each hand."

Mars waved for a waiter and ordered drinks. "I just visited Penny and Buck and the little bundle."

Michelle laughed. "They *are* cute. Buck is so attentive. Was Nathan there, too?"

"Not while I was there." Mars stared at the beautiful woman and wondered, again, how Herbie got so lucky.

"He's as bad as Buck," laughed Michelle. "Penny just has to blink and they panic. She says they're even worse than when she was pregnant. And Nathan has learned to change diapers." Mars laughed.

Herbie walked up to the table and possessively pulled a

chair close to his wife. "May I join you two?"

"Not now, Herbie," replied Mars, "I'm telling Michelle all the nasty stuff about you that she should have heard before she married you."

"Just remember," said Herbie, "when your day comes I've got plenty to report about you."

Mars sighed. "I'd be happy to be in that position."

"No word from Nancy?"

He shrugged. "Maybe I'll call tonight." He sipped his drink as he watched his old friend hold Michelle's hand and stare at her in amazement. No one in River Bend was as surprised as H. Lawrence that beautiful Michelle consented to marry him.

From Mars' point of view it was evident that Michelle never gave a thought to anyone once Herbie came into her life. Shit. It was no fun to be the last man standing.

~ ~ ~

Guiding Janet with his hand at her back to a secluded table in the park, Tim said, "You're pretty solid. Do you work out?"

"Is that a line or are you just curious?" She tilted her head back to look up at him.

"I'm curious." They stopped at a table and put down the food. "You're too smart for any of my lame lines." Tim found a small towel in Lynn's car and spread it on the table for a cloth. He took out his handkerchief and wiped Janet's bench, then helped her settle on the seat.

"I work out," she said after a long silence. "One of the women detectives told me that I better do something at my age or I would be sagging soon."

"You're not sagging." Tim pulled the straws from their

wrappers and inserted them in the drink cups. Janet handed him a napkin and a salt packet. They unwrapped their burgers and looked up. Finding Janet staring at him, Tim smiled. It shed years and made him look like his nephew, Jason.

Hanging her head, Janet toyed with her food, sighed and spoke, "I'm sorry my mother was so heavy-handed."

"I think she's concerned. She doesn't know me."

"At my age, you'd think she would stop." Janet played with a French fry.

"Have you thought about getting a place by yourself?"

"I had one and got into some trouble." She stared at the river. "I moved back home because I became frightened and unsure of myself."

"Unsure of yourself how?" Tim held his burger suspended as he waited for an answer.

Janet weighed her words. "Last year, I was dating a man who had ulterior motives. He wanted to marry me and marry into our family business. I assume he wanted to run it. My mother's family has an insurance business in town. One of my uncles is the manager. My friend was hired and thought marrying me would get him a fast track promotion and partnership in the business. He pursued me with romantic intensity, but he was always a gentleman – more or less."

Tim had a questioning look on his face. Janet understood, and nodded, "Now my comments Saturday night make sense." She referred to her drunken concern that Tim was after her money.

Tim nodded. "I guess the money thing won't work for me now." Janet scowled. Then he asked, "So you found out about his intentions in time?"

"Worse. While he was romancing me, he exploited my trust, but never demanded anything more than some heavy petting," Janet took a bite of her burger, chewed and swallowed. "Anyway, while we were having this idyllic relationship he was taking out other women in the community and raping them." Janet shivered as she finished her tale.

Tim gave out a low whistle. "No wonder your parents are keeping you close."

Janet thought about what he said. "You're right," she nodded, "I have to be reminded at times that they were as frightened and deceived as I was. They're just protecting me."

Tim took her hand and asked, "What happened to the guy, to you, to the other women?" For the rest of the evening Janet told Tim the entire story of last fall and winter. He asked questions and made comments while the night closed in and the park lights began to glow softly in the dusk.

When she finished the story, she said, "I was ready to do anything he asked. I got my eyes Lasiked and my hair restyled and colored. I redid almost my entire wardrobe. I was changing myself for him and he was only using me."

Tim stared at her across the table. "I like your eyes."

She looked at him shyly and he could see the park lamp reflected in her gaze. "Thank you."

"Do we need dessert?" he asked with his shy smile.

~ ~ ~

It had been an entertaining night sharing dinner with Michelle and Herbie. Mars checked his watch as he entered his loft. This was probably a good time to call Nancy. With the time difference and the day difference between River Bend and Sydney, Australia, he had to plan carefully to make his phone calls match her schedule.

"Hey, Nan," he sighed into the phone as she picked up. "I'm thinking about you."

"That's what you always say." Her voice sounded reserved. Mars thought someone might be in her office.

"Can you talk?"

"For a few minutes. I have to attend a presentation for some people interested in our work on preservation of aboriginal oral history and artifacts."

"Wow, Nan. You sound like a real expert when you talk like that."

"Are you teasing me?" she challenged him.

"No. I'm impressed. And you should be proud to be an American and respected for the work you've accomplished." Mars flopped on a chair and put his feet up.

"Thank you," she answered in a voice that carried the warmth and affection he valued. "It's interesting work, and it's turned out well for me."

"So are you on track to be home for Christmas?" This was the question he asked during every phone call. Nancy laughed but made no reply. So Mars asked another question about her work. "Will you be doing the talking at this presentation?" He covered a yawn.

"Yes, this is the first time my boss is letting me go solo. He says it's for people from out of town." She was silent a moment. "Mars, I heard that yawn. Get some sleep. I'll email you about my presentation. Kisses."

~ ~ ~

Arriving back at her house, Janet invited Tim to sit on

the porch for a bit. "Mother will turn on the lights as soon as she hears our voices, but you're welcome to sit and enjoy this lovely evening."

Tim walked with her to the stairs and said, "Let's sit here." He dropped down on one of the steps. "I can't stay long." They sat for a moment and true to her prediction, the porch light flashed on. In the light, Tim turned and smiled at her. "She wants to protect you."

"I'm thirty-seven," Janet whispered in a sad voice.

Tim took her hand. "May I visit you and your mother the next time I'm in town?"

"I guess," she shrugged. "No one else in River Bend has any interest in me."

"I'll make a deal with you," proposed Tim as he brushed his fingers across her palm. "I'll take you to dinner next time I'm in town, but I want us to talk about all of your good qualities."

"That's a condition that's impossible to meet." She took her hand away.

"One of the qualities I admire, even after our short acquaintance," Tim said in a gentle whisper, "is the warmth and kindness I saw as you sat with my father." He stood to leave. "I have your card, can I send an email?" She nodded. He kissed her cheek and left.

"Wait," she called and ran down to the street where the porch light couldn't find them. "Thank you for listening to me this evening." She kissed him quickly on the lips and turned to go. Tim grabbed her hand.

"I have to go in. Mother will get curious." She left him in the shadows and ran into the house.

Chapter Sixteen

Nancy frowned as she hung up the phone after saying goodbye to Mars. He was persistent. Someday she had to sit down and think about her relationship with him. But there was no time for thinking today. She finished packing her computer and the projector, grabbed her notes and crawled under her desk to find her shoes.

"Ready?" asked her boss as he rushed into her office. "I know Americans like to hear our accent, but I think they'll understand our work better if they hear it from you."

"Americans?" Nancy slipped her shoe strap behind her ankle.

"Didn't I tell you? It's some group from your State Department working on cultural exchanges." Devon Chuddely straightened his tie and held the door as Nancy carried the paraphernalia out to his car.

Once in the car, she asked, "Who will be there?"

Devon slipped through traffic, skirted around a bus and said, "A small group of Americans. I don't have names. Our Cultural Ministry is in charge of this affair. We're just one presentation during their visit." He pulled up at a hotel and handed keys to the valet. "We're on the top floor."

"They won't listen to me," chuckled Nancy, "they'll be too busy staring out at the activity in the harbor." Devon helped with the gear and they were soon on an elevator to the hotel's presentation room.

An aide from the Cultural Ministry met them in the hall.

"I have everything attached, love," he said to Nancy. She handed him her power point and he disappeared.

Devon took their gear. "I'll send this down to the desk." He waved at a hotel staff member. Nancy nodded and looked for a restroom to freshen up.

When she came out of the restroom, the hall was deserted. She walked toward the windows to view Sydney's harbor. It was a glorious day and the Opera House sparkled. She squinted and could see tiny people climbing the harbor bridge. It always reminded her of ants crawling up a log.

"If it isn't my old flame." The voice was deep and almost leering. She turned and faced her old boyfriend, Cory Estridge. He moved to her and gave her a quick kiss on the cheek. "What are you doing here?"

"I can ask you that, too." Nancy struggled to keep her voice light and keep her balance. Two years ago they had been engaged. It ended under circumstances that Nancy tried not to dwell on.

"I'm part of the cultural exchange. My wife's father suggested that the group needed an attorney." Cory pulled his shirt cuffs so that they showed evenly from the sleeves of his suit jacket.

"I'm making the cultural presentation," said Nancy, willing herself to smile.

"You work here?" Once Cory had dismissed her as his fiancé, he hadn't kept up with her life.

"I came to visit my father and found this job. It's very similar to the work I did to help organize Taft Manor and Museum in River Bend." Nancy moved away from Cory. He was standing too close, almost as though they were back in their old intimacy.

126

Cory responded to her body language by changing his tone to something more reserved. "I'm happy to see you again. Can we have dinner or something while I'm here?"

"You're married," she accused him.

"And my wife's pregnant. But you're here and she's in Maryland." Cory frowned at her. "Nancy, I only asked you to dinner." The sound of his voice indicated that he was insulted that she had read more into the invitation. "Let's talk after your speech." He took her arm and led her into the meeting room where he proceeded to introduce her to the American delegation, saying, "I want you all to meet an old family friend."

After the presentation, Cory handed Nancy a note as he left the room with the delegation. *"Great job! Pick me up at the hotel at 7. I'll take you to dinner. C."* Nancy stared at the note but was distracted as Devon called to her.

"I'm coming," she answered and rushed for the elevator.

~ ~ ~

"So we wasted another weekend," complained Scotch about their time in Mocksville. "That guy left town. The office girls have no idea where he is. Did you learn any more info from that redhead?"

Al had intermittently been dating one of the PFM office staff in Mocksville. But he didn't want to talk about his private life with Scotch. "She thought she knew where he might be, but it turned out to be an abandoned barn."

Scotch laughed. "Barns. That's where we seem to be this whole job. Why can't the boss send us back to Tennessee? I like that night life in Nashville." He took a nip from his flask as they sat in the bar of an old Mocksville bowling alley, waiting. The early morning bowlers all looked to be about eighty.

Rothman slid into a seat at their table. "I found that guy. He's got his payment. But he's two days late. Go pick up the money and worry him a little. Not too much. I want him healthy enough to make the next payment." He slipped Al a piece of paper with an address.

"When we finish here, then what?"

"Get back to River Bend. The girls at the office say there's another letter from that Bergman guy."

"Did you find out more about that guy?" asked Al.

"Not yet," replied Rothman, "but I know a guy who can give us some answers." He left the men and walked out of the bowling alley thumbing his phone. He tried to remember what Cory told him about the time difference in Australia.

~ ~ ~

At seven, Nancy drove to the front doors of the hotel. Cory walked from the building and settled nonchalantly in the passenger seat. "I love these backward cars," he said acknowledging the right side steering. "Where am I taking you?"

"I thought we could walk along the Quay and act like tourists."

He reached over and traced his fingers along her thigh. "I thought we could do something more in line with our ..." He trailed his finger up to her breast.

"You're married." Nancy was gripping the steering wheel. "Do I have to remind you again?"

"Oh, Nancy," he almost seemed to sob, "it was such a mistake. Leaving you, marrying her." He rubbed his eyes pressing his fingers into his sockets, trying to contain his tears. "I can't even be sure the baby's mine. And there's nothing I can do. The marriage is a political alliance. Mother needs her father's support in the Senate." He took her hand from the wheel and caressed it, bringing it to his lips for a tender kiss. "I'm so miserable."

Nancy strangled a sob as she drove through the streets of Sydney. "We can go to our place," she said in a whisper.

"Our place?"

"Dad and me." She turned down a street and said, "Here we are." As they climbed the steps to the lobby of the apartment building, Zachary Rawlings came out wearing his tuxedo.

"Dad, I met Cory in town today," explained Nancy. "We were coming by to eat and visit with you."

Zachary shook hands with Cory, saying, "I'm on my way to an embassy dinner this evening. It's last minute. I always get calls because I have a tuxedo. I shouldn't be out too late." Zachary smiled, nodded to Cory and walked toward his waiting car.

Nancy turned to Cory. "There's food upstairs. Our housekeeper usually fixes a meal before she leaves for the day." The ride up in the lift was uncomfortable for Nancy. She was bothered by Cory's earlier touches. And puzzled by why she had invited him to the apartment. To her relief the evening proved uneventful. Cory talked about his job, his family, and the many friends they had in common, never referring again to his marriage. He never stepped out of bounds and was ready to be taken back to his hotel by ten.

As he left her car, he asked, "Do you have time to show me around this weekend? Some of the team members plan to do some personal sightseeing before we head back on

Monday."

"What would you like to see?" she asked.

"The usual, I guess. How can I reach you?" She handed him her card and he smiled a polite good night as he climbed from the car.

~ ~ ~

Zachary Rawlings walked into the embassy dinner still thinking about his daughter. He was disturbed to see her with that Cory fellow. Though they had been engaged some time ago, Zachary had never been happy about the prospect. The young man was reputed to be involved with some unsavory characters.

Zachary had heard at Buck's wedding about some of Cory's dealings and actions that were borderline felonies. Those stories had been expanded with information shared by some recent visitors from the states. And he had left Nancy alone with the unpleasant young man. He shook his head to get those thoughts out of his mind and to set his face in the placid – meaning bland – look ready for another diplomatic dinner.

During the meal he chatted with a woman who wanted to relate intimate details of a family crisis involving her daughter and some gigolo. "I tried to tell her, but nothing worked. She thought she knew best." The woman daubed her eye. "We'll survive. We're far enough away from home that the story may take years to cross the ocean, but it was devastating. Fortunately, he was easy to buy off and made no fuss when we claimed the baby as ours."

"Baby?"

"Really, Mr. Rawlings, that's what happens," said the woman. "We'll return to the states with a baby and a story about a failed marriage. I'm certain there are those who would love all the details."

Zachary wondered why he invited such personal confessions from anonymous dinner companions. "Has your daughter learned anything since you stepped in to aid in her cover up?"

"I don't care what she learns," huffed the lady, "we have enough money to protect her until she finds a presentable husband."

The conversation caused Zachary to do a lot of thinking. What should he do about Nancy? Offer advice about her renewed relationship with Cory? Stand by silently? Hope it was only a one-time event because he was in the country? It was a challenge. He had failed himself and his children when he suffered in silence as his late wife carried on her sexual activities. He thought he did it for the children's sake. However, lately he had begun to suspect that his children had learned about their mother's reputation since her death. Would Nancy even listen to a man, namely her father, who had had no courage to stand up to his wife in the past?

Zachary excused himself as soon as possible and returned home. He was delighted when he bumped into Nancy in the kitchen, ready for bed. "I'm sorry I was in a hurry and didn't visit with Cory."

"We ate your dinner and he went home." She rinsed her glass.

"How long had it been since you've seen him?"

"A wife and child ago." She dried her hands.

"I hope your visit was pleasant." Zachary was relieved.

"Don't worry, Daddy," said Nancy, "he'll be on his way home soon. Good night."

I hope that's the end of him, thought Zachary. With that final wish he turned out the lights and went to bed.

~ ~ ~

As Cory watched Nancy drive away, he pulled his phone and scanned the messages Rothman had been sending for the last hour. It must be important. It was early morning in the states. He kept his evening with Nancy light and friendly, knowing he had to return Rothman's calls soon. Cory sighed. The money was great but this guy could be a pain in the ass. Cory thumbed an icon, "Yeah?"

"Where you been?"

"I told you I was coming to Australia. I'm here now. You got me at a meeting with some State Department people. You got my attention now. What do you want?"

"Tell me something about some people in River Bend."

"Like who?" Cory found a quiet corner in the lobby.

"Bergman."

"The old sheriff?" sniffed Cory. He was a politician's son and knew the influential pols around the state. In the old days Bergman was a guy to know.

"Yeah. He's supposed to be in a nursing home or something. Has he got a daughter that does computer stuff?" There was some paper shuffling.

"Yeah." Cory tracked through his memories of River Bend. "She's real vague. Forgets to tie her shoes, but is supposed to be real smart. I never saw any sign of it."

Rothman breathed into the phone for a minute and finally said, "This Bergman fellow is sending letters to our River Bend office asking questions about our services and who is our board of directors. He wants to meet with someone. In fact, I have two letters he's written."

"I thought you said he was in a nursing home?" Cory was confused.

"My guys are checking on it. So what do I do about him?"

"He won't go away on his own," advised Cory, "He may need to be encouraged."

"What about the daughter?"

"I'd keep an eye on her. In River Bend you don't want to hurt women, everyone gets crazy, especially the detectives." Cory glanced around the hotel lobby and saw a young woman sway into the bar. "I gotta go."

"Don't take so long to answer the next time." Rothman was gone.

Cory headed for the bar and the swaying hips of that young woman.

Chapter Seventeen

Dusty dashed off some email to his staff with some last minute instructions for the unit. He would be gone all day, moving Jason to college. Outside Lynn and Jason had the car crammed full of college supplies. Fortunately, Jason's dorm suite included a TV, microwave and refrigerator, because there was no room left for anything but Jason, Lynn and Dusty in the big SUV.

"I didn't know you owned this many clothes," Dusty commented as he scanned boxes labeled underwear, shirts, sweats. "You always wear the same three things at home."

"Girls," said Jason as if to explain his interest in a variety of clothing.

Dusty studied the bike tied to the top of the car. "Why do you need this?"

"I can't have a car until my sophomore year," explained Jason. "I might meet a girl who has a bike, too."

"Is there anything in here to help you study? Or is it all to help you meet girls?" Dusty asked. Jason grinned.

Tim and Will stood by the car. Jason gave his Uncle Tim a shy hug. Tim said, "Good luck, pal. You have my email."

Will gave Jason a slap on the back. "Take care. You got a lot more junk than Doyle." Will was driving Tim to catch his plane ride this morning, but in another day or two he was scheduled to drive Piper's son, Doyle, to college. The two men waved one more time and left for the airport.

"I think that's everything," said Lynn as she put a bowl

of water on the porch for the dog. The dog had been adopted last year. One of Jason's friends had to move to another town and the dog needed a home. Chips had been an easy fit in the family. A lovable black lab, he liked patrolling the yard and sleeping on the back porch, as Dusty pointed out, the closest porch to the kitchen. Although he was alone most days, he was always waiting by the door as the family returned. However, Lynn had a suspicion that Chips traveled throughout the town, making friends wherever he went. She was worried because River Bend had a dog leash ordinance. But Dusty assured her that the dog was smarter than anyone responsible for bringing in stray dogs. "We'll be back by seven," she told Chips, patted his snout and climbed into the car. The trip would be a nine-hour drive to campus and back. Lynn thought Chips would understand if his dinner was a little late.

She climbed into the backseat because Jason needed the space in front for his long legs. He was now about eight inches taller than her, coming in at six-three. He might even reach Dusty's six-five before the growing was over. She didn't remember when he got so tall, but buying clothing for college had been an adventure. He was tall and thin. Nothing seemed to fit correctly.

During the rest of the drive to campus she sat in the back and thought about her baby boy and how he had grown and how she was proud of the young man he had become. It was a melancholy trip.

~ ~ ~

Rothman glanced into the motel breakfast room located at the airport near River Bend and nodded to Al. "Finish up," Al told Scotch, "the boss is here." The two men

136

hurried to the back of the parking lot where Rothman was grabbing a smoke as airport traffic rumbled overhead. He handed a letter to Al.

"This is the letter I told you about yesterday," Rothman said as he blew smoke toward the motel dumpster.

Al read the letter then handed it to Scotch. "This guy sounds like he's serious."

"For a retired sheriff, he sure is nosy." Rothman smashed the remainder of his cigarette onto the pavement. "I got some ideas." They all climbed into his car and drove away from the motel. Rothman headed away from the airport and away from River Bend, finally pulling into a small, deserted church cemetery on a country road.

As they got out of the car, Rothman lit another cigarette. Al and Scotch followed him to a secluded area of very old grave markers. "Here's what I know," Rothman began, "this guy is in a nursing home. He has the same name as the IT chick that worked with Joseph. So I had our IT people look over Baikar's computer."

"Did they find anything?" asked Al.

Rothman exhaled and said, "They thought someone was trying to get into our system a few days ago. They also thought that someone might be the same as before. I can't understand what he was doing?"

"Who?" asked Scotch.

"The dead guy." Rothman lit another cigarette. "I think he had this freelance computer chick looking into our operation."

"Aah," said Al, "he musta found something. All those papers we recovered."

Rothman nodded. "It's a good thing those cops didn't

get a warrant." He shuddered at the thought.

"So what do we do?" asked Scotch. "We can't go to no nursing home. We don't even know where it is." Sometimes thinking through a problem was a challenge for Scotch.

Rothman looked at Al. "You know our other business allows us to … ah … ask some of our clients for favors. I got a kid for you to see. Tell him he's behind in his payments and we either break his legs or he helps us solve our problem with this Bergman fellow." He handed Al a photo with an address attached, tossed his cigarette toward a headstone and walked back to the car.

At the car Rothman said, "I want you boys to come with me, first. We got a new client. Some old guy. I gave him some money last Thursday, and we got to explain his payment schedule."

"I thought the office girls handled this stuff," said Al. He didn't like hassling old people. They reminded him of his grandfather.

"These old guys need a man's touch. They think the girls are flirting with them or something. You won't believe it but they pinch the girls and sometimes propose."

Scotch guffawed at the thought. "Them old guys don't give up, eh?"

~ ~ ~

After school, Piper drove to the country club to get her mother who had been playing bridge with several old friends. She found Glenda chatting with a gentleman at the bar. Piper smiled to herself. Her mother was getting back to her old self, interested in her friends and charming everyone in sight.

"Where are the girls?" asked Glenda as she joined her

daughter.

"They told me they didn't have time to wait for you to flirt." Piper jingled her car keys.

Glenda rolled her eyes. "Like Bart needs to flirt." She tilted her head toward the gentleman at the bar.

"He is handsome," Piper observed. "Daddy might get jealous."

"Bri doesn't have anything to worry about. Bart has a live-in companion," the older woman snorted.

Piper squinted at the elderly man. "He does? He doesn't look sick."

"He's not sick." Glenda scowled. "He had someone move in about two weeks after his wife died. I can't blame him." She wiggled her eyebrows. "He needed help because of his eyesight and she wanted someone to look after."

"So he hired a housekeeper?" Was that what Glenda was hinting?

The older woman gave another unladylike snort. "Is that what you young people call a bedmate these days?" She pushed her daughter through the lobby toward the parking lot.

Piper almost choked trying not to gasp out loud. Glenda patted her hand. "You go back to your office and think about sex and us old people. What about Jim and Marianna?"

"I surrender," said Piper. Jim, Lynn's father, had jumped into a relationship with Marianna Pruitt only weeks after they met. Piper admitted to herself that she still had a hard time with old people sex. Then she wondered about her parents' sex life and what Bri's surgery would mean, she gulped and shook her head, a change of subject might be in order. "How was your afternoon?"

Glenda frowned. "We had a discussion about old age. All my friends seem to be in the same boat – health challenges, kids worried, loneliness. What do we do? And at what age should we make life rearranging decisions?"

Piper threw an arm around her mother. "You know we're here to help."

"I know, dear. I don't think your father and I are ready to have this discussion with each other, let alone with you and Will."

"Can I help?"

"Just let me think on it a little more. I'm giving it a lot of thought and your father is trying to block it out of his mind."

"Oh, Mom, you shouldn't have to make the decisions alone." Piper helped her into the car.

"What decisions?" asked Glenda. "I told you Bri's not ready to even talk about our future, so," she swallowed a sob, "so I guess we'll limp along until something even more critical forces us to make a hasty, or unpleasant decision."

"Oh, Mom." Now Piper almost sobbed.

"As long as we have you and Will as our safety net and our conscience, I'm sure we'll muddle through." Glenda secured her seat belt. "You adult children can be pushy and intruding."

As Piper climbed into the car, she thought about aging parents. Today it was Glenda and Bri. Tomorrow it might be Jim and Marianna. How can parents get old and keep their independence and yet be ready for the inevitability of aging? She shrugged to herself. A good question, but she had no answers.

~ ~ ~

Rothman and his team drove back to River Bend and arrived at Wendell Sarkis' trailer. "Hello, Wendell," said Rothman as he walked through the door uninvited, followed by Al and Scotch, "Remember me. I loaned you money on Thursday and we came to talk about paying us back."

"Paying you back?" asked the old man. "I thought you was giving me a gift."

Scotch opened and closed a few drawers and cupboards in the small kitchen. Al just leaned against a wall and played with a light switch. Rothman stubbed out his cigarette and said, "I brought my friends here to help you understand. I will loan you a hundred a month and all you gotta do is sign over your life insurance policy to me." Wendell opened his mouth to object, but Rothman continued, "I saw the work-up Joseph did for you. I know you got a policy."

"That Joseph fellow didn't say he wanted my insurance."

"Joseph ain't here any more. Now you're dealing with us big boys," said Scotch as he looked over Wendell's small supply of liquor, uncorking a bottle and giving a sniff. "You drink this swill?"

"That's all I can afford," said the old man.

"Remember," said Rothman as he held the door for Al and Scotch, "we'll be back Friday afternoon and you make sure you got your policy here."

In the car Al asked, "How do we make money on him?"

"Easy, " he signs over his life insurance to us and when he dies we collect. Joseph already had done some research. This guy has ten grand in his policy, plus some military allowance. We get the ten grand and we keep giving him a hundred a month until he dies. Usually these guys die within the year."

"And you get ten G's. Nice work," said Scotch.

"They always pay?" asked Al.

"Sometimes they die before the paperwork is finished and we don't cash in. I just move on to the next guy," explained Rothman.

"I guess old age is risky," concluded Scotch.

~ ~ ~

"I feel so old," sighed Lynn as the college campus disappeared in the rearview mirror.

"You look good to me," said Dusty as he patted her knee.

She smiled and settled into the seat beside him. This was the first time since their marriage that they were all alone. "You know what I mean," she said, "I never thought that little baby would ever grow up. And look how he turned out, tall, handsome and ready to leave me."

"You still have me."

She smiled at Dusty again. "After his father died I was terrified that I wouldn't be able to manage to be a good mother." She ran the back of her hand along Dusty's cheek. "But you came in and helped me through the rough spots."

"But there were times when I was part of the problem," admitted Dusty. He was remembering last summer when he and Jason fought daily and then Jason got lost on the river.

"But we got through it," said Lynn, "and our families gave us so much support. Your mother taught him to cook - -"

"Only biscuits," Dusty reminded her before she rewrote history.

"Will taught him to repair – -"

"Flat tires," said Dusty, "that kid has no mechanical

sense."

"Dad helped him learn about life – -"

"Your father took up cohabitation with Marianna."

"I meant that Dad survived cancer." She poked Dusty in the ribs. "Jason has a lot of character and a lot of talent. He was an athlete. He scored soccer goals."

"He was the only soccer player I ever saw who could trip over a blade of grass." Dusty looked at her out of the corner of his eye. "I notice you're not taking any credit," he offered, "like what you showed him about dead bodies and murder investigations."

She laughed. "These last few years certainly took us down a different path than I expected, but it all turned out for the best."

"He's a little loopy, but he's got a good heart and he's smart," observed Dusty. "He'll turn into a good adult and we can all take credit for it."

They rode a few miles in companionable silence, then, "What do you mean loopy?" Feeling a little melancholy made Lynn slow on the uptake.

"You know, spacey, klutzy, loving, happy. Danny says it best. He says Jason never toppled a wedding cake at the bakery, not that he didn't try."

Lynn threw back her head and laughed. "Maybe we should warn the campus patrol."

"I already did." They drove along in a comfortable silence until Lynn's stomach growled. "Let's look for a place for lunch," announced Dusty as he took the exit ramp. "Well, I'll be, one of the towns where Personal Financial Management has an office." Dusty careened off the ramp toward Mocksville.

Lynn gave him her special look that challenged his
motives. It was the look she usually gave him when he
walked in the kitchen, smelled what was cooking on the
stove and suggested that he had been hankering (yes, he
said hankering) for pizza for dinner. "Don't play any games
with me," she said, "I'm not the attorney general. I'm as
curious as you are."

"Great!" Dusty patted her knee. "Anyone asks, I'll say it
was your idea." Without any more pretense, Dusty drove
directly to the financial office. "You do the talking," he
instructed Lynn.

"What am I looking for?"

"I don't know. Talk nonprofit stuff." He pushed the
door open and she walked into the reception area.

"May I help you?" asked the redhead at the counter.

"Yes, I'm working with a group in the next county to
help people in financial trouble." Lynn smiled at the woman.
"This is my board chairman." She indicated Dusty. "We
thought we could get some organizational help from you. I
understand that you're a nonprofit, too."

The young woman looked at her. She closed the file that
she had been reading on the counter. "We've been advised
to watch out for people trying to get information because of
the murder of one of our staff members at the River Bend
office. I'm afraid I can't talk with you unless our manager
approves your credentials."

"Is he here?" asked Lynn.

"Mr. Rothman will be here next week. He says I can
make an appointment for next Wednesday for anyone who
wants any information."

"I see," said Lynn. "Do you have a website where I could

study the by-laws and other organizational information?"

"Mr. Rothman will give you all the information you need, once he knows that you're serious about helping people organize their finances." The young woman pulled up a calendar on her computer. "Can I schedule a time for your visit next week?"

Dusty grabbed Lynn and dragged her out of the building. He placed her in the car and climbed into his seat. As she complained, "You didn't give me a chance. I would have gotten something."

"You wouldn't have gotten anywhere. That woman had us marked when we walked in."

Chapter Eighteen

Much to Lynn's surprise, Tim sent an email on Thursday saying that he had taken some time off and was driving to River Bend to spend a week or two. Too bad Jason's already settled in college, she thought, he always enjoyed his uncle's visits.

Across the parking lot, Janet was coming apart, at least that's how she felt. Tim was coming back to town, only a few days after taking her to dinner. She didn't need another flopped affair, another intrusion by her parents into her private life, another challenge to her self-esteem. Sitting in Kevin's IT offices, she looked out at the parking lot and saw a group of people leave the Philanthropies' office. Some committee meeting must have just ended. Maybe she could go over and talk with Lynn and put an end to Tim and his interest.

Janet walked over to the office. "Do you have a minute?" she asked as Lynn looked up. It was time for a break. She smiled at Janet and nodded.

Lynn motioned her into the conference room, then walked back out to the main office and spoke with someone Janet hadn't seen. She heard an outer door close and lock. "OK, we're alone. Nelda's off to make a bank deposit."

"You know why I'm here." It wasn't a question, but a statement.

"No," replied a puzzled Lynn.

"It's Tim," said Janet. "He says he wants to see me this

weekend when he's in town."

Lynn nodded, "He borrowed my car to take you out to dinner the last time he was in town, didn't he?"

Janet turned deep red. "And now I can't get him to leave me alone."

"Why do you want to be left alone?" Lynn thought a moment, "Or you just don't like Tim?"

Janet looked at Lynn with very sad eyes. "How can you ask me that? You know my past, you know about Christmas. You've heard stories about my dad always intervening. Everyone in town knows I have no people skills. I make wrong choices."

"Tim's not a wrong choice." Lynn was ready to fight on behalf of her brother-in-law.

"But he may be for me," Janet shook her head. "How would I know?"

"I've always heard you refer to that deputy your dad chased away, but that was, what, fifteen or twenty years ago? And then last Christmas. What about all the choices in between? Have there been other men?"

"No." Janet looked down at the tabletop. "Just me and my folks."

"You mean between nineteen years old and last year, there have been no other men?" The tone of Lynn's voice reflected her disbelief.

"I was in school for ten years."

"What?" More disbelief.

"You know, undergraduate degree, original research, dissertation, doctorate." Janet rested her elbows on the conference table and stared at Lynn.

"You have a doctorate?" asked Lynn, wide-eyed with

surprise. Janet frowned as though insulted.

"I'm Dr. Janet Bergman, intrepid expert in *Nanotechnology Regeneration Techniques and Network Security*." Lynn's mouth dropped open as Janet continued, "There were men. I had my share of guys who thought a little sex would convince me to help with their research or edit a thesis, or something else that didn't have anything to do with building a relationship. All they were interested in was their own academic advancement. I finally let word get around that I didn't mind sex, but I would charge a fee for academic assistance. That ended my social life. Most men aren't attracted to smart women."

"I thought you just ran a little website selling jewelry and worked with Kevin," said Lynn as she tried to get her image of Janet to coincide with this new information.

"I have a national reputation in my field and do a lot of consulting, but it's mostly secret, you know, for the government." Janet shrugged. "I moved back here when Dad started having health problems. I make a great living and rarely have to travel. I work with Kevin to keep busy." She stared out the window. "Since I came back to River Bend there hadn't been any men until last year. And now Tim."

"Have you looked?" Lynn was curious.

"I wasn't interested. And sometimes I think my degrees put men off."

Patting Janet's hand, Lynn said, "Tim's smart, too."

"I haven't told him about this doctorate stuff." Janet hung her head. "So here I am, nothing to offer."

"But you're smart and cute. You run your own business. All your friends enjoy your companionship and your sense of humor. How often have I seen you make everyone laugh?"

"I don't make people laugh on purpose. Things just come out mixed around." She shrugged and Lynn laughed at this pure Janet-ism.

Janet sat shaking her head. "I have no qualities that attract good men." It was a final statement. Janet slouched back in the chair and folded her arms across her chest.

"What?" Lynn's screech made Janet sit up. "You have everything. And when you were in those dresses Sonny gave you, you were a knock-out."

"I felt stupid in those dresses." Janet looked down at her khaki slacks.

"You really looked good in that little black dress. But maybe the Donna Karan was a little over-the-top for River Bend." Lynn thought back to the day the investment club and a few others had made Janet model several dresses. "Do you still have them?"

Janet nodded. "I couldn't part with them. Sonny was so special." Janet had received some gifts from the estate of Sonny Bosco. A famous Hollywood producer, Sonny chose River Bend for her final days as she suffered through a terminal illness. In her final bequests Sonny had given special gifts to many of her friends in River Bend. Janet received several designer dresses far removed from her usual dress code.

Lynn took Janet's hand. "Don't worry. Tim is a great guy. He's just what you need to see yourself in a different light."

"Nerdy," stated Janet.

"Sweet and smart," countered Lynn.

~ ~ ~

Al and Scotch sat in their motel room, reviewing all the information they had received on the Bergman family. "This Internet really works," said Scotch as he clicked through information on the screen. "It would have taken us days, and probably some rough stuff to get all this."

"So his daughter worked on the computers," said Al, "The boss had someone look into them to see what she did."

"What could she do?" asked Scotch. "Here's her photo. She runs a website to sell arts and crafts. What could she know?" He studied the items on sale on Janet's website. "Who wants this crap?" He pointed to some handmade jewelry.

"Everybody has different tastes," said Al. He thought the jewelry looked pretty. It would look even better on the redhead in the Mocksville office. Another night in the same room with Scotch and he would so appreciate his lady when they got together again.

"What do you have planned?" Scotch asked.

"We already sent that kid to take care of the sheriff. We're going back to the neighborhood where the Bergman family lives. We'll do a little recon and maybe have a serious talk with the daughter."

"I don't like hitting women," complained Scotch. "My mother wouldn't like it."

"We don't have to hit her," explained Al, "we can just threaten her or her family or her cat. Look at her picture. She'll faint and then promise anything. Let's go. I want to stake out her house."

~ ~ ~

Last night was the first time since their marriage that Lynn and Dusty had been alone. It had been very sweet.

151

Dusty had almost seemed shy, finding that he could initiate a romantic evening in the living room and not worry about someone, namely Jason or for that matter any one else in the family, barging in. Lynn smiled to herself. He had even opened a bottle of wine. When they got up this morning he promised more of the same, saying there were a lot more rooms in the house.

Ah, romance. Tim and Janet popped into her head. What an interesting couple. Maybe Janet was the type of girl Tim needed – quiet, smart and ... and, Lynn hoped, Janet was someone interested in Tim. She'd stay out of it. If he asked for advice she'd be helpful, but with restrained enthusiasm. Romance ... hmmm.

She better get her mind back to work she reminded herself. They had taken Jason to school yesterday and she hadn't done anything since coming back from lunch but think about Dusty and this evening. She was called back to focus in her office because she heard a commotion in the reception area. Nelda was talking in a soothing voice, trying to comfort or calm someone. Lynn rushed from her office and found Vicki Gillespie from the Council on Aging sobbing in Nelda's arms.

"Vicki, what is it?" Lynn took the young woman into the conference room as Nelda prepared a quick cup of tea in the microwave.

"He's dead," she sobbed, "Suicide. Bertram called because the meal volunteer found him dead in his trailer."

"Who?"

"Wendell Sarkis, a man who receives home delivered meals," Vicki explained.

"Have you called the police?"

Vicki nodded through her tears. "I had to see you because of the note."

"Note? The victim sent you a note?"

She nodded again. "Not to me, but left it on his trailer door. He said he had no money and couldn't pay those Personal Financial Management people so he took all of his medications with some whiskey."

"Does Dusty know about this?" asked Lynn as she placed the hot tea in front of the young woman.

"He took the note." She placed her head down on the conference table and sobbed.

Lynn walked to the outer office and phoned Dusty. "Vicki from the Council on Aging is in my office – "

"I'll be right over," interrupted Dusty.

Within five minutes Dusty and Teniquia were barging through the Philanthropies' door. Lynn led them into the conference room where Vicki had pulled herself together. Dusty and Teniquia sat at the table. He pulled a piece of paper from his pocket. "This is a copy of the note." He turned to Vicki. "How did you get it?"

"When the meal volunteer got to Wendell's place there was a note on the door addressed to me. It also said 'no meal today.' The volunteer, bless him, knocked anyway and looked through the windows. He saw Wendell slumped in his recliner and called Bertram. You know the Hunger Coalition delivers our meals now. Bertram told him to call 9-1-1." She paused to wipe her eyes. "Then Bertram called me and we met out at Wendell's trailer. He was dead. The volunteer gave me the note."

Lynn took the note from Dusty and read it. The old man had started it with a pen that seemed to run out of ink and he had continued writing with a pencil. It was a heartbreaking confession.

Dear Vicki,

You been kind and kept me from going hungry. You saved my pride not letting my daughter know my straits. I can't make ends meet even with your help. That Mr. Joseph tried to help but when I called his office, they said he quit. Some other fellows came to see me and gave me one hundred dollars but said I would have to pay it back real soon, or they wanted my insurance policy. That money is for my daughter to bury me. They tried to scare me, those other two men did. I told them to come back Friday because I had to get the policy out of the safety deposit box.

I give this a lot of thought. This is my answer. Thank you for everything.

Wendell

Dusty held up another paper. On it was reproduced a copy of Joseph Baikar's business card. "This was in the letter. I've got the techs out at the trailer looking for finger prints."

Lynn asked, "Vicki, what can we do for you?"

"Nothing. The police said they would contact his daughter. I told them I would help her out when she comes to town."

Teniquia said, "I've already contacted the daughter. They'll be in town tomorrow. They live near Sylva."

Lynn volunteered. "We can organize a small service for him."

"I know his meals volunteers would attend. I'm sure his daughter would appreciate it. She's having some difficult times herself. Wendell told me that her husband lost his job recently." Vicki hung her head overwhelmed by the sorrow facing Wendell's family.

"Are you sure it's suicide?" Lynn asked Dusty.

He nodded. "Pretty much. The glass by his chair, his prints, all his meds. I just hope we get some prints that belong to the men he referenced in that note." They all sat for a few moments while Vicki sipped her tea and wiped her eyes. Finally he said, "You work something out with Tee. I want to see if my techs found anything." He left the office.

"Is suicide unusual with your clients?" Lynn asked Vicki.

She nodded. "It's high and many suspect under reported because coroners try to protect the surviving family from the stigma. You know, an old person, they can always claim some health condition and the family doesn't face the guilt." Vicki shook her head. "And I'm sure many people think, so what, they were close to death anyway."

Teniquia agreed. "I did some research after the call. Suicide is high for the elderly and especially high for men like Wendell, over 85 and white. They seem to have lost their support systems, suffer depression and may be isolated or estranged from their families."

"Men like Wendell," explained Vicki, "worry about becoming a burden on their families. In his case, he knew his only child, his daughter, had her own problems."

The three women thought about Wendell and others like him. Vicki wiped her eyes and stood. "This is another issue I want my board to face at our retreat. I don't know the answer but I work with some good thinkers."

Lynn gave her a hug and walked her to the door. Returning to the conference room she asked Teniquia,

"What does this mean for the investigation of Personal Financial Management and Joseph?"

"That's a good question," replied the detective. "I think I can get a warrant for the offices now if we're lucky and maybe if we find some prints in the trailer, we can put names to some folks for our case and to help the AG with his big case."

~ ~ ~

Monthly bridge night at Millie O'Hara's was a great success. Who could imagine that since their last game night Glenda would have experienced so much excitement! Although the club was known among the bridge players in River Bend as a very serious crowd, tonight was an exception. No one could concentrate. Glenda told her story at each table as the evening progressed, and by time for dessert, everyone had questions.

"He was sleeping with you?" asked Thel.

Glenda frowned at the question. "He was sleeping in my attic. I didn't know he was there."

"Don't you have a dog?" asked Marianna.

"He died last year."

And that was how dessert went, more questions, more answers and everyone in a state of delicious, vicarious fear. "This is almost like going to one of those horror movies," twittered one bridge player.

"How's that?" asked Marianna as she helped Thel Bergman retrieve her pursue from under a table.

"All spine-tingly." The woman shivered as Millie helped her with her sweater.

The women laughed and one by one said good night to Millie who was always a generous hostess. Marianna and

Thel were the last to leave.

"I'm happy Glenda has moved in with Piper," said Millie. "She shouldn't be at that farm all alone."

"I think she frightened Piper and Will," confided Marianna.

"At least her daughter can be trusted to take charge and think straight," muttered Thel.

"What do you mean?" asked Marianna.

Thel shook her head. "Sometimes Janet is just out in space. It was endearing when she was young, but with Bergy ill, I could use her moral support and some help listening to the doctors."

"Doesn't she see Bergy? Doesn't she help out?"

"She's very attentive," said Thel, "to both of us. She just won't talk with me about our future, even though, it's her future too."

Marianna nodded. "We aging parents can be pretty scary. Maybe Lynn and I can help you."

"You and Lynn have an old age plan?" asked Millie.

Marianna gave the women a sheepish grin. "I guess I should take my own advice. Some day soon," she promised, "I'll talk with Lynn about our future."

"Then you and she can talk with me and Janet." With that last statement, Thel turned toward the door and crumpled to the floor.

~ ~ ~

Lynn wasn't certain what they had been watching on TV. She had fallen asleep in Dusty's arms. She woke up because he moved from the couch and was closing up the house for the evening. "I'm sorry I fell asleep," she yawned.

He kissed the top of her head as he passed by to turn

out a lamp. "It wasn't a good movie anyway. Let's go to bed."

She picked up the throw and folded it, then returned it to the arm of the couch. "I still keep thinking of that poor man. So sad, and dying all alone because he didn't know where to find help."

Dusty pulled her into his arms. "We found some prints at his trailer and I think some of them may be related to this murder case."

She rested her head on his shoulder. "This isn't what we had planned for this evening."

"I've been thinking," said her husband.

"What?"

"I think I'll enjoy growing old with you." He turned out the last light and pulled her toward the stairs. His phone rang.

~ ~ ~

Two men sat watching the Bergman house. They had seen the old woman leave but hadn't seen any sign of the computer chick. Suddenly they saw her race from the house and jump into a car parked in a garage. The car sped out of the yard and headed out of the neighborhood.

"Something's up," muttered Al.

Scotch just snorted because, as usual, he had fallen asleep. Al slapped his arm. "Wake up. We got to follow her."

"Who?"

"Never mind." Al started the car and followed Janet.

"The hospital," observed Scotch. "Maybe that old guy died and we can leave this town."

Al parked the car so that they could keep an eye on Janet's car. Then they settled in for another dull evening, this time at a different location, the hospital parking lot.

Scotch couldn't sleep much because of all the ambulance activity. Finally about midnight, with the hospital security getting curious, the two men returned to their motel room near the regional airport.

~ ~ ~

Late Thursday evening Mars called Nancy. "Is this a bad time?' he asked.

"No, I have a minute," came her reply from half a world away.

"I just wanted to hear your voice," he confessed.

"You have to talk, too. Tell me what's happening in River Bend."

"Not much. We still have this murder investigation going on. You know Thel Bergman, she collapsed at the O'Hara's tonight and is in the hospital."

"She's one of Uncle Nathan's friends." Nancy was glad Mars couldn't see her as she looked at her watch. She was late.

"Yeah, he came to the hospital. Her husband is in rehab. He had a stroke several weeks ago." Mars sort of sighed into the phone.

"Sounds very small town, Mars." She packed her briefcase and checked the time again. She was to pick up Cory shortly at his hotel.

"I like these people," he replied defensively.

"I know you do." She hoped her voice didn't reflect the horror on her face that she saw in the wall mirror. "It's a life I have a hard time understanding."

"But you will, won't you?" The question hung between the continents.

After the excitement of seeing Cory again after all this

time, it was more difficult than ever for Nancy to even think about a long, dull life in River Bend. "I'm always thinking about it." She looked at her watch and panicked. "I have to get to a meeting, Mars. Remember it's Friday here. Talk to you soon." She was gone.

He sprawled out on the floor of his loft. Nancy was changing and he didn't know what to do.

Chapter Nineteen

Nancy called for Cory at the hotel. He said, "I met a guy who gave me keys to his flat, don't you just love that term, a flat at the beach." Cory handed her an address. "Is it far away?"

"Not really," she said. "I can take you. There are buses to get you around, and even back to Sydney." Cory had called inviting Nancy to dinner and a little sightseeing. Now he was talking about staying longer? She was confused.

"Great." He looked around her car. "Can you take me to get groceries?"

"Sure."

And that was how it all began. Within a few hours Nancy was in his bed, crying that she had somehow encouraged his infidelity.

"It's not you. I'm so lonely and miserable in my marriage. Trapped by my mother's political future." Cory had made love to her in a gentle, sweet, sad manner always reminding her that he had married the wrong woman and that she was a comfort to him even for these few hours. In her turn she spoke of Mars' attention and her determination to not become a cop's wife. It had been a long time since Nancy had had someone with whom to share confidences.

During the long afternoon and early evening, Nancy also proved to be a valuable source of River Bend gossip. When she finally told Cory she was hungry, he told her to rest and he would run out to get something. Nancy had spoken to Mars for five minutes and got all sorts of useful information. He had to call Rothman.

"You know what time it is?" the man growled.

"I'm never sure," came Cory's reply. "I'm a day or half a day or something ahead of you. But I got information for you."

"Go ahead."

"Janet Bergman's mother fell and she's in the hospital. Janet is alone in the house. But don't hurt her," Cory warned.

"We won't. We're just going after the old man."

"Watch out for that cop, Mars. He's real protective of his people."

"He's one guy."

"Just a heads-up," Cory tried to pacify his client. "I'll call if I learn anything else."

~ ~ ~

As they got ready for work Friday morning, Lynn said, "Sorry I didn't wait up. Marianna called before you got home and said Thel was fine, just low blood sugar, or something."

"There was quite a party in the ER," explained Dusty, "Nathan showed up. Your father and Marianna. Janet. They almost had to sedate her. Dr. Rita got everyone under control and calmed down."

She finished flossing then said, "I forgot to tell you Tim will be here tonight, again."

Dusty dropped the toothpaste in surprise. "He must enjoy it here," the detective mumbled as he pulled his toothpaste out of the sink.

Lynn gave him a speculative glance as she left the

bathroom buttoning her blouse. "Janet thinks he's coming to see her."

As Dusty combed his hair, Lynn's voice came from behind him, very close to his ear, "Are you going to tell me about Tim and Janet?"

"What do you mean?"

"Something happened. He's coming back this weekend." Lynn ran a finger along his spine. "And Janet came to my office yesterday to tell me ... hmmm ... I'm not sure what she was telling me. But you know something."

He sighed. This was another of Lynn's interrogations. "Damn, can't anyone have a secret in this house?"

"I won't tell."

"I thought once you got all my secrets, I was safe," he complained as Lynn tickled his ear, he swatted at his lobe, then surrendered. "At Piper's party Janet, ah ... er ... ah."

"She made a pass at Tim?"

"How could you tell that by what I just said?" He was mystified.

"I saw that she was a little tipsy that night, and Piper said that Janet had once confessed to losing control with too much liquor." Lynn slid her hands over imaginary wrinkles on his shirtfront. "So?"

Dusty sighed again, he had to report what he knew. "She might have kissed him and things. So I told him to take her home and behave. Jason was there and I threatened him if he told you."

"Tim would behave. You didn't have to say that," Lynn replied, offended at Dusty's lack of trust.

"You didn't see what she was doing," he pointed out. "I told you she was kissing him and things."

"What things?" Lynn whispered with her lips close to his mouth. Dusty started to demonstrate. But Lynn thought of another question.

"Do you think they did anything the other night?" She hoped it was a short answer because Dusty was making the demonstration interesting.

"No." Dusty moved his hands down her back, "Neither one of them has a place of their own."

Lynn felt sorry for Janet and Tim.

~ ~ ~

Running late Lynn dashed into the coffee shop for an iced coffee and spotted Janet and Dr. Rita with their heads together. "Secrets?" she asked, always eager to stay in everyone's loop.

"Mom took a fall last evening," moaned Janet. "She was leaving Mrs. O'Hara's after their bridge game and stumbled on something. She's in the hospital."

"I know," said Lynn giving Janet a concerned squeeze. "Can I help?"

Dr. Rita patted Janet's hand. "Thel'll be fine. Everything will mend. She'll just be in the hospital for a few days of bed rest."

"I never thought they could be so fragile," Janet said in tears.

"They're getting older," said the doctor. "It happens to all of us. Once she's back to normal, you talk to her and Bergy about their future."

"I'm their future," cried Janet, "and I don't know what to do."

"There you go," said Dr. Rita, "you have time to figure things out. I have to get to my office." She patted Janet's shoulder, grabbed her iced coffee and went out to face the humid August morning.

"Can I help?" asked Lynn, again.

Janet played with the tea bag in her cup. "Dr. Rita's right. I have time to think this through. She says Dad's ability to speak will return soon and Mom's new medicine regime will have her back on her feet in no time. I'll just do what they tell me."

"That's not what Rita said," Lynn pointed out, "She said the three of you can discuss this challenge together. I know your parents won't want you tied down as a twenty-four hour a day caregiver. My dad did that once for my mother. You can't do it alone. You'll need your family and friends."

Janet opened her mouth, but Lynn held up her hand. "I don't want to hear that you have no friends." They sat for a moment then Lynn said, "I need your help. The office computer is acting up."

"You're just trying to distract me," said Janet as she gave Lynn a squinty eyed look.

"Is it working?"

Chapter Twenty

Tim knocked at Janet's door a little early for their date. His plan was to start to make friends with her mother. When Janet opened the door she was wearing Sonny's little black dress. The soft, sleeveless dress dipped low in front and lower in back. Without even trying, the cut of the neckline seemed to rest just at the roundness of her breasts, discreetly hinting at the hollow separation between two soft mounds. The clingy fabric, lightly gathered at the waist, dropped to the hemline just above her knees, accentuating a curving female form. Tim studied her with a look that made her uncomfortable, but pleased.

"I thought you said you were wearing a jacket and tie," she challenged as she stared out the door.

"I am." He walked into the house and spread out his arms.

"Oh," she said, flustered.

Tim looked around the room. "Where's your mother?"

"In the hospital." Janet gripped the doorknob, ready to leave. Tim took another appreciative look at her and closed the door. Then he turned out the overhead light in the entry hall. Swinging around he couldn't find Janet, but finally located her sitting on the edge of a chair in the living room. He walked over and turned out the light beside the chair. Janet darted to another chair. Tim followed her, turning out a floor lamp along the way. Moving again she settled on the sofa, sitting tensely on the center cushion with her hands clenched in her lap. Tim sat next to her and turned out the lamp beside him. Janet moved toward the opposite arm of the sofa. Tim slid across the cushions after her.

She was soon wedged between him and the sofa arm. He put one arm around her shoulders then reached in front of her with his other arm and turned out the last light. The room was now bathed in the warm dusk lighting of a late summer evening. Tim's movement resulted in Janet being pinned to the sofa wrapped in his arms. She tried to get away. He held tight.

"I thought we were going to dinner," she said in a belligerent voice.

"Then why did you wear that dress?" he breathed in her ear.

"What does this dress have to do with dinner?"

"You look too good to take out." Tim moved his lips along her neck.

"Lynn said this was a good dress to wear." Janet tried to move away.

"She was correct." Tim kept her in his arms and felt her tension. "We could sit here and talk, you know, get to know one another." He nibbled her ear.

"What do you want me to say?" There was distrust in her voice.

"What do you feel like saying?" A soft kiss on her neck.

Janet's eyes popped open wide. "What do you think you're doing? That's what I feel like saying. I want to know why you're picking on me? I want to know your ulterior motives."

Tim pulled her closer and ran his hand down her hip and thigh. "I want to get to know you. I like what I've seen of you so far."

She put her hands in front of her mouth as he tried to kiss her, and she challenged, "You haven't seen anything." He wiggled his eyebrows at her and the dress. She pushed at his chest. "You know what I mean."

Tim smiled at her. "I like the way you sit with Dad. You share your patience and kindness with him. You don't expect anything from him, yet you find time to give to him."

Janet's eyes stormed as her hands pushed against his chest. "Your father isn't trying to get something from me. What about you?"

Tim said, "I'm jealous. I don't understand why you don't want to sit with me and hold my hand the way you hold his, and why you don't want to know anything about me."

"In my limited experience with men, none of you stays around long enough to do more than ..." she shrugged, "... and you're not acting like you want me to hold your hand." She clamped her mouth shut and crossed her arms in front of her, angry, and now, silent.

Tim got to his feet and began to pace the room. "I thought I was a distrustful person. You have me beat by a mile." He continued to pace stepping on the light squares created on the floor by the streetlights shining in as dusk settled. "You're the first woman in three years that has interested me. And it's because you're kind to Dad."

"I have other qualities," she pouted.

"I know you do, I experienced some of them at Piper's party." Tim watched her as she slipped off her shoes and drew her legs up under her. She looked down at her hands. Tim sat beside her and, putting his finger under her chin, lifted her to face him. Janet still had a frown deep in her eyes.

Her voice was quiet as she talked almost to herself. "My father warned me that men only want my body, no one would appreciate my brain and my humor." Bobbing her head at Tim she said, "I can be pretty funny." Then her eyes seemed to focus on a distant thought. "Why haven't you dated for three years?"

Tim was startled by the change of direction in her thinking process. "I dated. I never got involved for more than a few dates."

"Why?" Her voice had an analytical tone.

"The woman I had dated for five years threw me out. It was very painful. I came back from sea duty and found another man in our bed."

"Were you married to her?"

"No. She had convinced me that marriage was for people who didn't trust one another." He shrugged.

"What's wrong with you?" Janet gasped then reframed her question, "I mean why did she leave you?"

"She said I was boring, that I didn't understand her and that she had heard I dated around when I was away from her." He blew out a breath.

"Did you?"

"No."

Janet sat back on the couch, still with her legs under her, thinking about what Tim had revealed. He sat beside her, with his legs thrust out on the floor and his ankles crossed. "Are you ready to go to dinner?" he finally asked.

"Are you?" she whispered, sitting like a statute in the corner of the couch. "I remember kissing you at Piper's. You didn't take advantage." Janet touched his cheek. Tim held his breath, hopeful about the direction this conversation was taking. The house phone rang.

Racing into the kitchen Janet grabbed the receiver from the wall phone. "Hello ... This is she." There was a gasp. Her voice carried worry. Tim heard it all the way in the living room and rushed into the kitchen. Janet was ending the conversation, "I'll be right there." Hanging up the phone, she turned to him. "Something happened to Dad. I have to go."

"I'll go with you." He was smoothing out his shirt and straightening his tie.

"I have to change."

"Why?" Tim grabbed her hand. "They want you there now. Come on."

~ ~ ~

Mutt Mason sat in a chair with a bag of ice on his eye, his elbows on the table in one of the nursing home conference rooms. His mother hovered over him as Dusty tried to make some sense of the situation. "Let me get this straight," he started, "you walked into Bergy's room and someone was wrapping a scarf around his neck?"

"Yes," sobbed Mutt, his dark skin turning darker around his eye. "I yelled and I jumped him. Not Bergy – the other guy."

"I understand." Dusty patted the young orderly on the shoulder as his mother hovered. "The doctor's checked out Bergy. He says there's no damage. You got there in time."

"Honey, you want me to make you some tea?" his mother asked.

"Please, ma'am," replied Mutt, "I could use something

to calm down." She hurried off.

"Does your mother work here?" asked Dusty.

"Yes, she's a cook. She got me this job." He shifted the ice pack around his face.

"You looked after Bergy tonight," Dusty patted his shoulder again. "Did you know the fellow who attacked him?"

"He looked familiar, Mr. Dusty." Mutt closed his eyes and thought. "He might have been in school with me, only older. He was a white boy with shaggy dark blond hair. He had a pierced nose. You know right here." Mutt ran his finger along his nostril. "When I yelled he threw a water pitcher at me, I ducked and he ran out. I chased him and he slugged me. Then he kept going, right through the kitchen like he knew his way around here."

"It wasn't someone who worked here in the past?"

"I don't know. I've only been here since graduation," said the young man who had graduated from high school in May with Jason. "I just work nights and weekends."

Mrs. Mason returned with tea for Mutt and Dusty. She sat at the table and Dusty asked her, "Did you see the attacker run through the kitchen?"

"No, I was out making certain the dining room was ready for breakfast. I was ready to go home." She was distressed at her son's condition.

"This is the second time he's been a hero," Dusty reminded her about that summer a year ago when Mutt helped rescue Jason. "You must have raised him right." She smiled. The detective clasped her hand and told Mutt to stay available for more questions.

"I'll be here," the young man replied, "we're short-handed tonight."

~ ~ ~

Arriving at the nursing home, Janet and Tim rushed toward the lobby to sign in and gain access to the patients' rooms. There was a patrol officer at the entrance, pacing back and forth, talking on his radio and glancing out into the night. "Good, you're here," he said as Janet entered. "Dusty wanted to know when you got here."

The information from the officer sent Janet into a panic. Tim placed his arm around her shoulders and could feel her quaking tension. The officer notified Dusty and they all waited until the detective came from the nursing wing to admit them.

"Thanks for getting here so soon." Dusty nodded to them. "Your father was attacked this evening." Janet sagged into Tim as he held her with both arms. "We're not certain what happened except that one of the orderlies surprised the attacker. We got called." Janet tried to speak, but Dusty made a gesture to be calm. "Your dad's fine, he's sleeping, but the rules here say that you have to be notified."

"They have rules for attempted murder?" Janet might be nervous but she could still follow a logical thought. Tim tried not to laugh.

Dusty sighed. "No, they have rules for general incidents when families should be notified." The detective stopped for a moment and looked at the woman in front of him. She looked pretty good in that sort of dress, and Tim looked really interested. Dusty wondered how long it would take Lynn to sniff out this little arrangement.

As he stood there thinking, Lynn and Piper came out of the rehab wing of the facility. "Dusty?" Lynn called, "What's going on?" He had forgotten that the two women were in the building visiting Bri. Then Lynn noticed Janet and Tim and decided not to ask any more questions. Piper, on the other hand, wanted answers now.

"What are you two doing here?" Piper stared at Janet. "You look great in that dress by the way." Then she looked at Tim with one of her elementary school principal stares. Tim looked at the floor.

Dusty motioned all of them to follow him. He knew that this might be an investigation, but Lynn and Piper would not be put off by professional standards. They were there and they were going to hear the story.

Once everyone was seated in the small interview room, Dusty began, "A few days ago, the sheriff," everyone knew the sheriff was Janet's father, Bergy, the man who had been sheriff for thirty years in James County and out of office for five, "sent me a message that he wanted to see me."

"He can hardly talk." Janet was following the story and indicated that it was not computing.

"Mutt called me."

"Can you trust him?" Janet was getting picky.

"Do you want to hear my report or do you want to argue?" Dusty glared at her. Lynn, Piper and Tim glared at him. Janet had more friends in this fight than Dusty so he changed his tone. "Let me finish, then ask your questions," he offered in a much kinder voice. Janet nodded. Tim took Janet's hand and Lynn lost interest in Dusty's report. Things were getting more interesting right in front of her.

"I got the message and told Mutt to tell Bergy I would be here on Saturday morning, that's tomorrow. In the meantime, I asked Mutt to keep an eye on him. Neither one of us knew what he wanted. It had been a struggle for Mutt just to understand the request to see me."

Dusty stood and closed the door to the room, then he described the assault that had taken place earlier in the evening. "I've got a guard at the room tonight and his wing is locked down. Anyone coming to see a resident is being advised that tonight and tomorrow visits will be restricted. Notices have been posted on the entry doors that there is a virus going through the facility. We promised the director that friends and family can come back after lunch tomorrow. But I'm keeping a guard in Bergy's room." He looked at Janet with a soft smile. "His old deputies are all volunteering to take a shift." Janet smiled back at the detective.

"Why?" asked Lynn. Dusty looked at her and she closed her mouth.

"All I know is that Bergy wants to see me. When he wakes up tomorrow, I'll be here." There was a knock at the door and Mutt Mason stuck his head into the room.

"Mr. Dusty, my man won't settle, he keeps trying to say your name." Then the young black man smiled at Lynn. "Hey, Ms. Powers, you working on this case, too?"

"This case, too?" echoed Tim.

Lynn smiled at Mutt. "That's Jason's Uncle Tim."

"Hey, Uncle Tim. You look just like Jason." Mutt opened the door wide as Dusty stood to leave.

"I'm coming, too," said Janet. Tim stood to follow her. Dusty gave one look at Lynn and she knew that she and Piper better stay seated as Mutt led the other three back to Bergy's room.

Chapter Twenty-One

The old sheriff's eyes lit up when Janet came into his room followed by Dusty. Then his eyes became curious as he wondered who the stranger was. Tim took a place against a far wall. Janet went to her father and kissed his forehead. His fingers were dancing on his chest and he was trying to speak, fighting against the aftereffects of a stroke still controlling his body.

"I'm here, Sheriff," announced Dusty as he closed the door to the room. "Janet came to help me." The sheriff's eyebrows contracted in a question. Dusty seemed to understand. "Don't worry we'll see that she's safe." Dusty nodded to Tim. "He's volunteered to keep an eye on her." Dusty saw Tim blush, as he confirmed Dusty's statement with a nod. Bergy's fingers continued to fidget.

"He's signing," said Janet. Dusty looked at her. She explained, "It's just the alphabet, but he's signing." Janet blew out her breath. "Get me some paper." Dusty handed her his notepad. She stared at her father's hand and jotted words on the paper. Making a settling gesture, Janet said, "Dad, let me repeat this message." The man seemed to nod. "Fraud. Company bogus. Losing life savings." Bergy's fingers jittered. Janet turned to Dusty. "He says that's correct and there's more." Dusty nodded and Janet held the notepad ready. The sheriff started signing again. Finally, she said, "He says that he has heard several patients and their families talk about losing assets to a fake financial management company."

"Does the name Personal Financial Management sound familiar?" asked Dusty.

"That's it!" Janet gasped as she watched her father's hand.

"What's he heard?" asked Dusty.

"He says they're doing the damage. I helped him send them two letters asking for a meeting," said Janet.

Dusty thought about what she said, and asked, "Do you have the information he's referring to?"

She shook her head. "He hears people say things, but can't ask questions so I helped him form a letter, or letters, sort of vague but asking questions about their lending practices. We haven't gotten an answer."

Dusty put his hand on Bergy's shoulder. "Thanks, Sheriff, it fits into another investigation we're working on. I'll keep you informed. You just tell Mutt when you need me." Dusty turned to Janet. "Visit with your father a minute, then see me before you leave." He left the room.

Bergy's fingers were moving rapidly along his bed sheet. "Dad, I can't answer that." Janet shook her head. "I'll come by and we'll talk tomorrow." She left the room and Tim followed.

~ ~ ~

Back in the small interview room Lynn, Piper and Mutt had been catching up. Mutt was a high school friend of Jason's. "You're becoming a nurse?" asked Lynn, delighted to hear Mutt's career plans.

"I go to the community college all week and work here on weekends and some nights." Mutt gave her a proud smile. "My mama works in the kitchen, so she keeps me busy."

"How long until you graduate?' asked Piper. Mutt had been one of her elementary school students.

"Longer than most." Mutt sighed. "I can't carry a full load and work. The program is two years, I might need three because I gotta work."

"I thought you got some settlement from Jason's assault?" Lynn was referring to last summer when Mutt and Jason's other friends helped save Jason's life and exonerate a suspect. The man, grateful to be free, gave each of the boys a reward.

"Momma says that's my future. As long as I can work the money stays invested." He shrugged.

"You'll have to come visit my school," said Piper, "to tell the kids about your career." Then she squeezed his hand. "I'm so proud of you."

Dusty walked into the room as Mutt was telling the ladies stories about his adventures in the nursing home. "I've finished with the sheriff. Mutt, I want you nearby when you're working here. I told him to give messages to you when he needs to see me." Mutt beamed.

"Makes me almost a detective like you, Ms. Powers."

"I think we both better keep our detecting to ourselves. Dusty doesn't like us amateurs solving his cases." Dusty grumbled a comment and everyone was laughing as Janet and Tim came into the room. "If you'll excuse us, I have to talk with Janet and Tim." Mutt understood and said goodnight, returning to his duty station.

Lynn and Piper, however, were glued to their chairs. Dusty glowered at them. They smiled, but sat. Surrendering to the standoff, he said, "Janet, your father may be in danger, and so might you if he was assaulted because of these letters." He decided to add more information for Lynn's benefit. "The sheriff has heard people around here talking about bogus loans and unfair, maybe illegal, financial dealings."

Janet nodded, "Do you think I'd be a target because I'm Bergy's daughter or because I adapted some code for that office or because I helped him write that letter?"

"What?" gasped Lynn and Piper.

Dusty rubbed his eyes as he digested the information. "Let me understand this. You work for these people?"

"They're one of Kevin's clients. Joseph hired me to rewrite some software to be more specific for their office." Janet then began a description of her modifications.

"Stop right now," ordered Dusty. "I don't care what you did. But I want to know about this letter."

"I typed two letters for Dad that asked to meet with the manager or board members about the rumors he had heard about people losing assets."

"What people?" asked Dusty.

"Dad didn't name names," said Janet, "and I don't think he got any reply."

"Do you think this insider software information puts you in danger?" asked Dusty. Janet shrugged.

"I don't want you alone," stated the detective. "I can send Mars over." Dusty studied Janet. "But he's too young to see you in that dress." She scowled at him.

"I can help out, Dusty," offered Tim, trying to look serious and concerned.

"Maybe Tim could stay with you a few days until we sort this out." Dusty couldn't look at Lynn and Piper as he made the suggestion. "We found one dead man at the Llewellyn's farm and we think he's related to this case. Now I have an attempted assault. So Janet, you may know nothing, but I want you safe." Dusty ignored the joy in Tim's face.

"She'll be fine," blurted Tim, "I mean I know how to run a protection detail, sir." He almost gave Dusty his best Navy salute.

~ ~ ~

After leaving the nursing home with a series of instructions from Dusty and curious stares from Lynn and Piper, Janet and Tim stopped at the grocery store for something to make a quick meal, and as Tim whispered in her ear, "Something sweet for breakfast," Janet almost dropped the carton of eggs she was holding.

Shepherding Tim through the store was difficult enough, but running into several acquaintances who were interested in her date and her little black dress presented additional challenges. Janet complained all the way to the car. "Doesn't anyone go to a movie on Friday night? What do people do, just go to the grocery store? No wonder we're a nation of fat people." She gestured wildly with one arm as she carried bags stuffed with donuts and bagels for Tim's breakfast in the other. "And how many breakfasts are you planning to eat with me?" She railed at him as her mother's bridge partner passed them in the parking lot.

"I think all those people just wanted to get a look at you in that dress." He carried several of Janet's re-useable grocery bags, brimming with enough food for about three weeks. Janet had insisted that the six-pack of Sierra Nevada go in one of the bags because she refused to carry it out of the store in plain sight. "You could be carrying an Uzi. They'd only notice the dress," Tim argued.

Unpacking and stowing the groceries in the kitchen went swiftly. Tim surprised her with his homemaker skills. He put all the correct foods into the refrigerator and left the pantry items for her to shelve. Janet walked around the kitchen as though hypnotized, automatically putting away bread and beer. He began to think she was distracted, maybe even frightened, by her father's assault. Considering that she may need consolation, Tim moved toward her and decided that he wasn't interested in food any more. When she stopped, he thought he had an opportunity to get her into his arms, but she opened the refrigerator door and hit him in the stomach.

"Ooof," he gasped.

"What are you doing here?" She looked at him with her beautiful brown Lasiked eyes.

"I was following you." He looked around the room. "I wondered if you, if we, if ..."

Janet stared at him as she processed his non-comment. "I'm thirsty." She poured some cold juice into a glass and drank it. Then she looked at him. "Are you?"

"Am I what?"

"Thirsty." He shook his head. She carried her glass to the sink, rinsed it and placed it on the dish drain. Tim followed her as she meandered through the house. When she finally sat at the dining room table, he turned on a light and sat opposite her. She stared at him.

He asked, "Did you say you worked for Dusty's dead man?"

"He's not Dusty's." Janet and logic, peas in a pod.

Taking a deep breath, Tim said, "I mean, you know the dead man and you know the company Dusty talked about."

"I know the dead man. He was my contact when I customized some office software."

"Do you think they were after Bergy to get to you?" Tim felt a chill. All of a sudden this wasn't a game.

"No." Janet drifted off in thought. Tim waited. She refocused on him. "I think Dad was targeted because he was asking questions; at least it appeared that he was asking questions. He can't talk and I don't know who else signs, or maybe it was a mistake and they confused him with some other old guy." She snapped her fingers. "That's it. It was a mistake." She sat back happy with her conclusion.

"He was making some sort of inquiry. No matter who wrote the letter, it was his idea, and he wanted to share information with Dusty." Tim was getting into this investigating thing as he offered an alternate conclusion.

Janet frowned, indicating that she liked her conclusion better. "I don't think any one is after me. They don't know who my father is, and when I worked for their office, I dealt with them through Kevin." She stopped again. Her eyes wide, she asked, "You don't think they'll go after Kevin and his family?"

"I'll call Dusty." After a quick conversation with the detective, Tim reported back to Janet. "He's sending Mars to spend the night."

Janet asked, "Would you like to watch TV?" She left the dining room and Tim followed her back into the living room where she grabbed the remote and turned on the TV screen. She waited for Tim to take a seat and she moved to the opposite corner of the room.

He got up from his chair and moved to her side. "Why are you so distrustful? I won't hurt you."

"I told you about last year," she replied, "and Dad always warned me that men might have ulterior motives. He and Mom taught me to be cautious and wary of men. You men don't always have my best interests at heart." She slid out of her seat and away from him.

"That's sex and exploitation," said Tim, "that's not a trusting affectionate relationship."

"Aren't they similar?" Janet stood at the doorway poised for flight.

"Affection is warm and trusting and fun."

"Fun?"

"How old are you?" he asked. "You sound like you're sixteen."

She frowned, "Sometimes I think sixteen year olds know more about life than I do."

He laughed. Her frown deepened as she said, "You have no idea how used and exploited I felt after last year. That's why I moved back to the house." He inched closer and placed an arm around her. She didn't resist.

"Love and affection are supposed to be fun," he explained.

"For who?" Janet stopped, thought, "Or should I say for whom. No, that's a question so I should ask, for whom?" She pushed him away.

"What are you talking about?" Tim was lost in her discussion.

"I'm asking for whom it should be fun." She walked away.

"Is that a question?" Tim was baffled by the conversation.

"For whom should affection be fun?" Janet asked as she

moved to another room.

"For everyone." He followed.

"You have sex with more than one person at a time?" Janet gasped.

"No, I mean for both parties involved." Tim frowned at her. "Do you always take everything so literally?"

"I'm a scientist," she announced proudly.

"Whatever," Tim muttered. He moved closer. "I mean both people in an embrace should enjoy it. Both people in a kiss should enjoy it." He moved his arms around her and kissed her. He didn't stop until he felt her respond as she relaxed in his arms. "See?"

"That was just an automatic response from my body." She worked to regain her footing as she tried to refocus her eyes.

"So your body was enjoying my kisses." Tim was triumphant in *his* logic.

"Try again," she challenged. He kissed her lips, her ear, down her neck, back to her lips, soft kisses, lingering kisses, kisses that included pressing his body into hers, wrapping his arms around her, and letting them explore her waist, her back, her ... He felt her relax into his embrace and stopped.

"Who's having fun now, you or your body?"

Janet stepped back and brushed her hand across her lips. She appeared to wobble. "You're cheating."

"How?"

"You used your hands. My body ignored me."

"I got more equipment to use. Want to see if you and your body can ignore it?"

"Now you're being stupid, not fun."

"But I was fun before?" Tim moved close again.

"Maybe."

"Which time? Which kiss did you like best? Want me to run through my repertoire again?" He had his arms around her.

She pushed him away. "Just your lips. Your hands behind your back. We'll see who's tougher." She pursed her lips and Tim put his arms behind his back. As he bent to kiss her lips he heard as small ding. The next thing he knew he was unbalanced and trying to stay on his feet while he kissed the air. Janet had disappeared.

He found her in the dining room, scanning the screen of her cell phone. He came up behind her, kissed her neck and ran his hands along her body. She never moved, but kept working on her electronic reply, thumbing on the keypad. Tim sighed and leaned against a wall, waiting for her to come back from wherever she had gone. Finally she put the phone down and turned, looking as though she were trying to remember something.

"Ready to try? Remember hands behind your back."

Tim frowned, "I already …. Don't you remember? You …"

Another ding. Janet was a captive of her phone again.

While Janet worked Tim secured the house, checking doors and windows. When she finally noticed him again he asked, "If I'm staying the night, could you show me where we sleep." Janet led him upstairs and pointed to a room at the back of the house.

"Is that our room?" he asked.

"Your room."

"How can I protect you?"

"Stay awake and guard the stairs." Janet walked into her room and closed the door.

Tim ambled into his assigned room and began to prepare for bed. He'd be sleeping in his underwear. He hoped any intruders would understand. He located the bathroom to wash up and borrowed what he presumed was the sheriff's razor and shaving cream. Being optimistic, he brushed his teeth with extra vigor, using his finger, and swished a double dose of mouthwash. Ambling back to his assigned room, he heard a muffled clicking sound. Walking to the top of the stairs he listened for sinister noises that might indicate danger. Nothing. He listened more intently, holding his breath, and traced the sound to Janet's room. Poking open the door, he couldn't believe his discovery – she was working at her computer!

She sat cross-legged on the floor in her bra and panties, absorbed in her laptop screen, the computer balanced on a storage chest. To Tim the sight was surreal, a young woman, clad only in lacy underwear, bathed in a silver reflected haze, totally lost in the gibberish on the screen. He leaned against the doorjamb and studied the tempting figure. Clueless, Janet kept typing, sometimes muttering to herself.

Taking a deep breath, he watched her in wonder. Who? Why? Questions floated through his mind. This slender, unfocused, literal, computer phenom had his attention. She had done nothing all evening to encourage him. Often, he felt as though she forgot he was nearby. And yet, there was something so intriguing and tantalizing about her. After fifteen minutes of observation Tim knew what he thought needed to happen this evening. He approached the woman, studied the screen then reached around her and typed, "*House on fire. We'll talk in the morning.*"

"What?" sputtered Janet as she turned. "You can't do

that."

"Who was that?" He looked over her shoulder at the screen.

"My client."

"At midnight?" He pulled her to her feet.

"They're in Hawaii. It's only five or six in the evening there."

"But it's Friday night." Tim knew what he would be doing in Hawaii on a Friday night.

"I work with computer geeks. They don't see any difference between night and day or days of the week."

"Do you?" He was holding her and rubbing her back and gently moving down her back to massage the part of her body covered by the lace panties.

"Do I what?" She was going limp in his arms.

"Do you know what night it is?" He felt her relaxing, moving to the rhythm of his touch.

"What night what is?"

He kissed her and unhooked her bra.

"What if someone tries to kill me?" she mumbled as she swayed in his arms.

"He'll have to wait his turn." He stepped out of his shorts.

Tim slid her panties off her hips. As her underwear slipped to the floor he looked at the woman in front of him. He studied the outline of her trim shape in the soft bedroom light. He looked again into her brown Lasiked eyes. Although his body was ready, he held his breath, realizing that this small woman, serious and quiet, was someone more than he had expected to find.

He cupped her face in his hands. "Why so somber?" He

kissed her. "I told you this should be fun." Janet stared at him with her probing beautiful eyes. He coaxed, she shivered at each soft, intimate touch. Their mouths came together as he lifted her and she clung to his neck. When she wrapped her legs around his body, he entered her.

"Hold on real tight," he rasped as he lowered them onto the bed. Tim was on top of her and kept whispering, "Hold tighter." He had been waiting since that night at the party. Finally, here they were and he kissed and caressed, ending with a rush of passion that unbalanced him. Janet began to relax her grip and he said, "I'm sorry. Next time we'll come together."

"We are together." Janet and logic, no matter the situation.

He rolled off her and whispered in her ear, "You'll see what I mean." The glow from the streetlights cast a warm iridescence around her face. He looked into her puzzled eyes and smiled as he began a soft exploration of her body. Janet slowly and shyly began to respond to his seduction. Her body arched. He pulled her on top of him and entered her setting a rhythm as he moved his hands to caress her body. He watched those eyes that seemed to go from questioning to enjoyment and finally to rapture. Again Tim climaxed but this time Janet was attuned and responsive in his arms. She called his name and collapsed on his chest as he ran his fingers along her spine.

Finally her legs seemed to lose the ability to stay wrapped around him. As she rested her head on his shoulder, he could feel her heart beat as though it were trying to escape from her body. She spoke in short gasps attempting to catch her breath. "I think ... you have a lot more ... experience at this than I have."

He eased her on her back, gently putting a pillow under her head, pulling the sheet up around them as he stretched out beside her.

"I think someone could be sneaking in here right now to murder me and you'd be worthless," she said as she turned and nuzzled his neck, murmured in appreciation and rested her arm across his chest.

Chapter Twenty-Two

As the Saturday morning sun came into the bedroom, Tim said to Janet's one open eye, "No one came to murder you. Ready for breakfast?" Janet threw a leg over him and moved her lips along his chest and neck until finally reaching his mouth. Tim drew a quick breath and said, "That's my girl," and they replayed last evening.

As Janet fell back onto the bed, she said, "That's what you meant by together." She was sweating and Tim was breathing heavily. He kissed her forehead as she rested her head on his shoulder. "Why did that other woman leave you?" she asked.

"I told you. She said I was boring." He kissed her forehead again.

"I guess I need a whole lot more time with you to see what she meant." She ran her hand across his chest and down his thigh.

"Can we have some breakfast first? Remember we never had dinner?" He lifted her hand to his lips. "And we can invite that guy who's outside watching the house."

"What?" Janet screamed. "Someone's watching? You mean some guard knows you spent the night? What will the neighbors say? What will Dad's old deputies say? Let me see who it is?" Janet said all this as she grabbed a bathrobe and peeked out the bedroom window. Dropping the curtain as quickly as she lifted it, she whispered, "That's not anyone. I mean he's not a patrolman or one of Dad's guys." Tim moved over to the window and slowly pulled back a corner of the curtain and snapped a photo with his cell. He then called Dusty.

"There's a guy out front and Janet says he's not one of yours." He handed the phone to Janet.

"No one I know. The car is a black SUV ... I've never seen it ... We'll send the photo." She ended the call and said, "Dusty's on his way over." Tim grinned and kissed her then started to hunt for his clothing.

When Dusty arrived the car was gone. He knocked at the door and Janet let him in. She was dressed in her usual khaki slacks and polo shirt. She handed him a cup of coffee and invited him to share the morning donuts and bagels. Tim came into the kitchen dressed in a pair of jogging shorts and an old T-shirt. "Where'd you get those clothes?" asked Janet.

He grinned, "I found them in Dad's room."

Dusty buried his face in his hands and shook his head sadly. "You better tone down that grin," the detective told Tim. "I could hardly keep Lynn and Piper from coming here last night with their own stakeout."

Janet moaned. She rested her head against the pantry door and began her list of complaints, "There's no privacy in this town. Someone has probably already told Dad. Mom's probably trying to escape from the hospital to get here."

"Quit lying to Dusty," warned Tim. "I read your father's sign last night."

"What sign?" asked Dusty.

"When he asked Janet who I was and said she finally hooked up with a winner." He grinned again. Janet looked at him ready to deny all when he sent her a message using the signing alphabet. She turned a deep red.

Dusty groused, "I don't even want to know what's going on. I'm just warning you. Lynn's hot on the trail of this little romance." Taking the high road he concluded, "All I'm trying to do is find a killer." Dusty focused his attention on Tim. "What's your rank again? Ensign?"

"I'm a commander."

"Then act like one," growled Dusty as he tossed the commander a small duffle.

"Thanks," said Tim as he checked out the clothes and supplies that Dusty had spirited away from The Heights.

~ ~ ~

By Sunday evening in Australia the lovemaking between Nancy and Cory had become more like their previous affair, with Cory encouraging experimentation, including drugs and alcohol. Nancy said, "I can't do these things and be ready for work tomorrow."

"Why are you working anyway? You have loads of money." He offered her another drink with a pill chaser, which she declined.

"I enjoy my work." Nancy crawled out of the bed. "I have to leave. Do you want a ride back to town?"

"I'll stay here and sleep this off." He grabbed at her as she moved away.

Soon Nancy was on the road to town wondering why she had let this weekend happen. But after a lot of thought, she finally admitted to herself that she would take Cory on any terms. She loved him without reservation, but she was happy that he would be leaving the country in the morning. One visit every few years might be good for her and him, but that was that. If Cory were to stay, Nancy knew that she didn't have the willpower to deny him anything. She had learned that about herself this weekend. Only her job, something she loved almost as much as Cory, kept her steady and got her home.

Chapter Twenty-Three

"**W**e got prints," said Mars, preempting Dusty's Monday morning question.

"Whose?"

"We got several. Over at Mr. Sarkis' trailer we got prints like someone looked through his cupboards and some cigarette butts. It looked like the old guy tried to clean up before he took his meds. Tabletops were wiped. The prints were on the high cupboards. We found the cigarette in his trash."

"I knew those guys were pros," nodded Danny.

"Guys?" asked Dusty.

"This just feels like a two man job to me," observed Danny. Mars and Teniquia snickered. "Wait and see," Danny challenged his partners.

"How many prints do you have?" asked Dusty.

"Three or four sets. The techs are eliminating the victim and the people who deliver meals," Mars explained, "but the cigarette will take a little time." Here he looked at his colleagues. "I'm still waiting for the analysis on the towel from Glenda's bathroom. Lynn had a good idea about the seat being up and that the vic wouldn't do that and make Glenda curious. Don't you think our vic would have always put the seat down so Glenda wouldn't notice?" Everyone nodded. Mars continued, "I think one of the hoods used the john and our techs think he wiped his face and hands and wiped down the faucets. They sent a hand towel to the state regional lab in Henderson County. They thought there were things on it and the new lab has the latest equipment. I'll let you know when we get the results." He grinned in triumph.

"Do we have names to go with the prints from Sarkis yet?" asked Dusty.

"We have to wait for the report." Now Mars' triumph was gone. "The techs say a few days. Something about Internet traffic."

"I stopped in to see Bergy this morning," said Dusty, sort of explaining why he was a little late. "Do we have any more information about his attack?" Everyone stared at the floor or any place that was not Dusty. "Tee, do a canvass of security cameras on the nursing home campus and look at some of the cameras in the area, you know, ATMs and stuff." She nodded and began jotting some notes.

"What about Janet and Thel?" asked Danny.

Dusty ran his fingers through his hair. "You know the court has all these translators on contract?" Everyone nodded. "I found a sign language person in Madison County. She joined me at Bergy's this morning." Dusty shuffled some papers showing his discomfort at outlining the discussion.

"He's mad at us? Thinks we're inept?" asked Danny.

"No," said Mars, "he probably thinks we're amateurs."

Dusty shook his head. "First, he didn't see his attacker, but he says it's related to these finance people. I told him what we've been doing and about the AG. He's on our side. But, he ... " Dusty ran his hand through his hair again as he tried to find the words.

"He thinks we're too slow?" Danny tried to help out.

"No, he had a whole lot to say about Tim and Janet,"

Dusty finally confessed to his team. "I think he embarrassed the translator. He was pretty graphic."

"He's mad at us for sending Tim over there?" asked Tee.

"No." Dusty heaved a sigh. "He had Dr. Rita in his room this morning and they seemed to have cooked up a plan to keep Thel in rehab or someplace so that Tim can stay with Janet." His staff laughed. "Tim told me that Bergy liked him."

"That's a whole lot of liking," offered Tee.

"Bergy's a smart guy," said Danny, "if he thinks Tim is the guy for Janet he's got no problem helping things along."

"I bet Tim is happy with the arrangements," said Mars, "But I know Janet, and if she finds out Bergy meddled, she'll get even." Mars had formed a close attachment to the Bergman family during his youth.

"So what does all this mean, Chief?" asked Danny.

"It means we solve this crime," predicted Tee, "and get ready for Janet to go crazy and Tim to be sent back to the Navy in a body bag."

"It means," concluded Dusty, "we keep our focus on our murder and let Bergy take care of his family."

~ ~ ~

"We sat there most of the night," complained Al, reporting on last Friday evening, "for nothing. She brought a boyfriend home and they got together."

"What about the wife?" Scotch asked. He hoped the women were out of the picture.

"She's still in the hospital," scowled Rothman. "My source says she collapsed from low blood sugar or something. Caused some sprains or something." Rothman paced the motel room.

"Maybe the family's not important now. I got the letters." He sat at the small motel room table. "That guy died. That dumb cop tried to get a warrant again on the office."

"What guy died?"

"The old fellow from the trailer. He killed himself." Rothman stood and paced. "I'm out a hundred bucks."

Al was puzzled. "What does a warrant have to do with a suicide?"

Rothman shook his head. "The old guy blamed our office. And the cop tried to make it a big deal. My attorney said he must not have any hard evidence, because the judge denied the warrant." He looked smug as he sat on one of the beds. "I told you he came to the Mocksville office and tried to act like some do-gooder. Fortunately one of the girls was smart enough to grab a picture." He held up his phone for Al and Scotch to see a grainy photo of Dusty.

"Yeah, he don't look smart," agreed Scotch.

"What about that attacker for the other old guy?" asked Rothman.

Al and Scotch had approached a man who owed money to the organization. He was offered the opportunity to clear his debt by attacking Bergy, the old sheriff.

Al swore. "What a jerk! I don't know what he did. I didn't see anything in the paper about the old man dying in the nursing home."

"What's our plan if he's still alive?" asked Scotch as he scratched his head. "Why we worried about old people now?"

"I say we just leave the old guy alone," replied Al. "Talk around town is that he had a stroke and can't talk. Besides, without that letter no one knows we're involved. I mean no one knows he's interested in us. It could just be seen as an old grudge, you know, someone he arrested once." Al shrugged as the other two men thought about his suggestion.

"You might be right," agreed Rothman. "Let's lay low. Another murder and that dumb cop might convince a judge to sign the warrant for our office."

"What about that jerk?" asked Al, referring to the man they had coerced into attacking the old sheriff.

"He owes us some money since he didn't finish off that old guy," said Rothman. "It's just another collection."

"Good," said Scotch. "I thought he was dumb as shit."

Rothman thought for a moment and came to a decision. "Go visit that asshole who couldn't murder a bedridden man. Just work him over and tell him you'll be back for our money in a week." He handed Al a piece of paper. "Show up at the Mocksville office tomorrow. I'll have them give you some cash. Take a little vacation. Things'll cool down and you can come back to River Bend Friday."

Al grinned to himself, a few days with the redhead. Maybe he should order that jewelry he saw on that website.

Rothman walked to the door of the motel room. "I'm going to be in Tennessee for a few days. There's some rumors going around that some investigator is snooping into our business. I gotta check it out."

Scotch volunteered, "You need us to work someone over?" Al held his breath. He wanted to spend some time with the redhead.

Rothman shrugged and shook his head. "I just gotta do this quietlike. See if someone is just nervous. You guys have a good one." He was gone.

Al was already texting his lady as the door closed.

~ ~ ~

Tim and Janet had spent three days together. Each day was an adventure. In Tim's opinion Janet was a genuine intellectual. Her mind jumped from one topic to another in mid-thought. Starting a conversation on where to go for dinner might end with a discussion of binary code as the salvation of the world. At least that's what he thought she talked about. Tim was discovering that Janet was probably the smartest person he had ever met. She was certainly the smartest person he had ever bedded. That led him to a whole different set of thoughts, and he walked into the kitchen to see if she was busy.

Stopping at the doorway, he realized that Janet was talking with someone, someone also in the kitchen. He frowned. He hadn't heard anyone enter the house – some guard he was! Peeking around the doorjamb, he saw her leaning with her elbows on the kitchen counter, focusing on her laptop screen. "I said erase that line of code and redo it my way." She stared at the screen and a voice replied.

"I did. It still doesn't run. Give me another idea."

Janet looked up from the screen and saw Tim. "Let me think about it." She hit some keys and the screen went blank.

"Am I interrupting your work?" Tim sat at the table and pulled her to his lap, ready to enjoy the afternoon, and enjoy this new serendipity in his life.

"Yes, you are." She fell into his arms. "How much code do you write?" She kissed him as his hands explored her body. "I'm having a problem."

"So am I," Tim said, "You aren't paying attention to me."

"I can't concentrate on you until I solve this problem,"

said Janet as she stared at the blank screen on the kitchen counter. Tim hung his head. He knew enough after three days to stop and help Janet with her software problem. It had to be solved before she would focus on anything else.

He pushed her off his lap and stood up. "Show me." Janet welcomed his interest. Working at her laptop she brought some lines of code to the screen. Tim scanned the characters. "You do much more sophisticated work than I do." He looked again. "Which line is it?"

"If I knew that, I'd be having sex with you right now." She was staring at the screen as she spoke.

He laughed. "No, I mean which line did you just change?" Janet brought it up and pointed out the way she had edited the code. "I can't tell if that's a comma," he squinted at the screen.

"It should be," Janet frowned at the screen. "Hmm. That's not the problem, but," she kissed his cheek, "you did find my error." She quickly retyped the line in a mysterious code that Tim didn't understand, then reconnected with her client and said, "Here's the solution." They talked for a few minutes while he corrected the software on his console.

"It works." The face on the screen smiled. "You the new boyfriend?" The face looked into Tim's eyes.

"Yep, I'm the new boyfriend."

"Has Bergy met him?" asked the pixeled face on the screen.

"He thinks I'm a keeper," bragged Tim. "So go away. We have plans for the rest of the day." The screen went blank. "Who was that?" Tim asked.

"That was Kevin. I help him in his business." Janet was unbuttoning his shirt. "Now you have my attention."

Chapter Twenty-Four

Just after lunch an elderly woman walked into Jim Hoefler's office demanding, "Where is that rotten lying robber?" She shook her cane at the receptionist.

"Does the robber have a name?" asked the secretary in her very professional voice. Fifteen years at this job showed.

"That Hoefler."

"If you'll be seated, I'll let him know you're here." The secretary ducked into the back office to warn Jim. Spying him at the coffee pot, she said, "Psst, Jim," in a hoarse whisper, "there's a very angry woman out front looking for you. I think she's about ninety."

Jim tiptoed to a small two-way window to scan the waiting room. "Oh, no," Jim shook his head. "I think I know why she's here." He took a piece of paper from his pocket and scribbled something. Handing it to the receptionist, he said, "Get me this file, then bring her to my office."

Hurrying back to his office, Jim cleaned his work from his desk and arranged the chairs at his small worktable so that his client could sit comfortably. He knew that her hip gave her problems and she had to sit on sturdy chairs.

"Adele," Jim rushed to the door to greet her so that he could help her to the chair. She raised her cane and struck him. He stepped back as she swung again. She started to lose her balance and tried to get her cane back to the floor to steady herself, but she couldn't move fast enough and began to tilt. Jim and the receptionist rushed to her side and helped her sit down. With a nod from Jim the receptionist left the office, but not before putting the cane out of reach.

"How did you get my house?" she demanded.

"How did you find out?" Jim sat on the other chair.

"Never you mind," spat Adele. "I asked you first."

Jim blew out his breath, sucked it back in and began. "It was about ten years ago. Remember when you had the kidney problem? Your husband needed money. He didn't know where to turn. I bought the house and he used the money to pay your bills." Jim looked at Adele. She was crying.

Jim reached across the table to hold her hand and she batted him away. "He died, remember, right after you were on the mend. He never paid me back and I never told you. Frankly, I'm surprised at how long you've hung around."

She scowled at him. "Why didn't you tell me when he died?" She was furious. "I would have cleared his debt."

"I didn't need your money. He left you comfortable as long as you had no debt." Jim shrugged. "I guess I could have told you, but I didn't think we had anything to gain." The elderly woman stared out the office window, running her hand along the edge of the table. "Why is this important now?" he asked.

Adele sniffed. "I need some money and I was going to get some money from that new place, Personal Financial Management. They advertise that they loan against your house. When they figured out where I lived they told me that I didn't own the house." She wiped her eyes. "They were so rude when they found out."

"Why do you need money?" asked Jim softly.

The woman looked at him then looked down at the table. "I need it for my great-grandson. His parents have thrown him out and he needs money."

"As much money as your house is worth?" Jim was puzzled.

"He has some debts." Adele's anger was all gone and was replaced by fear. "He says someone will kill him."

"Is he living with you?"

She nodded.

"Can I ask Dusty Reid to help us?" Jim asked as he held her hand. She shuddered as a sob escaped. Jim called Dusty.

~ ~ ~

Carl Reid walked into the Philanthropies office with rolled up blue prints under his arm. "My guys said you have some changes." He growled because as a contractor he hated changes. "And nobody told me." He also hated people directing his workers to make changes without his knowledge. He gave Lynn a look that said *I thought you knew better*.

"I haven't made any changes," she offered in her defense. "Tell those men not to listen to anyone. You have all the details we agreed on." She gave him a dark threatening look. She knew it wasn't his fault. One of her board members was trying to take over the office expansion forcing everyone to accept Early American as the office decor. At the last board meeting there had been an argument among several building committee members over those suggestions. It had been an ugly meeting.

"Got anything cold?" Carl asked as he slumped against a wall.

Lynn smiled at him and tilted her head toward the conference room. Once inside she closed the door. Carl threw his blue prints on the table as Lynn opened a refrigerator and asked, "cola or beer?"

Carl gave it some thought. "Cola." He sat at the table. "This is a great plan. You people were smart to buy the office next door, expand on this floor and finish the upstairs. You'll like that work space and privacy." He drank from the can. "I hear Tim has moved in with Janet."

Lynn laughed. "You're as big a gossip as everyone else in the family."

"And you notice I know who the best source is." He winked at her.

"We haven't seen Tim since Friday night." She helped herself to a soft drink. "Marianna heard from Thel yesterday that she'd be recuperating away from home for a week or so."

"Recuperating away from home?" asked Carl. "What does that mean?"

"Piper thinks it means that Tim and Janet are an item and Thel and Bergy like the idea."

"See, I knew I came to the right source." Carl took another drink. "That Bergy, I can see him doing that. He's a master manipulator. Did Mom ever tell you about how he got Thel to marry him?"

"He arrested her?"

"Close," admitted Carl. "He threatened to put down her cat. The cat liked to prowl behind the Sheriff's office. That was back before the new buildings." Lynn looked puzzled. "The old Sheriff's office was next to the insurance office, where the bakery is now, and Thel worked there as a teen. You know her family owns that insurance company, right? Anyway, Bergy went by every day going to work at the Sheriff's office, and the cat always tried to attack him. He told Thel she better date him or he was going to shoot the cat." Carl grinned. "The rest is history."

~ ~ ~

Dusty walked into his father-in-law's office and the receptionist ushered him through. Knocking on the office door, Dusty turned the knob and walked in. "Hello, Adele," he said. "Are you Jim's problem?"

"You know Adele?" asked Jim.

Dusty frowned at Jim. "I know as many people as you do."

"And he's nicer than you," added Adele. She turned so Dusty could kiss her cheek.

After placing a quick peck on her cheek, Dusty stood and waited for Jim to offer an explanation. Jim indicated a chair. Dusty took the cane leaning against the wall and handed it to Adele, then he sat down, stretched out his long legs, leaned forward and put his elbows on the arms of the chair.

"Adele," began Jim, "says she needs some money to help her great-grandson, Nevada Utley, and that if she can't help him pay his bills, someone's going to kill him."

Dusty took as deep breath, rubbed his eyes and threw himself back in the chair. "She's correct. He's in debt to some mean people that he hasn't made any effort to repay and keeps gambling."

"Nevada doesn't gamble," stated Adele.

"Yes, he does. He plays the ponies and visits a traveling poker game that shows up in somebody's barn in Portage every couple of months."

"Why don't you stop those games?" Adele challenged the detective.

"We do," explained Dusty, "that's why they have to keep moving. But your grandson always finds them. He has no sense, and he keeps giving out his markers. He's tried to sell your house to someone, but there was something wrong with your deed."

"He wouldn't sell my house. I live in it."

"He has your power of attorney," Jim reminded her. "We drew it up when you had pneumonia a few years ago, remember?"

"Yes, I remember," she snarled. "So what are you saying, he would have sold my house to pay his bills?"

"Yes," said both men together.

"You're just lucky I own the house, or you would be living in the streets," said Jim. She hit him with her cane.

"So how are you going to protect my great-grandson? He's all I've got." Adele sank back in her chair, seeming to surrender to all the bad news.

"Did he tell you who threatened him?"

"He won't say a word," sniffed Adele. "He says they would hurt me, too."

Dusty took her hand. "If he'll tell us who's after him we can intervene in some way. We'd appreciate some help shutting down that game permanently."

"That's too dangerous," said Adele. "They would come after him just for speaking with you."

"Let me work on that," said Dusty. "Where is he now?"

"He's at the house. If I can't give him money, he said he'll hide so I'd be safe. He's a good boy."

Then Dusty had a thought. "Who was going to buy this house?"

"You mean who did he try to sell it to, or who did I try

to sell it to?" asked Adele.

"You tried to sell it, too?" She nodded. Dusty pulled out his notebook. "Who were *you* dealing with?"

"Those people over at Personal Financial Management. They were real nice until they found out that I didn't own my house." She glared at Jim. "They talked about giving me a hundred per cent of my tax value from the county assessment records, as long as there were no impediments to the deed. I guess me not owning the house was a real big impediment." She poked Jim with her cane again. "Who was going to buy my house from my grandson?"

Dusty put away his notebook and started pacing in front of Jim's desk. "I suspect the same people. He probably talked to them first. That's how they knew you didn't own it." Dusty stopped as a thought grabbed his attention. "Once they saw your address, they knew they couldn't make a deal." He stood and paced Jim's office. "When did you learn Jim owned your house?"

"Today. I just came right on over to see this bum." She glared at Jim.

"Nevada still at your place?" Dusty asked.

Adele nodded. "Waiting to see if I get money." She sniffed and wiped away a tear.

A lot of interesting information swirled around in Dusty's head. He stopped pacing and said, "Let me look into this. We'll make sure Nevada's safe." He hurried out of Jim's office.

~ ~ ~

Dusty walked back to his office along Main Street after that bizarre meeting with Adele Utley. Thinking about unsecured loans, murder, and assaults, he started to wonder about ways the group, whom he now thought of as Rothman's bankers, could loan money and collect payments. Maybe Nevada was told he could erase part of his debt by performing some service for Rothman. Adele's grandson knows Bergy, he knows his way around town. Adele had been in and out of rehab at the nursing home and Nevada had surely visited her there several times. He stopped at the bakery for a coffee and cannoli. He needed something to help him think.

Would Nevada murder? Dusty shrugged, as he licked the cream from his cannoli. Depends on the alternative, he told himself. Rothman employed people who could murder. Nevada probably had two choices – his death or Bergy's. And, Dusty shrugged to himself, Nevada was not the brightest bulb on the tree.

While all these suspicions swirled in his mind his phone rang. "Chief, Mrs. Utley called for you to say we're too late, someone beat up her grandson," Teniquia reported.

When she finished he said, "Get a photo of Nevada Utley and show it to Mutt Mason ... I don't know where he is. Just find him and show him the photo. And send Danny to pick me up by his uncle's place. I'm on foot. Tell him we're going to Adele Utley's. And send an ambulance there."

Danny found Dusty pacing in front of the bakery. He jumped into the car as soon as it stopped, already issuing instructions to Danny, "Get to Adele Utley's," and talking on the car radio to dispatch.

The car raced from the curb and Dusty continued barking instructions into his phone. "Tell Mars to bring a tech team over to the house. Unless that fool kid is dying, I want him to stay at the house until I get there."

Adele Utley lived in the same neighborhood as Danny's grandparents. He was able to arrive at almost the same time as the ambulance. "They'll kill me," cried Nevada. "They said they'd hurt my gran, too." He was trying to get away from the EMT when Dusty walked into the house. Adele was sitting on a chair wiping tears from her eyes.

"Your gran is going to take a little trip. She's not happy with the trouble you've caused her, but she'll cooperate." Adele nodded silently. The chief of detectives then stared the young man down. "Did you attack Bergy?"☐

"They made me. I owe them money," whined Nevada. "I didn't do it to be mean. You gotta help me."

"Here's how we'll help you. You're going to jail for assault. No phone calls, no complaining or we'll just cut you loose right now."

"Nooooo," groaned Nevada. "You gotta hide me."

"My way or no way."

Nevada moaned, sniveled and finally nodded agreement.

"Fine. Then we all agree," said Dusty as he sat on a sofa while the EMT worked on Nevada's bruises. "How many guys?"

"Two."

"They're names?"

"I don't know," Nevada wailed, as much from the antiseptic being applied as from his terror.

"You don't have to tell me anything about them," said Dusty in as calm a voice as he could manage. "Just show me where they might have put their hands, or left some blood or something."

Nevada thought, something Dusty was certain he didn't

do often. "The bigger guy wiped some blood off his fist and dropped a tissue in the waste basket." He pointed to an overflowing container in the corner. Dusty asked the EMT for a bag and placed the container in it.

He turned to Mars. "Get him to lock up." Then he handed the young detective the trash bag. "Tell the techs to find a bloody tissue."

Teniquia came rushing into the house. When Dusty spied her, he instructed, "Get Adele someplace safe, some place she can stay for a few days."

As they walked from the house Mars caught a glimpse of a black SUV tucked behind a van in the next block. He hassled Nevada to make the arrest look real. They made a little parade to the jail, the two patrol cars parking in the jail lot and the car with the prisoner driving into the sallyport. As the doors closed on the sallyport, Mars received a call that Nevada's attorney was waiting for him in front of the magistrate, ready to post bail.

Nevada heard that discussion and wailed, "I ain't got no attorney."

"I know, pal," replied Mars. "Your friends were watching your place."

"They think I'm talking to you," groaned Nevada.

"We'll make sure everyone knows you wouldn't cooperate and we're throwing the book at you for trying to kill Bergy. We can hold you for awhile before you have to be charged." Nevada slumped in the back seat of the patrol car.

~ ~ ~

When Dusty returned to the office he made lists, assigned tasks, secured backup and other resources he thought he might need as he awaited for his team to reassemble.

Teniquia returned first. "Ms. Utley is staying with my mother for a few days. They're old friends. Mama helped when Mr. Utley was ill."

She checked some notes on her desk. "Before you ran us so crazy, I got a photo to patrol and asked them to check with Mutt.

Danny walked in and asked, "Can we go home now?"

A text came through for Teniquia, *Mutt says it's the guy.* And Mars walked into the office with Chinese food.

"Here's the dinner you ordered," he announced.

"Dinner?" Tee and Danny had other plans.

"Let's get this organized and then you can go," said Dusty.

Within the hour Chinese food containers covered Mars' desk. Dusty stood at the whiteboard using a chopstick as a pointer. "Based on Mutt's positive ID," he said, "I think that Nevada is –"

"A loser," snarled Teniquia. She was angry to be missing dinner with Lonzo who would be working evenings the rest of the week.

"– in debt to Rothman for a loan to pay off his gambling losses. I want the kid kept in jail for his protection as well as to question him." Dusty played the chopstick on the board as though he were a rock star drummer.

"Now we're crook nannies," griped Danny. He wanted to be home to play with his son. Just this morning the baby smiled at him and grabbed his finger.

Dusty turned to Mars. "How long before the techs have any information?"

Mars stacked the carry out containers. "They found a

tissue with blood and they want to see if it matches that towel from Glenda's or that cigarette butt from Sarkis. We're closing in on these guys."

Dusty dropped his chopsticks on his desk. "You can all go home." Tee and Danny looked at the dinner remains scattered around the office.

"I'll clean up," offered Mars. "You can all go home." With that all the married members of the unit dashed for the door. Mars wiped the duck sauce from the white board, wishing that Dusty had better control of his chopsticks.

Chapter Twenty-Five

"What have we got?" Dusty asked as he rushed into the office this humid August morning. "This case is taking too long. Tim has to get back to the Navy in another week."

"Did you visit Bergy again this morning?" Tee asked as she sipped her coffee.

"He thinks things are moving too slow."

"What does he expect ..."

Dusty shook his head. "Janet and Tim are moving too slow. I don't know how he figures. He must have his old deputies watching the house."

Three detectives just stared at him from their desks. They were curious about Tim and Janet, too, but decided it was in their best interests to focus on the murder instead. Mars spoke first, "The prints from Mr. Sarkis got a hit. Former Army guy named Angus Dewar, aka Scotch. Has a rap sheet. Dishonorable discharge. Runs with a partner named Al Bonaventure."

"So we know they visited the old gentleman. Do we know where they are now?"

As he was speaking a phone rang. Teniquia answered and spoke quietly to the other party. The tone of her voice made the others stop and listen. She smiled at them and nodded.

Finally she said, "Chief, results from some DNA test of the towel from Glenda's. It's our guy Angus."

"Angus again. He must be an enforcer," suggested Danny.

"And we found his blood on the tissue at Mrs. Utley's. Angus must have wiped his fist after he flattened Nevada on the carpet." Tee hung up the phone. "And they had one more item to report. Remember the cigarette from Sarkis? It has DNA from Rothman." She was delighted. Rothman, the man who had worked to deny the warrant, was in the thick of the investigation.

"Take your time putting together the warrant. I want the judge to see good police work connecting the dots."

~ ~ ~

Tim woke up and found himself alone in Janet's bed. He had been enjoying her early morning interest in his body for the last week. Grabbing an old T-shirt and a pair of jogging shorts he quickly dressed and went looking for her. Hearing voices from the kitchen he thought Kevin must have arranged an early morning discussion. After all, Tim had to admit that he was monopolizing Janet's time, and her work might be suffering. Entering the kitchen, he found Janet sitting on a stool at the counter talking into her laptop screen.

Tim poked his face in front of the computer screen to say good morning to Kevin and found himself face to face with a man in uniform. Realizing he had intruded on a more professional discussion than Kevin, Tim quickly ducked away from the screen, diving under Janet's stool, but not before being noticed by the client.

"Tim, is that you?" came the voice from Janet's computer.

"Huh?" Tim slowly raised his eyes just above the

countertop and peeked back at the computer image. "Sir." Tim snapped to attention, sending a cyber salute to General Vanderstaad.

"Are you acquainted with Dr. Bergman?" asked the general from the laptop screen.

"Doctor?"

"How do you know Kyle?" Janet asked Tim. "I thought you were in the Navy." She and Tim looked at one another while the general watched from the laptop.

"Kyle?" asked Tim, puzzled.

"Yes, Tim?" answered the general.

"No, sir, I mean, I'm confused." Tim turned to Janet. "I worked with the general on a joint services project a few months ago." Tim turned back to the screen. "Is she," he nodded to Janet, "the consultant who solved our software problem?"

"Yes," answered General Vanderstaad. "Now why are you there?" His eyes scanned the edges of the screen. "In her kitchen?" He looked around again. "It is your kitchen, not your office?"

"Yes, Kyle," sighed Janet, "it's my kitchen."

The general folded his hands, rested them on his desk and looked out into Janet's kitchen waiting for an answer. "I'm in town, ah, here in River Bend, visiting my family," offered Tim.

"You're related to Janet?"

"No, sir."

"It's mighty early to be visiting," suggested the general as Janet and Tim looked over the general's shoulder at a clock on his office wall which said '08:00.' When no one replied the officer continued, "Are you consulting with Dr.

Bergman? Are you working on some other project?" Even across the ether, the general saw them both turn red. "Hmm," he concluded. The general rearranged papers on his desk for a moment as he seemed to debate with himself whether a good offense as a good defense should be his policy, or a quick retreat to fight another day held more promise. Finally, "I'd like to give you some time to look at my problem, Janet. Can I call you back about this next week?" Then he looked at Tim. "That won't interrupt anything you have planned?"

Tim got redder than the general thought possible while Janet turned pale. "Sir," stuttered Tim, "we'll wait for your call. I'm certain Dr. Bergman will be prepared with her solution." The general nodded and the laptop image dissolved to screensaver.

They stood in the kitchen too frozen by embarrassment to speak until Tim found his voice and asked, "Doctor Bergman?"

Janet stared at him. "You were part of that cyber team and you acted like you couldn't understand my code?"

Tim gulped. "But I couldn't. That's why you had to be called in to clean it up." He closed the lid of the laptop to make sure no one else checked in, then he moved closer to her and took her in his arms. "I missed you this morning." He began to greet Janet as he would have had she been in bed. She responded happily to his encouragement. Tim led her back up to the bed.

"You promised the general I'd have a solution soon," whispered Janet, "So you better be really inspirational today."

"I'll do my best."

~ ~ ~

Dusty and Mars settled with Nevada in the interview room, the young man was in tears. "I been thinking. I can't talk. They'll kill me."

Mars responded. "Not in our jail. We'll keep you here and keep you safe until we wrap this case up."

Dusty cleared his throat and began. "I already talked with Adele and she's upset that you tried to give away her house. But she's your grandmother and wants to help you. So I want to know who loaned you money."

"Some guy over the phone," sniffled Nevada, "he said he heard I needed money and that he would loan it to me."

"How did they find you?"

"You know the ruckus about Gran not owning her house. I was talking about it at a bar, you know, that after I asked those personal finance people for money and they said they'd help and then didn't. Maybe someone heard me. 'Cause the guy on the phone seemed to know I had tried to borrow against the house. So I borrowed his money. I was late with the payment and they said I could do this job instead."

Dusty made notes as Mars asked, "Who beat you up?"

"Them guys, the ones who said they would take care of my debts if I did the job." Snivel. Sniff.

Dusty slipped two photos in front of Nevada and he gasped, "That's them. They said I didn't do the job."

"What job were you supposed to do?"

"I'm confused about that," whined Nevada. "First they said I had to do one job, tell them who was the retired sheriff and where could they find him. When I did, they sent the loan money to pay that guy in Portage. A few days later they called and said I missed a payment on that loan. I said I only had the money for less than a week. They said it was their rules and I was late. To wipe the debt I had to off Bergy or me and my gran would disappear."

"So you went after Bergy?"

"I had to. I figured he was real sick and wouldn't mind checking out." Nevada sniffled. "I attacked Bergy but he survived, 'cause that nurse guy butted in. So them guys came to the house and told me I had to pay the loan and interest within twenty-four hours. Then they beat me up so I would know they was serious." He sniffled again and ran a sleeve under his nose. "Gran found me on the carpet when she got home."

"What now?" Mars asked Dusty.

"I want to solve my murder," groused Dusty as he slapped the tabletop, "and I don't want to have to worry about Adele and her fool of a grandson."

In a speculative voice Mars suggested, "We can ask the AG to include the River Bend murder in the charges on Rothman. He'll point the finger at those two real quick. Right now, if all three states have enough proof, it'll be white collar. He'll spend some time in a federal country club. Let's face it. He hasn't scammed as much as some of those big con artists, so he's probably looking at three to five. They add murder, he's looking at a real prison and real time."

Dusty acknowledged that was a possible scenario. "Let's hold Nevada on attempted murder and see if anything pops."

"Murder?" screeched Nevada. "I didn't murder anyone."

"That's why it's called attempted murder," replied Dusty, "but I could always send you home."

"Noooooooooooo!!"

"Attempted murder it is."

~ ~ ~

On a late afternoon in Sydney, Cory called. "Nancy, I'm staying for a few more days." She was silent on her end of the phone. "Don't you want to see me? We can do some tourist stuff. Can you get away?" His voice was so tempting, and just thinking of the past weekend made her dizzy with desire.

Finally she said. "I can take off a few days. Call me back at four." She hung up and made plans with Devon to be out of the office for a few days.

By the end of her impromptu vacation with Cory, Nancy was delirious with love and passion. Cory had pledged his devotion and promised that if she returned to the states, he would find time for her, no matter what his schedule.

"It can only be this way, Nancy." He held her in his arms and pressed his naked body against hers. "We'll have to steal love when we can. Having you near makes me able to face my wretched life." He held her, made love to her and pulled passion from her that she had never experienced before.

On the final morning Cory said, "I turned in my plane ticket and was able to get a business class ticket for tomorrow. Can I borrow ten thousand dollars?"

Nancy looked at him, clearly surprised at the request. "Why?"

"I have to pay for my ticket. The delegation traveled coach. I can't go on a fifteen-hour flight in coach again. My delegation ticket doesn't cover the extra cost." Cory walked up behind her. "Aren't I worth that much to you?" She turned to face him and he knew the money was his. "Will your father be upset?"

"He doesn't ask how I spend my money," said Nancy. "I never spend much of the cash that comes into my account routinely. My financial adviser always teases me."

"It's just sitting there?" Cory wished he had known this sooner.

"Buck sometimes asks if I want to put money into something; so does my advisor. He cautions me about too much cash that isn't working for me."

Cory stared out a window. "I have investment opportunities that may interest you. Would you mind?"

Nancy walked into his arms. "I'll listen to all of your propositions."

~ ~ ~

Marianna arrived at the retirement center in time for the bridge game. She had stopped to get Thel Bergman at the rehab facility on the other side of the campus. "I can't believe they're letting you out," marveled Marianna.

Thel looked behind her to acknowledge the CNA pushing her wheelchair. "I'm not out. I'm being wheeled from one building to another because I've been behaving myself."

"And you keep on doing it," muttered the CNA, "or you'll be put in solitary."

Marianna laughed and Thel rolled her eyes. "This will be interesting," observed Thel. "In all our years, our club has never met anywhere except our homes."

"Times are changing," said Marianna as she held the door open for the wheelchair parade.

Annie was waiting in the lobby. "Everyone else is here. Let me show you our new setup." They followed her to a small, tastefully furnished room. A sign at the door said "Game Room," and on the note board was written, "Reserved 2 to 4 pm today." The room looked out on the small lake and landscaped property of the retirement village. Against one wall was a small buffet with cups, saucers and a tray of cookies and nuts along with a coffee pot and hot water for tea.

Annie pointed to the refreshments. "That's part of our service. We just had to reserve the room and they provided this. Isn't it great? They said if we wanted more food, there's a charge. I told them my friends were cheap and would be content with what was free."

This afternoon eight women would be playing bridge. They were the remaining members of a club that had been meeting together for forty-five years. As the newest member, Marianna felt privileged to be welcomed into the group. She enjoyed the gossip and the friendship, but most of all she enjoyed the quality of play – these ladies were experts.

As everyone settled there was a quick exchange of gossip and news, but once the cards were dealt, silence. Between games members seemed to be in a rush to talk and comment, but silence quickly returned as the cards were dealt.

As the afternoon of games ended, some of the women hurried off to other duties, but Marianna, Glenda and Thel stayed behind to visit with Annie.

"How long have you been here?" Thel asked Annie, as she thoughtfully studied the room.

"About three months," replied Annie as she poured herself more coffee. "It was a tough decision, but I have a small one bedroom apartment and it includes one meal a day and all the folks I want to talk to." She grinned.

Thel nodded her head. "Bergy and I need to make some decisions. How did you decide that this was the best option for you?"

"I hope you have a magic solution," pouted Glenda, "Bri and I can't seem to reach any conclusion. We just argue." Marianna patted her hand.

"Finding a dead man in your barn," observed Marianna, "certainly added to your stress."

"I heard about that," said Annie. "News like that travels around this place like a cold."

"Tell us your magic solution," Glenda reminded Annie. "I need help."

"So do I," admitted Thel.

Annie sipped her coffee and took the last cookie on the tray. "It started out as a family feud." Everyone gasped. "My sister, Emmy, told her kids that she needed help with their father. He has Parkinson's. Three kids and three excuses why they couldn't step up to the plate. And the reasons were valid – jobs, their own kids, and one of them lives in Vancouver. The daughter living here in town went crazy and stated flatly that she and her husband weren't going to take the burden. That's what she said – burden."

"Taking care of someone is hard," said Marianna. "Those months taking care of Sonny were challenging. I couldn't have done it without all of you helping."

"Bri's grandmother lived with his family," said Glenda. She hung her head. "Bri's mother said she would never put that burden on me and Bri. She saw it as a burden, too. As she aged we offered time and again to take her in and she refused. She finally consented to rent a room to a lady so she wasn't living alone."

"That's right," recalled Thel, "she offered a place to a woman who had been widowed. She was from South End and had no family or resources."

"It worked out well for both of them," said Glenda. "Mother had a companion, we didn't worry, and the lady had a home. Mother was able to die in her own bed."

"What happened to the lady?" asked Marianna.

Everyone was silent. Glenda finally said, "I lost track of her. We let her stay at the house for a time. I think she found another placement rather quickly."

"She was probably filling a need that no one had thought about before. After all, grandparents and elderly relatives usually just moved in with the next generation," said Annie.

"But what happened to your sister?" asked Marianna bringing everyone back to the original question.

"She came to me," said Annie as she continued her story, "and told me what had happened. She was upset because her children had acted so selfishly, and she was upset that they had misunderstood. She wasn't looking to them for help, she was looking to them for advice and guidance. I sat down with her and her husband and listened to their concerns. Then I began to do some research and look at their finances. I paid a visit out here and to the facility in Indian Hill."

"Did you like that one in Indian Hill?" asked Thel, "Bergy likes that area, but I think it takes us too far out of town."

"You have to first decide if this is the kind of life you

want," Annie told her. "Emmy and I talked for what seemed like days. We looked at every option within a hundred miles. Then we laid out the pros and cons and brought her husband into the discussion."

"What were they?"

"What were what?" asked Annie.

"The pros and cons."

"Mine won't be the same as yours," replied Annie, "but I can give you some idea of our thinking. Emmy wanted to stay in River Bend because she likes their doctors and she wanted to be close to their church and the other things they enjoyed, including her children. She can still drive and they lead an active life, even with her husband's health problems.

"There are a lot of living arrangement choices here," Annie swung her arm around to encompass the facility, "studio apartments, one or two bedroom apartments and even free standing cottages. After studying their finances they chose a two-bedroom apartment and feel satisfied that they're well situated for all levels of care, from independent living to assisted living to nursing home care.

"When we finished all this research," Annie concluded, "I agreed with them and got myself a small apartment. I'm still pretty independent, I still drive, and, now, I'm safe."

"No bodies in the barn," nodded Glenda.

"The best part," said Annie, "is that I'm with my sister. We haven't lived this close since high school. And we have fun. We usually have dinner together. I'd forgotten how funny my brother-in-law is. Her kids are starting to make tentative apologies, in small ways, for their behavior, and Emmy and I laugh a lot."

"I don't have a sister," said Glenda.

"I told you," Annie reminded her, "that my thinking might not fit your case."

"What are you both thinking?" Marianna asked Glenda and Thel. "Someday Jim and I may have to consider other living arrangements."

"Lynn would take you in," said Glenda.

"I have my own children," said Marianna, not certain why she dismissed Lynn so quickly.

Glenda cleared her throat. "Bri and I just argue. He feels so helpless and he can't put his frustration aside and concentrate on solutions for our reality. I don't want to bring Piper and Will into the discussion because they'll just take over and Bri will be angry that we're not making our own decisions."

"Will *can* be stubborn," observed Marianna.

"And so can Bri," shrugged Glenda.

"I can only say that talking with your family helps you find the best solution," said Annie. "I suggest that just you and Piper have some girl talk before you bring the guys into the discussion."

"Why?" asked Thel.

"Glenda can make sure Piper understands Bri's concerns. Talk to her like she's a professional, not like she's your daughter," said Annie.

"I can't do that with Janet," moaned Thel, "she's a flake."

"Janet's not a flake," said Annie, "I taught her in school, remember? She's really smart."

"The way she's hanging around Tim," observed Marianna, "I'd suggest you or Bergy talk to him."

"What do you know?" asked Janet's mother. "Bergy's spies can't figure anything out. I'm getting tired of staying out of her way. Dr. Rita is running out of reasons to keep me in rehab."

"I don't know anything for sure." Marianna gasped, as she thought about Thel's comment. "You're setting up your daughter?"

"We have to do something," explained Thel. "He's perfect. If Bergy could leave his bed, things would be resolved by now."

Annie scowled at Thel. "You can't just throw two people together and expect things to happen. What about mutual attraction? Or even love?"

Marianna smiled at her. "I suspect that Tim's got his own game plan."

"You do know something," challenged Thel.

Marianna shook her head. "It's just a feeling. I've heard Tim brag that Bergy and he get along." She gave her listeners a knowing nod, "And I can see how Janet feels about him."

They all nodded their understanding. Bergy's plan was working.

Chapter Twenty-Six

Cory didn't get out of Sydney as quickly as he had hoped. Business class reservations were tight. He explained as much to Rothman during one of their conversations. "I can't get out until tomorrow. What can I do for you now?"☐

"Are you sure these cops are dumb?" asked Rothman. "They seem to be getting close." Dusty's staff had convinced the judge to at least let them search Joseph's desk at the PFM offices.

"Dumb luck," snorted Cory. "Last time I was in River Bend these guys were trying to solve a murder and that Mars fellow ended up on stage handcuffed to some gay guy dressed as a woman. And their chief, a guy named Reid, a tall skinny guy, his wife was hit in the head while she was chasing some other guy through some trees. It was an embarrassment to all law enforcement."

"You sure about them?" Rothman didn't want trouble in River Bend because he was already putting out fires in Tennessee.

"I saw it with my own eyes." Cory assured his client. "Just relax. I'll be back in the country soon."

One reason Cory was glad to delay his departure was to secure his relationship with Nancy. He was very interested in getting her back to the States, her and her money.

On their last evening together Cory showed Nancy how easy it was to search the Internet for jobs. "You could be in the states in a matter of months and we could be together."

Cory always found her easy to convince if they were in bed and naked. "What kind of work could you do?"

Nancy snuggled closer and said, "I have good credentials for museum archive work. Organizing historic displays, researching." Cory typed on his laptop, then took time to nibble her ear while the computer did a job site search.

"Look at these," said Cory as he got back to the screen. "There seem to be jobs everywhere."

Nancy took the computer onto her lap and began scrolling. "This one," she squealed, "It's just what I did for Lynn." She squinted at the screen. "It's in Wisconsin." She frowned.

"But it would get you home, closer to me." Cory tossed the computer aside and began his seduction. He wanted Nancy and her trust fund closer to him.

~ ~ ~

Piper pushed through the doors at the Philanthropies office. Late afternoon was her time to claim Lynn's attention. There was so much to think about these days, and she needed advice from her best friend. "Lynn in?" she asked the receptionist.

Nelda nodded toward the stairs. "She's looking over the new construction."

Climbing to the second floor renovation project Piper called, "I'm here. Where are you?"

"Come see my new office," called Lynn from behind some boxes.

Piper walked to the back of the second floor and found Lynn studying a floor plan balanced on a cardboard box. "This will be my office with enough space for a work table.

I'll have two extra offices up here and a lavatory and small kitchen, and this common area for gossiping and stuff." As she talked she gestured in all directions. The Philanthropies office was an end unit in the business park. They had just purchased the unit next to them to allow for expansion. Part of the plan included moving Lynn's office upstairs – the unfinished portion of both units met overhead.

"Some new office," groused Piper as she surveyed the dust and disorder.

"When it's finished, it'll be great." Lynn frowned. "Carl has so much else to do that he does this in his spare time, you know, while he waits for deliveries for other jobs and stuff. He says it's a good way to keep his guys busy and not lay them off for a day or two every week."

"Is he going to do his usual great carpentry?" asked Piper. Lynn's brother-in-law, Carl, had a reputation for his finish work that always included artful storage and shelving. "Won't you be out of the way of the action, spending your days up here?"

"I hope so," replied Lynn, "between you and Nathan and a dozen others, I never seem to have time to do Philanthropies work. Someone always seems to be hanging around."

Piper walked over to the dormer and looked out into the back parking lot, the street beyond and a glimpse of the hills toward the country club. She sighed.

"What is it, honey?" Lynn asked her best friend.

"My parents." Piper hung her head.

"I thought you all were figuring things out."

"My parents are fighting," she said. "They have these private talks and neither one will tell me what they've decided. Mother comes home from visiting Dad all red-eyed and if I ask Dad, he just swears. After my talk with Dad I thought we would be ready for them to make a decision. He gets out of rehab at the end of the month and we're nowhere near a solution."

"Do you have any idea what ..."

"If I knew what," growled Piper, "I'd solve this problem."

"Maybe that's it," replied Lynn. "Maybe they want to work this out themselves, like adults, not like they're your children."

"That doesn't make any sense."

"They want to be in charge of their own lives. They don't want to burden you, nor do they want you to take over. Maybe my dad could talk with them, you know, oldie to oldie."

Piper scowled at her. "Then they'd be mad at me for talking about our family problems to strangers."

"I'm no stranger," argued Lynn.

"I know, but you know what I mean. Dad's so private. He wants to figure things out on his own. If he wants help from me and Will, he'll want to tell us exactly what kind of help and how he'll repay us."

"Repay? Will won't take ..."

"I know." Piper shrugged as she leaned against the wall. "You should hear Will on the subject. I know they're frightened. They're coming to terms with their age. It has to be scary – admitting their mortality. Dad's always been independent. Mother's always been able to work right along with him. This scare about memory loss has Mother very nervous. She keeps asking me if I think she's forgetful or confused. I don't know what to say. I think she is sometimes, but if I say so I'll upset her."

"There are no really good answers," agreed Lynn, "The challenge is to find a solution that lets them feel in control and still able to live a full life."

"And what would that be?"

"Who knows?"

~ ~ ~

"We got another problem. When the cops picked up that Utley kid Friday, I had a guy there to spring him. They won't let him make bail." Rothman announced all this to Al and Scotch as they downed the motel breakfast. "I think that detective, a guy named Reid who stopped at the other office, is behind this. He might get Utley to ID you guys."

"Want us to stop him?" asked Scotch.

"The cop?" asked Al. Scotch nodded.

Rothman put his cup down. "You could threaten him. Rough him up a bit, threaten his family. Tell him to stay away from things that aren't his business."

"A cop?" asked Al.

"He a small town stiff. He'll panic." Rothman was confident after his conversations with Cory. He had to solve his problem in River Bend so he could concentrate in bigger problems. "Maybe just some sort of accident so he's out of the picture for awhile."

"Won't it get him curious?"

"Not if you do it right." After some thought he continued, "Watch him for a day or two — when you can get him alone, do it." The other men nodded.

Chapter Twenty-Seven

Lynn felt restless and didn't know why. Mr. Sarkis' funeral caused her to do a lot of thinking. Making life good for everyone meant paying attention to those who were not safe. But so many people were hurt by PFM and many of them were elderly. And it had been very clear at this funeral that the community had failed the elderly gentleman.

She grieved for the man's daughter. The woman had sobbed and asked, "We told him to come and live with us. Why wouldn't he?"

Vicki had tried to explain, "As folks get older they want to maintain a level of independence. They don't want to be a burden."

"He wouldn't have been a burden," the woman had wailed. "We loved him." Her husband had taken her in his arms, even as he contained his own sorrow. It was evident to all that this couple had sincerely wanted to have the older man in their lives. Why had he been so stubborn?

All these thoughts wove through Lynn's mind along with the images of Glenda and Bri and Bergy. Old people – how did families make them feel loved, and nurtured, but still independent? Somehow it almost felt like the relationship she had worked to develop with her son – independence with a safety net of love and affection. Lynn smiled to herself. At her age she wondered if she should be dealing with older parents just as she dealt with her son –

ready to be there just in case, but not holding the reins too tight.

Lynn walked out of the small church into the hot August afternoon and looked around for Dusty. She had seen him at the back during the service, but she had lost sight of him. She got into her car and drove to his office. Danny was working at his desk.

"Hey, Lynn, Dusty's at a meeting."

She flopped into a chair beside Danny's desk and blew out a sigh. He smiled at her. "I hope you aren't here for marriage counseling."

She smiled back at him. "I do need advice. We were at that funeral and it got me thinking. Something is bothering me and I came to talk with Dusty." She looked around the empty office and then back at the detective. "But you'll have to do."

"Good thing I don't have an ego," he teased, "or I'd be a quivering, useless heap of manhood now."

She reached over and patted his arm. "It's about getting old."

"Who? You, me or Dusty?"

"No, I mean about old people." She shook her head as though organizing the ideas inside. "I've been giving some thought to all the older people we've been dealing with lately. Vicki at the Council on Aging has made me aware of all the challenges and dangers facing old people here in River Bend. Scams, elder physical abuse, family exploitation." She blew out another breath. "How can we let our elders be so unprotected?" □ Danny nodded. Lynn knew that Dusty called him the social worker of the unit. Maybe he was the right person to talk with.

He blew out his breath mimicking her frustration. "I know what you mean. We get calls sometime. But we never get any evidence. A son or daughter may get power of attorney and skim money out of an estate. The other siblings get wind of it and they all fight." He shrugged. "But there is that power of attorney and the parent, if still alive, may not want to say anything because she's frightened, or usually unaware. You know, in a nursing home, or under some home care situation with the suspected child in charge."

"Can't we do anything?"

"I guess we can start now to warn the elderly to have their lives in order before they get ill. Some people won't listen because they don't think they have enough of an estate to be concerned." He shrugged.

"What about scammers who aren't relatives?"

"That's different in some ways but the same in others." He got up from his desk and walked to the center of the room. "People don't realize they've been scammed until they find they have given information over the phone and money has disappeared from their bank account. Or they paid for a re-roofing job upfront and never see the workman again. By the time we get called by a relative, usually, there's no trail to investigate. You'll notice the Sheriff tries to get that sort of warning in the paper and on the local radio as quickly as he can to alert other potential victims."

"But what can we do?"

"From our office, I think we do all we can. And the folks in adult protective services seem to be working as hard as they can to respond to cases."

"I have heard those announcements on the radio and

seen stories in the paper, but they never meant anything to me until these last few weeks."

"Maybe that's why there's a problem," suggested Danny as he leaned against his desk, "No one really hears the warnings until after the fact. Somehow people should hear these things sooner."

"But how?" asked Lynn. She got up and began to pace. "Maybe I should talk with Vicki. Maybe she's already got ideas."

"That sounds like a plan. She knows what old people need."

Lynn looked at Danny. "You have a lot of old relatives in town. Maybe you should be talking to Vicki."

"I already have a job," he said. "You have to deal with my boss."

Lynn looked thoughtful. "I have some ideas. I'll talk to Vicki first. Then I'll talk to your boss."

~ ~ ~

It was a few days before Nancy's father, Zachary Rawlings, learned that Cory had extended his stay in Australia. Checking a calendar he tried to remember when Nancy had gone for that short vacation.

Had she told him where she was going? Had he even asked? He turned his attention back to the young banker who seemed to know something about Cory.

"You were asking if I know Cory Estridge." Zachary reminded Crandall Haug-Barten.

"Yes, sir." Crandall straightened his tie as he spoke. "I met a fellow from the U.S., a Cory Estridge. Do you know him?"

"I do. He attended school with my son." Zachary held

onto his placid, relaxed face. "Is he still in town? He was here with a cultural delegation last week."

"I believe he left this morning. I saw him at the airport. You remember that I had to escort Mr. Tao to his international flight." Crandall preened at his good fortune, escorting a wealthy Chinese client. "He said he had spent some time with a lady."

"Mr. Tao?" Zackary gasped.

"No, Cory Estridge."

"I hope you weren't gossiping on company time," chided Zachary.

"No, sir," Crandall rushed his reply. "This Cory fellow seemed real eager to tell one and all that his girlfriend had wanted him to stay a few days and had purchased a first class ticket back to the states as a reward for his service."

Zachary had an ugly feeling.

~ ~ ~

At dinner Nancy seemed tired and listless. "Are you feeling ill?" Zachary asked his daughter.

"I played too hard on my vacation," she yawned. "I'll look better with a little more rest. We're preparing for a visit from a representative of the royal family. One of the princes will be here on an official visit in ten months. Isn't it amazing how far in advance they plan these visits?" She yawned again.

"You like your job, don't you?" her father asked.

"Yes." It was a solid, excited response. "I do so many interesting things and I enjoy all of my colleagues. It was a good idea to apply for this job."

"Does that mean you plan on settling here for a good length of time?"

"Good length of time?" Nancy laughed. "What a term! I plan to keep this job until it's not fun or until I get another, better offer. Do you plan to stay here a good length of time?"

"I don't know." Zachary was thoughtful. He wanted to return to America, but he had a hunch he should remain here with Nancy to guard against more incidents with Cory. On the other hand, he cautioned himself, she may not have been with Cory last week. "I've been looking for a position back home."

"In River Bend?" she asked.

"No, I've been looking everywhere in the states. I haven't had any nibbles yet. It may take some time. I'm not as young as others looking for work." He patted her hand. "What would you do if I returned home?"

"That's a good question." Silently Nancy played with the food on her plate. "I couldn't afford this place. Well, I could if I use my money, but not if I want to live on my salary."

"Do you live on it now?" asked Zachary.

"Don't you know?" she answered.

"No. You're an adult. Your funds are your business, but I'd be happy to work with you any time you ask." Zachary mentally estimated the size of her funds. "Your advisor at the Jameson Group is a good man, but I'm always available for an opinion. And so are your brother and your Uncle Nathan."

"Thank you." Nancy toyed with her food some more. "I think I'm happy with my advisor. He tells me I could spend a little more on myself."

"I'm happy to hear that," smiled Zachary, "It means you aren't being reckless. I have confidence in your judgment." He pushed his plate aside and stood. "I think we need a dessert. Let's walk down to that tea shop."

Nancy smiled back at him. "That's a great idea. I'm not as sleepy as I thought if we're talking chocolate."

As they walked toward the tea shop Zachary said, "Where would you settle if you returned to the states?"

"I don't know. Maybe D.C. It has all those museums."

"Do you have friends there?"

"I'd make friends there, just as I have here." She looped her hand in her father's arm. "Cory told me quite a few of our old friends have jobs there."

"Does he?"

"I think his job is there and his family lives in Maryland. His wife's parents have a place on the bay near St. Michaels."

"Do you know the woman he married?" asked Zachary, trying to remember whom Cory had married.

"No. She's a bit older," Nancy huffed, "I think her family was desperate for a match."

"I heard his job kept him in Sydney longer than I thought." Zachary didn't look at her but lightly held her hand on his arm.

"I wouldn't know." Her voice seemed to sing.

She's lying, he thought. Just like her mother, the same tone of voice. He always knew when his wife was lying – her voice seemed to hold a note a little too long. Was Nancy the girlfriend Cory had boasted of? Had she given him money for a plane ticket? Zachary was miserable, but he kept his placid demeanor and treated Nancy to a chocolate pastry while entertaining her with stories about the people he had met at his latest diplomatic dinner.

He shared the story of the young woman who had given birth. "Oh, Dad," chided Nancy, "no one gets pregnant these days unless she wants to." Then she laughed. "Don't worry, I won't run off and leave you with twins." She laughed again and he laughed with her.

~ ~ ~

"Dusty," Lynn said as she placed a bowl of his favorite dessert in front of him, "I was talking with Vicki at the Council on Aging about elder issues."

The serving of fresh, warm apple crunch draped in whipped cream, caramel sauce and nuts shimmered in the bowl. He held his spoon in mid air because he knew this dessert was coming at a price. He thought he would wait for the grand total before sampling it. "Get to the bottom line."

"You know me too well," she grinned. "I've learned so much about aging and the dangers out there for those who have no family or have disinterested or almost criminal family involved. Those folks need help. And I talked to Danny today and he explained that sometimes making a criminal case is very difficult for any number of reasons." She sat down and sampled her dessert. Dusty took her cue and dove into his.

After two great tasting spoonfuls, he said, "I know you have some cockamamie proposal."

"It's not cockamamie," she licked some caramel syrup off her finger. "It's a great plan. Vicki is having a board retreat and I thought Danny, because he has so many old relatives in town, could give her board some idea of the dangers elders face with scams and abuse and how local law enforcement tries to help and reasons why it doesn't always work."

"Then what? We'd just look bad."

"No, that's where I'm going. You could make Danny a

person to liaise with the Council on Aging and you could both share information and maybe," she wiggled her eyebrow, "evidence." She put her spoon down and rested her elbows on the table. "That way, both of you would share information quickly and Vicki could warn her clients of scams and Danny could hear about issues that might be criminal in nature."

Dusty ate more dessert, drank some milk, handed Lynn his empty bowl with a nod. She took the bowl and refilled it. "That's not bad," he said after taking a spoonful, "And I think you have the germ of an idea, too. Law enforcement has some role, social services has a role, maybe even some local attorneys and doctors who have elder clients." His tongue darted out to catch some caramel sauce on his lip. "Danny can work with Vicki, but I think I'll challenge her board to manage the effort and to include as many other interested parties as possible in this early response effort."

"What a great idea!" Lynn bounced in her seat. "Early response for elder safety!" She kissed Dusty on his cheek, then wiped the whipped cream off. This was a dessert that always managed to leave evidence.

Chapter Twenty-Eight

Shelby Bowman was sitting on a bench along the walkway in front of the Philanthropies office. It was early Monday morning. Lynn greeted her with warmth. "I hope you came with good news."

"Yes, ma'am," beamed the youngster. "The community college counselor helped me so much. He even said I could apply for a campus job once my classes begin. Mama is so relieved." She frowned as she looked at Lynn. "I think she's going to leave her husband. I think she only married him so that we would have a home when I was little. She said we could make it on our own if we both work hard."

"I'm sorry to hear about her marriage."

"She's never been happy. He's not a mean man, just not interested in our life." Shelby wrinkled her brow as she tried to gather her thoughts. "He did his share by giving us a home and food, and we cooked and cleaned and never caused trouble. Mama got a job with Amelia's Maids last year and she got me part-time work there. We studied our finances and think we can manage without him. I don't think he'll care."

"I'm sorry." That seemed to be all that Lynn could think of to say.

"Don't feel sorry for us, Ms. Powers. You've given us a whole new path to follow." Then she grinned. "The man at the community college told Mama she should enroll in evening classes. He said in a few years she could be a bookkeeper or learn medical record keeping. He said there were jobs in the area and he might even find her some tuition help." Shelby threw her arms around Lynn. "We'll leave as soon as we find us a place. Everything's smiling for us and it's all because you helped."

Lynn invited Shelby into the office and indicated that she should take a seat and wait for a minute. Then Lynn slipped into her office and closed the door so that she could make a phone call, remembering the discussion last week with her friend, Gary, about looking for a renter. "Gary, I think I found someone to rent your mother's cabin." She knew by his confused mumbling that she had gotten him out of bed.

"Someone for what? You're not matchmaking, are you?"

"No, a renter. The mother of one of our scholarship students needs a place to live. Her daughter is going to use her scholarship money at the community college, so it will be the two of them. Is it still available? Is the place big enough for two?"

"Yeah. Do you think they would take care of Mom's dog? All the folks in this neighborhood already have a pet. I've been trying to figure out what to do with him."

"I'll give her your phone number and you can work it out."

"These are people you approve?"

"Yes." When she got off the phone she stepped back into the reception area. Shelby was sitting quietly with a distressed look on her face.

"Is something wrong with my scholarship, Ms. Powers?" asked the young woman in a panicked voice.

Lynn sat beside her and took her hand. "No. I had to get

some information before I made a suggestion to you. If you and your mother are looking for a new place to live, I have a friend who wants to rent a place. I told him I recommend both of you as good tenants."

Tears came to Shelby's eyes. "How did you know? Mom will leave her husband as soon as we can get organized." Shelby got out of her chair and began pacing. "We have so much to think about and we want to be settled as soon as we can. School starts in a week."

"Just call my friend. He has some conditions, but I think it will work out for all of you." Lynn stood and hugged the young woman.

Another day and Lynn's social engineering paid off again. She walked Shelby to the door then did her celebration dance around the office.

~ ~ ~

Janet was cleaning her bedroom muttering to herself about how sex can mess up a room when she found a box marked 'Accessories.' She remembered that Marianna had delivered the box along with the dresses Sonny had bequeathed. Janet had never been curious about the contents — accessories were foreign objects to her. When she received the gifts, she had determined that she would never wear any of those dresses. But it had been a strange weekend and stranger week. As soon as Dusty's investigation into Bergy's attack was complete life in River Bend would go back to normal — except here in my bedroom, she thought.

Inside the accessories box, she found a DVD. It was clearly marked 'For Janet Only.' She took the DVD to her laptop on the dining room table. As the video came up, Janet saw Sonny as she had looked during her last days. She began to speak, "Dearest Janet, yesterday we dressed you up and made you feel uncomfortable in your own skin. It's beautiful skin, and your new eyes are worth your investment. Most Hollywood starlets would be delighted to have such a metamorphosis at so little cost. I'm giving you several dresses. Wear them and enjoy them. I don't know the man claiming your time who prompted your changes, but I can tell you that he is not the man for you. He doesn't make those eyes glow. He doesn't make you laugh. You have the best comedic timing of anyone in River Bend and make some of the snappiest comebacks. A real asset on stage. If your man doesn't bring out these qualities, he's wrong for you. Keep looking. You'll know the right man when you can laugh and love in the same breath with his hand at your back to guide you along the way." At this point in the narration, Janet started to cry. "Are you crying?" asked Sonny's image. "I hope so because that means I'm correct. You've found your man, haven't you? I hope he has seen you in the little black dress. I love you." Sonny's image stayed frozen on the screen as Janet put her head on the table and wept.

Tim had been standing in the doorway watching the DVD. He came into the room and placed his hand on her back. Janet rose from the table and he enveloped her allowing her to cry on his chest. "I've never watched this DVD in all the months that I've had it," she sobbed.

"She must have sent me to you," he whispered as he held her.

"Sonny was so kind and cared about all of us." Janet had

stopped crying and wiped her eyes on Tim's shirt.

"I hope it's only your eyes that you're wiping," he growled. Janet pretended to blow her nose on his shirt. Tim picked her up and kissed her. "She meant me," he bragged. It was a definite statement.

Love and laughter. Janet understood.

~ ~ ~

"How hard can it be to scare a small town cop?" asked Scotch sitting in the passenger seat of the black SUV with dark tinted windows. "He probably never deals with anything more than drunks and hookers."

"Whatever you say, Scotch," replied Al. He thought this was a dumb idea and wondered why Rothman was pushing for action. Maybe the rumors he heard from the redhead in Mocksville were true. Rothman was on someone's radar. She didn't know why he was, but she had been talking with staff at other locations. "We just gotta find him first. Some guy named Reid. I got kind of a picture." He squinted at his phone screen. They were sitting in the parking lot at River Park watching some unusual activity.

"Is that a TV camera? We better move," said Scotch.

"Look at the name," said Al as he pointed to a chalkboard at the edge of the production unit. "It says *Reid video*. Maybe that's our guy."

"Let's go take a look." They left the car and wandered over to join the other people watching the videotaping. A crewmember was announcing that everyone was welcome but please be silent until the taping concludes. The crowd cooperated and the scene finished with no problem.

As the crew packed up, the two men wandered closer to listen to any discussion and were rewarded for their caution.

"Mr. Reid," asked the host of the program, "When we get to the mansion I understand you have quite a story about robbery and murder. Do you think that would be interesting?"

"It will. I can show you where some old-time bank robbers buried jewelry in the house and, also show you where we found blood from an unreported death that happened almost eighty years ago." Carl Reid ran his hand through his short hair. He had gotten the haircut his wife insisted he needed.

The show host directed Carl toward a van as they continued their discussion. The two observers walked back to their car. "I think that's our man," said Scotch.

"Let's look at that picture to be sure," cautioned Al. Back at the car they studied the grainy photo on Al's phone as they took quick looks back in Carl's direction. "Skinny, tall and that short haircut."

"I agree. Let's tag along and see if we can get him alone. I don't want to spend the night in this town." Scotch stretched before climbing back into the car.

The black SUV followed the crew to Palmer Mansion where they spent the rest of the day doing whatever film crews do. The men in the car didn't care. They just wanted to have a word with that Reid fellow.

"What's our plan? Scotch asked after yawning for the hundredth time.

"I think just an accident," shrugged Al, "you know, he kisses our bumper and is down for the count while Rothman cleans out the offices."

"Good idea," Scotch agreed. "My hand's still stiff from the last guy." He flexed his fingers.

After an hour a patrol car arrived at the mansion and a young African-American woman hopped out. She greeted Mr. Reid, confirming his role as chief investigator in the minds of the two men in the black SUV. The host of the show talked with her and they all moved into the house again. In another hour, the crew was back outside and the woman left in her patrol car.

As the crew began to pack up their equipment, the two men went on alert. Their opportunity would happen soon. Mr. Reid hopped into the van and the crew caravanned out of the Dancing Creek neighborhood.

Chapter Twenty-Nine

Lynn's last meeting of the afternoon was about money and the Rape Crisis Center. She wasn't certain about the agenda. Trudi, the executive director of the agency, had called and asked that Lynn help talk with a donor. In walked Trudi and Lee, one of the Rape Crisis Center volunteers. She met them in the reception area and asked, "What's this about?"

Janet walked through the door. "Why did you call this meeting, Lynn?" From what she had heard, Lynn was surprised that Tim let Janet out of the house. But she suppressed a smile.

"We're all here," said Trudi. "Can we sit in the conference room?"

Lynn led the way, issuing a few instructions to Nelda, "Lock up and go home."

"Thank you, dear," came the comforting reply.

Lynn sat at the table and waited. Lee smiled, Trudi shrugged and Janet looked lost – a normal look for her.

Trudi began, "Last year the center received an anonymous donation from Janet's family to support the three known rape victims of that man." Lynn nodded. "We have since identified three more woman." Janet gasped. Last year Janet had unwittingly dated a man who was assaulting women in River Bend. Although his victims were reluctant to report the crime to the police, several women sought help and counseling at the Rape Crisis Center.

Eventually the man was murdered by one of his victims. During this hurtful time Janet's family made a donation to the center to aid the man's victims.

"Do you need more money?" Janet asked.

Trudi smiled at her. "We could use more. Let me tell you what we've done with the original donation. We hired a therapist to meet with each of the original three women every Friday. They each have a private session. One of the women has wanted to advance her education. We've used some of the money for tuition support and fees. Not the whole tuition, just something to help. But now we have three more women and we need to provide help for them." Trudi looked at Janet. "We've tried to follow your instructions to assist his victims."

"How much more do you need?" asked Janet.

Lee took over the conversation. "One of the women was pregnant. She gave the baby up for adoption. We would like to help her because she's trying to pay off her medical expenses. She lived with a relative out of town for several months and lost her job. After she works with our counselor, she'll need some financial aid to help her in her new life."

"How much do you need?" Janet asked again.

"We're not certain," said Trudi. "This woman who had a child may require a substantial investment."

"I think," said Lee, "that we can help her if we start working with her now." By the sound of her voice, Janet and Lynn understood the urgency of the meeting. "We didn't know she existed until she came back into town a few weeks ago. Someone encouraged her to talk with us."

Janet took a deep breath. "There will be another ten thousand tomorrow and then let's meet again after

Christmas to see if you need more." She smiled at the women and Trudi jumped up to hug her.

"Why did you need me?" Lynn asked Lee.

"I'm not sure."

"I'm glad I could help," said Lynn as she smiled at the happy threesome. This was one of the secrets of fundraising that she learned. A committed donor only had to understand the urgency and need to increase their donation. And fundraising was very personal, one person, one ask at a time.

~ ~ ~

The video production van pulled into a small business park and Mr. Reid climbed out. After a few words with the passengers he watched the caravan leave the parking lot and he turned toward one of the offices.

"Now," ordered Scotch and the car sped to intercept Carl.

Lynn was closing her office as Janet, Lee and Trudi, the people at her last meeting of the day, hung out waiting for her to lock up. As they stood in front of the office saying their goodbyes, Lynn glanced out at the almost empty parking lot and saw Carl stepping out of a van.

"Carl," she called, "Salley left a message." He cupped his ear as though he couldn't hear her. She walked into the parking lot to explain her message. As she got closer to him, she was distracted by a dark SUV racing across the lot, apparently aimed at Carl. Running to him, she grabbed his arm and dragged him behind a parked car. The SUV swerved and an arm with a weapon came out on the passenger's side. By this time Carl understood Lynn's panic and pushed her around the parked car as she shouted back to Lee and Janet to call for help. Then she raised her own cellphone and began to snap photos of the attack vehicle.

"This way," gasped Carl, as he pulled her toward his truck. The SUV had circled the lot and was coming at them from another direction. It sideswiped Carl's truck causing Lynn and Carl to dash in another direction. The SUV spun in a tight circle and charged at them again, the passenger continuing to aim and fire.

Carl tripped and Lynn tried to help him up. The SUV stopped as a man jumped from the passenger's side holding his weapon. Carl didn't move and the man kicked him in the face, then turned to Lynn and said, "Give me that phone." She looked at him and threw it across the lot. The man slapped her and she fell to the tarmac. Carl tried to rise showing his indignation and the man pointed his gun at Lynn. "Move and she's done."

Carl sank to his knees, holding his bleeding nose. The man hit Carl on the side of the head with the gun. "Get in the car, both of you," he growled gesturing to the SUV, as people stepped from the offices to watch the assault. "You and your husband are out of luck."

"He's not my husband," said Lynn as a parade of police vehicles with sirens and flashing lights barreled into the office park. "That's my husband."

Dusty jumped from a car with his weapon at the ready. The attack SUV peeled rubber in an attempt to escape the police, leaving the gunman behind.

After some quick maneuvers by the patrol cars and a final crash into a parking lot lamppost, the SUV and its driver were surrounded.

Dusty kept his attention on Lynn's attacker. Mars had

already disarmed him. Carl and Lynn were holding onto one another while they sat on the ground as the police rounded up the suspects and brought order back to the parking lot.

Wiping the blood from Carl's face Lynn said, "It's all right. An ambulance is on the way. Try not to move."

"Try not to move!" Carl exclaimed in an angry, indignant croak. "My head must be split in two. I can't see with all this blood and you say don't move?" Then he sighed and closed his eyes. "What happened?" he whispered.

"They thought you were Dusty," Lynn explained.

"It's this hair cut. I'll never cut my hair again, no matter what my wife says."

"She'll probably agree with you after this," said Lynn as she waved to the arriving ambulance.

Listening to Lynn speak to Carl, Dusty said, "I don't know how they could confuse us. I'm better looking." He was kneeling beside Carl, trying to mask the concern in his voice.

Lee and Janet came rushing to Lynn's side. "Thanks for calling Dusty," she said.

"That's the car that was outside my house last week," gasped Janet.

Dusty waited for the EMTs to take over Lynn and Carl's care. He then confronted his suspect. "I got some evidence that says you fellows have been in town for awhile." He looked at the gunman. Danny had taken control of the driver in the SUV. With a nod from Dusty he put his suspect in a patrol car and headed for interrogation. The man standing with Mars said nothing. Dusty nodded and Mars pushed the man into another patrol car.

"You know what to do," Dusty said, "I'll check on Lynn

and Carl then join you." Mars nodded.

~ ~ ~

"Lot of arrests," Danny commented as he took a seat opposite Al in the interrogation room and opened a thick folder.

"Nothing took." The man looked bored.

Danny scanned the papers in his hands. He didn't want to look around the room. TV detective shows made their interrogation rooms look so stark and scary. Any perp would break down. The James County jail had those kinds of interrogation rooms. But the unit's offices in the basement of the courthouse had a different kind of interrogation room. It had been a part of the Guardian ad Litem suite until about three or four years ago when they moved that office to a place more inviting for children. Someone had tried to cover up the flowers and bunnies painted on the walls. But after a few years the forest creatures were trying to reclaim the room. Bambi and Thumper seemed to be laughing at the threat of interrogation.

The detective didn't have much hope of gaining information from a person as experienced as Al, but he said, "We got a picture of your car parked outside of the Bergman house. That's the same car you were driving when you and your pal attacked Carl Reid, a local contractor, and Lynn Powers, wife of our chief of detectives."

"I want my lawyer." Al sat back in his chair. He knew the drill and he knew his rights.

There was a tap on the two-way mirror. Thumper smiled at a butterfly. Danny closed the folder. The interview was over.

~ ~ ~

Mars sat in the interrogation room with Scotch. They were late getting started. Danny had gone in first because Dusty thought Scotch looked dumber and he might talk if he was allowed to stew a bit. Then they had to wait while dinner was served in the jail. Great! Scotch had dinner and Mars was missing a meal at Palmer Mansion with Buck and Penny.

"We've got some DNA from a bathroom," the detective announced.

"A guy's gotta piss. That against the law?" asked Scotch.

"From the bathroom in the house where Joseph Baikar was hiding."

"Who's he?" Scotch yawned and scratched his shoulder.

"I also got a bullet found in the chief's tire. The bullet someone used to flatten a tire out at the farm where Joseph Baikar was hiding."

Scotch looked around the room. "What is this place, a kindergarten?" A faded little bunny seemed to be perched on Mars' shoulder.

"Same bullet that tests for your gun. The gun you threatened those people with in the parking lot."

"That guy was hurting that woman," explained Scotch. "Al and I were helping her."

"Carl Reid is a local contractor and brother of our chief investigator." Mars studied a faded butterfly that seemed to be flying above Scotch's head. "And the woman is Lynn Powers, wife of that same chief of detectives."

"So they were having a family feud." Scotch was pleased to have all the answers to explain the situation. "She needed help."

"No." Mars gave him a look of certainty. "I got witnesses who heard you threaten Carl and Lynn. I got witnesses who saw you point a gun."

Scotch yawned.

"I got tire tracks near the farm where Joseph Baikar was hiding. I got foot prints in the field across the road from the farm." Mars sighed. "And I got a dead body."

"I want a lawyer."

There was a tap on the glass.

Chapter Thirty

After the attack on Carl the detectives were able to show a connection between the assault and the murder case and the judge signed the warrants for the offices of Personal Finance Management. "This Rothman guy is pretty interesting to me," said Danny in response to Dusty's early morning question. The staff had spent yesterday combing through the Personal Finance offices and computers. "He's listed as executive director for each one of the offices in all three states. He seems to control several businesses that are not nonprofit, but it's the usual complex corporate shelter."

"You mean like we usually see in organized crime and Ponzi schemes?" A man in a dark suit strolled into the office. Mars coughed, Tee squeaked her chair and Danny dropped his stapler. Dusty turned around to look at his guest, the guy from the AG's office.

"Look what the cat dragged in," Dusty greeted him. "They throw you out of Raleigh or you drive here?"

"I came on the state's plane, so I can get this information back to the office fast." Buddy Beazor was a long time investigator from the AG's office. He had survived through six different attorney generals and countless governors. Everyone wondered what he held over all those people. Because, everyone, especially Dusty, knew that he had no talent or skill in law enforcement.

The over weight man rocked back and forth on his feet. "You got Rothman all wrapped up for me?"

"You getting the collar?" asked Dusty, challenging the request.

"I thought I'd let the AG take the credit," Buddy grinned through a shaggy moustache. "He's running for re-election. So, is Rothman all tied up?" He stared at the four silent detectives. Dusty nodded to his staff.

"In spades," nodded Danny. "This guy looks guilty on paper, even if he's not doing anything dishonest."

"What about his employees?" asked Buddy.

"All the people who work for him are semi-clean."

"Semi-clean?"

"They all seem to be hoods-in-training," replied Danny, "People with misdemeanors, usually white collar related. Rothman must recruit from a court docket. But in each office he has at least one clean person who has some business background."

"Like Joseph?" asked Tee.

"Yeah, like him."

"What about that muscle you corralled?" Buddy asked. He made himself comfortable on the edge of Mars' desk.

"We found that Rothman was staying at one of the Shaw County airport motels and had two rooms on his credit card," replied Mars. "In fact, it was his personal credit card, not the agency's, or another company's. One of the rooms listed a black SUV as a vehicle, no license given. They were all in town when our vic was murdered. Rothman stayed in town long enough to stop our warrants last week. The other room stayed another week until after the assault on Bergy. They were back in town again before Carl was assaulted."

"They attacked your brother?" Buddy was concerned. "I

like that guy."

"So do I," said Dusty. "These guys thought he was me."

"He all right?"

"Yeah. It was how we captured them," said the detective. "They attacked my wife, too and all the witnesses called 9-1-1. The muscle came to deliver a message to tell me to stay away from the case. Carl didn't know what they were talking about."

"I hate when family gets hurt." Buddy seemed really concerned about Lynn and Carl. He pulled up a chair at Tee's desk, handed her a small package. "I heard you got married."

She looked at him in surprise. "Yes, I did."

"That's for you."

She accepted the small gift with a soft smile at this kind gesture from a colleague.

"Now gimme everything you got so I can get back home for dinner," he flicked some imaginary lint off his wrinkled sleeve, "in my private jet." The Buddy they all knew was back.

Dusty handed him a notebook. "Do you want me to go through it?" Buddy nodded. The unit began to explain all the information collected in the crime notebook.

"Did they commit your murder?" he asked.

"We can place them at the house, but nothing more. We can place them at another scene, but it was suicide. And we have witnesses to their assault on Lynn and Carl. In addition, I have a fellow in jail who has ID'd them as the guys who asked him to kill Bergy and they would erase his gambling debt."

Buddy read through the notebook, checked the pages of

forensic reports, then said, "People at the other sites are checking to see if these guys did collection jobs there and if anyone will testify. I agree with you. Our tri-state investigation can probably prosecute on white-collar loans and get a conviction. Your murder is too iffy. But, it's a great threat to have against Rothman. Maybe he'll flip on his boys."

They reviewed the files and information for the rest of the morning.

Finally Dusty said, "It's all yours. Our DA agrees, we don't have a great case and with all the other charges from your investigation, they'll do some time. I just hate to give them up."

"Now don't you whine," said Buddy, "we'll see that everyone knows how you sewed up this case." He collected all the information and with a nod to the staff walked out of the office.

Dusty started to swear in a low rhythmic tempo. The rest of the unit laughed.

"He's probably already forgot that we helped," said Danny, "and he's not even out of the building."

~ ~ ~

Thel helped Marianna clean up after the bridge game. They folded chairs and folded tables and folded score pads. "Thanks for picking me up today. Not being able to drive yet keeps me chained to the rehab center," said Thel.

"I'm delighted that you all asked me to join this group," said Marianna. "This afternoon group is more relaxed than Millie's evening group, and the gossip's better."

Thel nodded. "It's the judge. She plays for keeps. This afternoon group takes a longer view." The two women bustled around the bungalow that Marianna and Jim shared. It had been Dusty's old place before he married Lynn.

Marianna had learned a lot today about some of her new friends in River Bend as she thought about the afternoon talk among players. "Did Millie's brother really serve time in jail?"

"He sure did," replied Thel. "He tried to steal some assets from his father's business, take his share before the old man died. Millie's husband took him to court because he was watching the business as something his kids could inherit."

"How did that get her brother in jail?"

"It seemed he wasn't just stealing from his father, he was cheating some of their customers and some of their suppliers. As a result he went to jail, and now one of the O'Hara boys runs the auto parts store and the grandfather is delighted to have a place to hang out and not worry about his own son cheating him."

"Living here so long has everyone embedded in your life," mused Marianna, "I feel like a fresh tablet ready to make note of all your stories."

"And I feel like I have too much life, too many things." Thel huffed and plopped on the sofa. "With Bergy sick and Janet finally with someone we like, I don't know what to do with all of life that I've accumulated. There's Mother's china collection, photo albums, five generations of furniture. What do I do with all of it so Janet can go off with her young man and I can size down to something I can manage alone?"

"Janet will leave River Bend? Is this a really serious relationship?"

"I don't know. They aren't telling us what their future is. But Bergy and I have been clear, to Tim, at least, that we don't want him to worry about us." Thel crossed her arms as punctuation to her statement.

"I don't think Tim and Janet could build a happy life if it didn't include you and Bergy," observed Marianna.

"It can include us, but Tim still has some professional obligations in the Navy to complete. I want Janet to step into married life as soon as possible."

"They're getting married?" Marianna concentrated on this information. "They've only known each other a matter of weeks."

"He's perfect." Thel grinned her approval at Marianna. "Bergy and I are ready for him to propose. That's why I've been staying out of the way." She blushed as she admitted to the matchmaking scheme.

Marianna laughed. "I know you told me last week. Does Janet suspect anything?"

"No, but she worries about us. With Bergy so debilitated, and needing so much assistance, she thinks she has to stay with us. I want to find a way to show her I can handle it and that Bergy and I will be fine at the assisted living center. I'll get the help I need at the retirement center. James County Senior Living is just what we need to free Janet to have her own life. And we haven't really talked about this. Tim hasn't proposed and Janet is still ... you know ... Janet."

"So Janet isn't the only problem?"

"No. And on top of everything else, what do I do with all of life that I've accumulated? It's my legacy to Janet, my mother's things, Grandmother Bergman's things."

"Doesn't Janet want them?" asked Marianna.

"I don't want to ask her because she might use it as another excuse to put off a life with this young man." Thel hung her head. "And our house. My family has lived there since 1920."

"Thel, you're just talking about things," said Marianna. "How important is it really that the house stay in the family?"

Thel sighed. "It's important enough to me that I delay going into the retirement center just so I can cling to it as long as possible. On the other hand Bergy says we could use the money to cover our expenses in the retirement center and not touch other assets that we'd like to leave for Janet."

"So the question is, do you leave Janet money or a house and old furniture as her dowry?" Marianna patted the other woman on the shoulder.

"When you put it like that I can sell my house."

"I'm home," shouted Jim. He walked into the dining room. "Thel, what a surprise! You look great."

Thel tilted her head. "Jim, when's the last time you acted like a real attorney and gave me some advice?"

"It's been awhile," he said.

"Maybe we should have a talk," said Thel as she glanced at Marianna.

"I'll get the wine," offered Marianna.

"Sounds serious," said Jim. The women nodded.

Chapter Thirty-One

"Sorry, Mr. Bergy," smiled Mutt as he popped his head into Bergy's private room, "I thought you were alone." He gave a smile to Tim. "You guys are so quiet when you use that signing talk."

Tim stood. "I was just leaving." Bergy's fingers flashed.

"I think my man's got more to say," said Mutt. "I'll be back in a few minutes." And he closed the door behind him.

Tim looked down at the old man in the hospital bed. "You had plans for me from the first time we met." Bergy nodded and smiled. Tim continued, "She may fight this. Can I count on you and Thel helping me out?"

Bergy grinned and moved his fingers. Tim laughed. "You're spelling is horrible, but I got you. I'm on my own. I have to go, Sheriff." Tim patted the old man on the shoulder as Bergy signed another few words.

"I remember," replied Tim, "Goodbye, Bergy." He brushed his lips across the old man's forehead.

Walking out to the parking lot Tim sighed deeply. How was he going to lay out Bergy's plan to Janet? She would go ballistic. She had a right to be angry. All the decisions were made without consulting her. But Bergy was right. She was too caught up in her computer world and needed someone in her life to direct things.

Tim sighed again. He needed advice. He needed to talk with Lynn. Checking his watch he smiled, thinking he had just enough time to catch her. He'd try the house first, because he wondered if she was still recovering from that assault in the parking lot. He shivered. Everyone had been so frightened when they all gathered at the hospital a few days ago.

Tim had been doing a lot of thinking. He hadn't intended to find Janet during these last weeks. He needed advice and decided to talk with Lynn. Now he smiled. It had been right in so many ways to let Jason and Lynn back into his life. It was paying off in more ways than he had ever expected. All the new people he had met within the last few months now included him in their family circle. He belonged.

Driving into the yard in The Heights, he waved to Lynn as she enjoyed the sun while lounging on her front porch.

"I could use some help," she said as she tried to sit up to greet him. He kissed her cheek and helped her sit a little straighter on the lounger.

"I could use some advice," he replied as he took a chair beside her. He winced as he saw the scabs on her arms. Summer clothing didn't offer much protection against asphalt.

"Do you love her?"

"You get right to the meat of the discussion." He frowned as he pushed his sunglasses to rest on the top of his head.

"Well?"

"Yes."

"I needed that information first," she responded, "now I can listen to your problem."

"That's not the only relevant information."

"Yes, it is." Lynn handed him a cookie and pointed to a

pitcher of iced tea.

pitcher of iced tea.

"Every time we talk about our future, we talk in circles." Tim attacked the chocolate chips. "We have three parents who need attention. I have to go to sea in two months. She has a business here." He was now standing at the porch rail, throwing his arms out to the privet hedge. "If she comes with me, she'll be alone in two months and have to return and take care of everyone alone. And when I return from sea duty what do we do?"

Lynn leaned forward and stared at him. "You know we'll help her if she's here alone. You know we'll all pitch in if she follows you to Norfolk for a few months. You know that ..." Tim held his hand up in surrender.

"I know all of those things. But it's what do we do when I return from sea duty?" He stared off toward the river. "When I return, I'll be reassigned to another port. Norfolk is convenient, but something on the west coast or abroad would be challenging."

"Have you talked to her mother and father?" Lynn watched him as he struggled with his thoughts.

"They tell us to leave and enjoy our life together." Tim looked at Lynn. "We can't do that. Mrs. Bergman shouldn't live alone, but she's too healthy and active to go into a home of some sort, isn't she? Bergy needs more care, even when he can move back home, and my dad doesn't even know where he is." The dilemma of all these aging parents weighed on Tim's mind.

"I think I'll have the same problem in a few years myself," frowned Lynn. "Dad and Marianna are healthy and mobile, but there may come a time when Dusty and I have to face the same questions. Helping you work through this will be good for all of us." She patted Tim on the shoulder. "Piper and Will are having the same discussions about her parents. Come over tonight. Maybe we can all share ideas."

~ ~ ~

Three couples sat around the table in the kitchen in The Heights. Lynn had invited Tim and Janet to talk over parent issues with Will and Piper.

She was explaining, "You all have the same problem. I thought talking with each other might help you figure things out." She threw her arms out to them. "I don't think there's any one answer, but talking might help sort things out."

"Besides," added Will wiggling his eyebrows at Tim and Janet, "You two probably get too distracted when you try to talk by yourselves." Piper hit him in the arm and Dusty laughed. Tim and Janet stared at the tabletop.

"Piper, why don't you start," encouraged Lynn.

Piper sighed, "Daddy comes home from rehab in two weeks. Mother can't do all the work necessary to tend him and work the farm. They're too healthy and independent to move to assisted living and they aren't happy considering a retirement community." She sighed again. "So far my solution is to take them into our house and figure something out."

Lynn laughed. "Isn't it interesting that in these last few weeks we've learned all these new terms – nursing home, assisted living and retirement community. Each one defines a different level of care and support."

Her audience mumbled in discontent.

"How do you all deal with your mother, Dusty?" asked Tim.

Dusty thought for a moment. "Two of my brothers live within sight of her house. We have moved her bedroom to the main floor so she doesn't have to go up stairs and we don't let her cook for Sunday dinners every Sunday." There was a general sound of sadness. "I know," he responded to the group, "that Sunday dinner held the family together, but she doesn't have the stamina. All my sisters-in-law work and no one can handle that kind of meal on the weekend. So she cooks one Sunday a month. She says that's the only way she can count on seeing us."

"But how do you share the responsibilities?" asked Will.

"That's a good question." Dusty drank his beer. "I stop by at least twice a week. Lynn and I take her to dinner or to some activity at her church or something the kids are doing. My other brothers do the same."

"What about you, Lynn?" asked Janet, then she added, "and Will?"

"We seem to have younger parents," answered Lynn. "Dad has been ill, but appears to be healthy now. We see them a lot. My concern is that Marianna keep her children aware of her health."

"Is she sick?" gasped Piper.

"No, but I hope her children know her wishes if she becomes ill." Lynn looked at them. "Even though I see her often, I'm not the person who should make decisions as she ages."

"You've met her kids," said Piper. "Do you think they would ignore her?"

"No, I don't think so, but she has to let them know her health conditions. Does that make sense?" Everyone nodded. "I don't want to have to rat on her if she needs help."

Everyone nodded agreement again.

"What about you?" Dusty looked at Tim.

"Dad's not going anywhere." Tim shuddered. "He may have another year." He took Lynn's hand. "I appreciate your help so much. This would have been devastating to me, to have to cope alone." She stood up and kissed his cheek before checking on the food she was preparing.

"That leaves me," said Janet. "Thanks for letting me hear that I'm not alone." Tim took her hand and she sniffed. After a moment she began, "I'm an only child, with two aging parents. Dad will need care to the end." She sniffed again. "Mom is my big problem. She's more or less healthy. This recent hospitalization was minor. She has a full life here. Her friends are aging, but everyone continues bridge and lunches. However, I don't think she should live alone. The house is too big for her. The upkeep is beyond her stamina. And what do I do with … ?" she gestured toward Tim.

There was a shuffling on the kitchen porch as Jim and Marianna walked in. "A party without us?" challenged Jim. He pulled a chair to the table for Marianna, then grabbed one for himself. "We were visiting Bergy, and he said that you were up to something."

"What?" gasped Janet. "He can barely talk."

"Easy," Jim waved his hand to calm Janet. "He can communicate and he's still a great detective." Jim took a beer from Dusty. "Bergy says that you all need advice about dealing with older parents." Everyone at the table gulped. "Just as I thought, you're trying to solve our problems without us parents participating."

Janet turned to Tim, "You told him," she accused. "You

pretend to sit there so quietly. You've been signing with him." It was as though she had exposed him as a snake oil salesman.

Tim blew out his breath. "I needed help. You needed help. I thought he would have some ideas." He slumped down in his chair as though he feared an assault.

Dusty started to laugh. "Bergy always has a solution. So what is it?"

"By the looks of all of you, Bergy isn't the only problem looking for a solution." Jim turned to his daughter. "So why don't you start? What are your old parent issues?"

Lynn turned bright red and stuttered. "I, we, I feel a certain responsibility for Marianna and I don't know how I should deal with her children." Lynn looked at her stepmother.

Marianna asked, "What do you mean?" Her voice was challenging. "I'm not your problem." She sounded hostile.

"In the context of our discussion," Dusty intervened, "We all spoke of the people close to us who might need care in the future. Bergy and Bri are two examples."

Marianna said, "I gave my future care a lot of thought while dealing with Sonny. My children have my instructions." She looked at Lynn, then softened her voice. "I guess I should have a talk with all my children." She turned to Jim. "Maybe we should talk with our children some day soon."

"I'll buy dinner Saturday night." Will gave the discussion the priority it deserved.

"So what about the rest of you?" asked Jim.

Piper shuffled in her seat. "Mother and Daddy can't stay out at the farm alone."

"Have you spoken with them?" Jim asked and Piper shook her head. "Maybe that should be your first step in finding a solution."

"I've tried, Jim," moaned Piper, "but they still think I'm ten. Or they act as though we're being pushy."

"Are you?" asked Marianna.

"What's pushy?" challenged Will. "We ask if we can help. We offer money. We ..."

Jim held up his hand to halt Will. "Maybe I should join you as a referee."

"We're not that bad," pouted Piper.

"I know. How about I join you as an interested, neutral friend?"

"That sounds better," agreed Will. "It just might get us moving."

"What about you?" Jim turned toward Janet. "Bergy said you needed some help with some decisions, too."

"He can't talk." Janet snapped. "You're making up things." Jim turned to Tim who tried not to look guilty. But Janet saw the exchange. "What do you know about my parents?" She had been holding Tim's hand and quickly let go.

"Bergy said," began Tim.

"Bergy? You call him Bergy?" Janet was furious.

"He said to call them Bergy and Thel," Tim said as he looked around the table for support.

"Bergy and Thel? When have you gotten so chummy?" Janet had her fist clenched.

"I visit him when I visit Dad."

"And do your secret signing?" Janet looked disgusted while Tim looked miserable and guiltier.

"Let's calm down," cautioned Jim. "Bergy and Thel asked me into this discussion. Your father wants help in making his decisions and so does your mother." He walked over to Janet and looked kindly at the young woman, placing his hand on her shoulder. "They want you to have your life and not worry about them."

Now Janet was crying and shrugging off any attention from everyone. "He couldn't tell me? He didn't think I could figure things out? He still treats me like a child." Tim sat silently, waiting for Janet to allow him to speak.

Jim stepped in to lead the conversation. "Bergy has some ideas that he wanted me to propose." He looked at Tim who nodded, so he continued. "Bergy says that he and Thel have been thinking about moving to the facility where he's staying now. It's a place where a person can have an apartment or cottage or nursing bed or any care in between."

"They don't trust me to care for them," sobbed Janet. "If they move, where will I live?"

"With me," said Tim softly. Janet cried harder, sitting alone and resisting any of Tim's touches.

"It seems he's sold the house," said Jim. "They can use the money to cover their living expenses at the retirement center when a placement is available. The money, as he's invested it, will support them with a monthly payment that will cover what their retirement income doesn't. They also have a nice nest egg from their share of the family insurance agency in case they have some big problems."

"I don't even have a home?" Janet spoke in a soft sad voice, curling herself up on the chair. "When do I have to move out?"

"Never," said Tim. This time he spoke with more force.

"I bought the house for us. Thel's staying there until they have an apartment available for her and Bergy." Janet gasped.

"What other plans have you made without any input from me?" Janet turned to face him. "What else have you and my parents planned for my life?"

"I'm sorry. I love you," he said as Janet sat sobbing into her hands and shrugging off his attention. Tim stood, nodded a silent goodnight to every one and left the kitchen. They heard him climb the stairs to his bedroom. Everyone was silent.

"If I had directed this movie, it would have ended on a happier note," commented Marianna, the Hollywood professional breaking into everyone's thoughts. She stood and walked over to Janet gently stroking her hair. Placing a hand under Janet's chin, Marianna lifted her face and looked into her eyes. "If I had directed this movie, my heroine would have been cheered by the love of a marvelous man who wanted to help her face some of life's most desperate issues. My heroine would have understood his clumsy, but loving, attempts to make her happy and to ease her worries about her family." Marianna pulled Janet to her feet and led her toward the stairway, as she coached, "My heroine would have gone to her lover and thanked him for his devotion. She would have understood that he wanted her life free of worry and filled with love. She would have gone to him to make him see that all of his efforts made her heart burst with affection for him and that with him at her side, there would never be anything in life to fear. Together they would solve all problems and love one another until the day they died." Marianna gave Janet a push up the stairs and watched as the sobbing woman slowly climbed the stairs to Tim.

As she returned to the kitchen Marianna thought about the discussions she had had with her friends during the last several weeks as they talked of dealing with aging and dealing with their children. She had even implied that she and Lynn could be helpful in any discussion. It wasn't true. Marianna had never talked with her stepchildren. She said, "If I had directed this little drama," sweeping her arm around the kitchen, "I would have behaved better." She kissed Lynn's cheek. "I would have shown my new children that I value them as much as my old children." She tousled Will's hair.

Tim and Janet came into the kitchen, smiling. "We're going home," he announced. Then he turned red as he said, "We ... ah ... er ... Thel comes home in a few days. We have to clean the house." They were out the door.

Everyone turned to Marianna and applauded, shouting for the director to take a bow.

~ ~ ~

Driving back to the house, Tim said, "I'm sorry that I acted without consulting you." He reached out and took Janet's hand. "But sometimes you seem to be oblivious." She looked at him and frowned. "I guess I didn't say what I mean," he said responding to her look. "Bergy and I know how smart you are, and we know that your mind is always so busy that sometimes your body is here and your mind is someplace else." She frowned deeper. "I'm not hitting the mark, am I?" Tim closed his mouth and sighed with relief as they pulled up in front of the house.

"Is this my house or your house?" Janet asked.

"I want it to be our house." He had spoken softly and Janet brushed her finger along his cheek. She opened the car door and climbed out.

Following her into the house, Tim said, "See your key

still works."

Janet sat on the couch and stared up at him. "I don't know what to make of this," she sighed, "you and my father planning my life. I seem to be going from one keeper to another. I want autonomy, freedom."

"You can be as free as you want with me," offered Tim as he sat beside her. She got up and walked to sit on a chair. "Did I say the wrong thing again?" He stayed on the couch waiting for her to continue the discussion.

She began to pace the room. "I want to make decisions. I want to ..." She stopped in mid-sentence and rushed into the kitchen. Soon Tim heard the clickety-clack of her laptop keys. He got up and walked into the kitchen. Janet was focused on the screen as she scrolled through some code. More typing, a slow study of the screen, then she turned to him, "I want to ..." She stopped. "That's what you meant."

"What?"

"I get distracted?"

"Yeah." He took her into his arms.

"But there are so many things swirling in my mind – ideas, solutions, connections, sometimes just enjoying the elegance of theories and designs." Her eyes stared at the dish drain, but they were seeing something far-off.

Tim moved closer and began to kiss her neck and glide his arms across her body. She responded by turning to face him and offer her lips. "What are you thinking of now?" he whispered.

"What?" She was going limp in his arms as he turned her to walk upstairs. Then she focused. "Should we go back to The Heights so I can apologize for my behavior?"

"No, I think they figured it out."

Chapter Thirty-Two

When the General Vanderstaad connected with Janet for his appointment, he was treated to a domestic scene. He could see Tim washing dishes at the sink. The general watched him stack dishes, clean the table, put away food, a very homey tableau. He cleared his throat, "Janet, what have you got?"

She began her review of the software problem and her suggested solution. The conversation was technical and crisp. At the end of thirty minutes, the general said, "Thank you, Janet. I'll have the staff work on these suggestions and let you know what happens." Then he seemed to look over her shoulder into the kitchen, "Tim," he called.

"Yes, sir." Tim ran to the laptop and stood at attention. He was in his T-shirt and jogging shorts.

"We've tried for months to get Janet to come to the labs for a good week long work session. Do you think you might convince her to visit us?" The general had decided to play to his team's strength. "We could get a lot of work done and we promise to give her time off in the evenings."

Tim blew out his breath. He turned to Janet. "Can I talk privately with the general?"

"No." Janet sat on her stool with her arms crossed in front of her.

Tim looked back at the screen, took a deep breath and said, "I was hoping she would be coming back with me," he gulped, "after our wedding."

"Wedding?" screeched Janet while the general nodded. "You leave in three days!"

"Bergy said it was a fine idea," argued Tim.

"Who's Bergy?" asked the general, finding this diversion better than the afternoon soaps he sometimes secretly enjoyed.

"You decided this with my father?" Janet raged at Tim while the general nodded his understanding. "First you buy my house and now you've planned my wedding?"

"I was going to talk with you but we never seem to ..." he stopped and looked at the laptop.

"Go on, boy," ordered the general. "You were making plans without her because talking takes up too much time when you're alone together?" concluded the romantic brigadier.

"Kyle," Janet looked into the screen. "When did you join this party?"

"Janet," the general replied, "I've told you for months to come down here and I'd find you a good man." He looked at Tim.

"You what?" Tim was outraged. "That's not how you treat a professional."

"How have you treated her?" asked the general. "Planning her wedding for her ... with her father?" By his tone of voice the general let Tim know that the Army didn't handle things that clumsily. He stared out of the laptop.

Tim frowned at the general as Janet said, "Kyle, ----

The general nodded. "I'll let you know how these suggestions work." He dissolved on the screen.

"Can we talk now?" Tim asked Janet.

"No, I have another client checking in in twenty

minutes." She looked forlorn. "Go visit your dad and mine. We can talk at lunch." She walked out of the kitchen.

~ ~ ~

"Take the plea bargain," Cory advised Rothman. "You'll get less time, and don't cop to a murder charge. Make certain they know you only sent those bums to find your confidential files or something. You never said anything about murder."

"Yeah, yeah." Rothman was worn out. Interrogations by three AG's had him numb. "That attorney you recommended is doing all right. I also brought in some big guns. Just making sure everyone keeps their word."

"My mother had me appointed as a liaison among the three states and federal prosecutor. I'm in charge of closing down the Personal Financial Management offices in three states. Let me know if I can handle anything while you're away."

Rothman chuckled. "Sounds like you got my back."

"That's what you pay for." Cory ended the call.

And that's how it all worked out. Rothman copped to white-collar crime and explained that he never ordered any murders, he said his staff always followed company policy about collections.

Of course, when asked about seeing the company policy, he asked for his attorney.

Much to Adele Utley's delight, Nevada never had to testify regarding his relationship with Al and Scotch. The James County DA charged Nevada with assault on Bergy and sentenced him to five years probation so that he could take care of his great-grandmother.

Cory read all the news using his River Bend Chronicles

app as he sprawled across the bed in his motel room, his latest conquest attacking the room service cart after a vigorous sexual workout.

~ ~ ~

When Tim returned from his errands, he found Janet sitting at the table staring out the kitchen window. He saw tears in her eyes when she turned to look at him. He was on his knee at her side with his arms around her as he asked, "What's wrong?"

"I'm pregnant." She sniffed and ran her finger under her nose. "I shouldn't be surprised," she said as she began one of her speeches. "Weeks of unprotected sex, multiple times a day." She stood and stared at Tim who had remained on his knee beside her chair, but she pushed him away. "What are you, insatiable? Don't you ever tire? Are you stocking up before sea duty?" She was now pacing the kitchen. "What will I do? What will my parents say?"

Tim stood and cleared his throat. "Bergy was wondering what was taking so long. He wondered if you were over the hill or if my guys couldn't swim any more."

Janet spun around, then grabbed her stomach and sat on a chair. "My father? You've told him about our sex life?" She was turning pale and gripping the edge of the table. "You discuss me, us, with him?"

Tim looked pained and insulted. "He's just hinted that something should be happening if I was as eager as I looked." He stared at the floor.

"He asked you?" Janet was trying to be outraged, but the room seemed to be tilting.

"He said you looked pale and unsteady the other day." Tim went to her and took her hand. "He was real excited.

He said that he hopes the baby brings us as much joy as you brought to him and Thel."

Janet glared at him, as she burped. "Why does he tell you all these things? Why can't he tell me?"

"Well, he said that you're so smart he's never known what to say to you." Tim pulled her up so that he could hold her in his arms. "He said that I'm just another dumb guy and he can talk to me." Janet tried to move away but Tim held her tightly. "He said we should tell Thel and he'll act surprised when she tells him." Janet threw up on his shirt. He sat her down and found a towel to clean himself. He slipped off the dirty shirt and rolled it together with the soiled towel. Before taking the items to the laundry, he checked the floor for any mess. Finding nothing he kissed her cheek, handed her a napkin and a glass of water, then carried away his dirty clothing.

When he returned with his clean shirt he knelt beside her chair and asked, "Will you marry me?" He held his breath as he held her hand.

"Yes." Her beautiful brown Lasiked eyes were filled with joyous tears.

He pulled her to her unsteady feet, kissed her gently and said, "Let's go tell your mother."

~ ~ ~

It had been a lot of work wrapping up this case. Mars was too wound up to sleep, so he sat in his loft drinking a beer and rereading the email that had arrived from Nancy today. He blinked.

Her email was uncharacteristically long and newsy. She said that she was sorry for the length but she had so much information for him. She was applying for jobs in the U.S.

285

He was not to get his hopes up, because she was looking everywhere. She was using his name as a reference so she included her resume as an attachment.

After reading and rereading the email, Mars flopped on his couch and tried to determine what her news meant. She was coming back to the states, but not to River Bend. She wanted his help to land a job. Did she want him for anything else? He thought about harried weekends to meet her around the country. Then he smiled. For a few months that might be a great way to carry on a romance – no routine, no boredom. His grin broadened as he thought about making love to Nancy from coast to coast.

He decided that the email was a good omen. She was coming back to him.

Chapter Thirty-Three

Lynn joined Piper's investment club for their Saturday morning brunch and gossip. She was learning a lot about finances, but more about the lives of everyone in town. She told herself that this wasn't really gossip but information gathering, a necessary function in her role as executive director of the Philanthropies. After all, she had to be aware of people's personal lives so she didn't seat two enemies at the same table at the annual dinner or ask two feuding women to co-chair a committee, or invite two business competitors ... what was she trying to prove? She shook her head. She knew. She came for the gossip.

Which is what Annie, the oldest member of the club said as Lynn walked through the door. "Need your gossip fix?"

Lynn had the courtesy to blush.

"I'd tell you anything good, you don't have to come and listen yourself," said Piper as she poured coffee around the table.

"I want it fresh," replied Lynn and the others applauded.

"Are you the one who told Salley to ask us about helping her clients?" asked Piper.

"Yes," admitted Lynn, "Can you?" Several weeks ago as Lynn tried to do some detective work regarding Joseph's murder, she had suggested that Salley ask the investment club to help tutor domestic violence victims in basic financial management and budgeting.

"I think it's a great idea," said Annie, "I'm working up a lesson plan."

"Once a teacher," smiled Lynn. "They'll love you." She took a cookie. And asked Janet, "How's Thel?"

Janet seemed vague, as though she couldn't remember who Thel was. Finally she brightened. "She's fine."

Annie patted Janet's arm. "Everything will work out."

The investment club smiled at Janet. They knew Tim was going back to Norfolk tomorrow morning but had told Lynn he would return in two weeks. Janet and he were being tight lipped about their future.

"So what's the latest gossip?" Lynn prodded the group.

They looked at Bev, owner of Bev's Spas. She had the most current dish. "Not much has happened since our last meeting. Except that murder and since Lynn's in the middle of it, what can I say?"

"I'm not in the middle of it," Lynn protested. "It's solved."

"There is the talk about Janet," added Bev.

"What talk?" demanded Janet.

"That black dress at the grocery store late on a Friday night." Bev and Annie waited for an explanation.

Piper decided to help. "She was called to the nursing home because Bergy was attacked. And she had to get food for Tim because he was going to guard her."

Janet turned bright red.

"Guard her?" Annie sure knew how to put suspicion into a question.

"I heard he came back a week after their first date to spend more time," offered Bev.

"And I heard he makes a show of staying with Lynn but

sleeps," here Annie wiggled her eyebrows, "at Janet's. All for her protection."

"I thought Dusty caught those killers?" asked Bev as she looked at Lynn to verify that the case was closed.

"He did," said Piper. They all looked at Janet.

"And I don't know why people read those novels anyway." Janet could always be counted on to change the direction of a conversation.

"What novels?" No one understood the shift in topic.

"Romance novels," replied Janet.

"You read romance novels?"

"I don't know why," Janet moaned, "they're so misleading. All the heroines have freckles on their noses." She crossed her eyes to try to see her nose. It was a good nose, a plain, unfreckled, two nares, just where it should be nose. She sighed. "And they're always new-bile, newbeul ... how do you say it?"

The investment club members just stared at her.

Janet was on a roll. "Anyway, she's always newb ... you know what I mean. Never experienced or unvirginy."

"Unvirginy?"

"And the women always have long curly, amber, russet or white blonde hair." She pulled at her dark, straight, short hair. "And," she ran her finger under her nose, "There's all this electricity. OK, maybe that part's true. But all that other stuff." She threw up her arms. "I'm thirty-seven and live with my parents."

The investment club continued to stare as her mind took one of its random turns, "And just what are these men? Always tall and handsome and with sculpted bodies, rock solid. I guess that's why they look sculpted." She thought about that idea a moment. "Anyway, very little hair on their chests and thick eyelashes. Or is it thick chest hair and thin eyelashes?"

She took a drink of water, took a cookie from the plate, turned it over in her hands, then continued, "The guys always have money and they make it by being their own bosses, you know, dentists or freelance terrorists."

"Terrorists?"

"Something they can do when they feel like it but not do if some newb ... you know what I mean, comes into their life in some outlandish, sexy way – interrupting their bank robbery or bleeding to death in their carport. Something to get a hot guy's attention."

She frowned at the group. "All I'm saying is no matter what they do or how they meet or whether they have sex on page six or six hundred there always seems to be a condom within easy reach. Do men always carry condoms when they're robbing a bank or extracting teeth or walking their dog?" Janet took a sip of her drink. "Those romance novels can't be right," she said, "That's not what men are like."

"Tim isn't romantic?" asked Lynn ready to defend her brother-in-law.

"You read *romance* novels?" Piper was still distracted by Janet's other comment.

"Someone has to." She shrugged. "Besides my social life needed the jolt."

"The jolt?"

"You know, learning what happens to beautiful people in sexy situations. How can so many women find love in just a week? Maybe it's because I don't have freckles."

"Freckles?"

"All the women have freckles when the men look real close."

"Janet, those are just stories," cautioned Bev.

"In a week they're in love and almost married and using condoms. And the man always has a hard body and great muscles. Tim is skinny.

"But he uses condoms." Lynn wasn't delicate. The whole family knew what Tim and Janet were doing.

"No." Janet stared at the floor.

"What?" The investment club had an ugly feeling.

"I'm pregnant."

Lynn's mouth dropped open. "Can we help you? Does Tim know?"

"He and Dad planned it."

"What?" This conversation was getting really strange. No one was going to be talking about investments this morning.

"How can we help?" asked Lynn.

"I came to invite all of you to our wedding." Janet sniffed. She turned to Lynn. "Will you stand up for Tim? It's only fair because I want Mars to be with me because he's almost my brother so it's only fair that you be there for Tim, but he didn't say you had to, but he smiled when I said it should be you if it was Mars." Janet took a deep breath after the run-on sentence.

"Mars?" Then Lynn remembered the long history Mars had with the Bergman family. "I'd be delighted to be in your wedding."

"Will you be my sister-in-law, too?"

"Of course." Lynn pulled Janet into her arms and gave her a congratulatory embrace. Piper ran to her kitchen to get some wine for a toast – for everyone except Janet.

~ ~ ~

"What … did your … friends … say?" The words rasped out of Bergy's mouth at barely a whisper. Janet, Tim and Thel sat in his private room straining to hear.

"Everyone is thrilled." Janet blushed. Thel fussed over her and grinned at Tim. He blushed, too.

"Not as thrilled as us," said Thel. "A baby and a good husband, that's all we ever wanted for you." She brushed Janet's hair back from her brow – a gentle, loving gesture.

"But what about the two of you," moaned Janet, "I can't desert you."

"Sure you can," replied her mother and Bergy nodded vigorously.

"We're not deserting anyone," said Tim. He moved away from the wall and stood in the center of the small room demanding everyone's attention. As Bergy began to sign and Janet opened her mouth to speak, Tim raised his hand for silence. "I think it's time we make some plans beyond our wedding. And I mean all of us. Janet and I will still need your help." Bergy and Thel nodded. Tim began to outline the issues. "I'll be going to sea right after Christmas. I would like Janet to come to Norfolk until then. Once I leave though, I hope she considers coming back here to our house where you both can look after her. Although Bergy, you can't get up the stairs, I bet we can build a ramp at the back door, and maybe Carl has some ideas about a lift or chair on the stairs. I've seen them advertised. Then when Janet is living back here she won't be alone. Or if you want to settle in the retirement center, maybe you know someone who's looking for a room to rent. We've got time to think about this, so I bet we can come up with a solution."

Bergy was signing. Thel finally spoke. "He and I have been thinking the same thing," said Thel. "We're thrilled you want us to be a part of your life and we'll do whatever we can."

They all looked at Janet. "What?" she asked.

"You're always telling us that we make all your decisions for you," replied Tim. "I think the ball is in your court. What do you think will work?"

She rushed into Tim's arms. "Anything, everything. We can make it all work."

~ ~ ~

Jim Hoefler's children and their spouses met for dinner. Getting old was the topic for dinner conversation. Jim raised his glass. "Here's to Tim and Janet. I got a call from Thel." They all raised their glasses.

Lynn said, "I'm the best man at the wedding and Mars is the maid of honor."

"Janet doesn't do anything normal," said Piper. "Don't you just love her?"

"But we're here to talk about us," said Will, getting the family discussion on track.

"I'm sorry," said Marianna, "I lost my temper and accused my two favorite step-children of being thoughtless. What's even worse, I told Thel and Glenda that Lynn and I could help them work through these same issues with their daughters." Marianne sniffed and Jim took her hand.

"I'm no better," admitted Lynn, "I told Piper that Dad would talk to Bri about -"

"You said they could talk oldie to oldie," offered Piper as she claimed a roll from the breadbasket.

"Oldie to oldie?" challenged Jim.

Lynn hung her head and Dusty laughed. When he saw Piper take a roll he grabbed one for himself. He had seen her put away food.

"You're only laughing because you solved your case," groused Will. He didn't feel very hungry. Talking family stuff was tough – he'd only been acknowledged as Jim's son for three years. "I don't see anything funny about all the challenges with Bri and Glenda."

Piper kicked him under the table and he yelped.

They all looked at one another and started to laugh. Jim wiped tears from his eyes with a napkin and said, "This is how family discussions should be, putting it all out there, a little combat and, eventually clearing the air."

Marianna tilted her head toward his. "Your children are trying to take over by distracting us. They probably want all your money."

"That's all right." He took her hand and kissed it. "I have you." He looked at the others. "And we have you. I'm grateful that you care enough to worry about me in my old age."

"And we've learned enough these past weeks that we have to pay attention to the future," Lynn spouted.

"I hope you're not getting ready with some growing old in the bosom of your family homily because I'm hungry," said Dusty.

"I agree," chimed in Piper. She turned to Jim. "And when we finish this discussion maybe you can talk to my parents, you know, oldie to oldie."

"It has to be easier than dealing with Bergy and Janet and Thel." He took a sip of wine. "The only practical one in that crowd is Tim."

Marianna kissed his cheek. "I think you helped them start on the road to some compromises and solutions. I guess Bri and Glenda are next." She winked at her husband.

Discussion at the dinner table exploded.

~ ~ ~

"Dusty," murmured Lynn as she snuggled close. "Janet talked about romance novels and the premise that all the heroines seem to find their one true love."

She moved closer. "I don't know how I feel, if I even believe in a one true love." She turned on her back to stare at the ceiling.

"Because?" he prompted. He felt her shrug and pulled her into his arms. "Is it because you love me and loved your husband and now you wonder if you deceived one of us?"

"How did you know?" She propped herself up on her elbow. "I don't mean deception or anything, but is there only one true love? I mean you both have my whole heart."

He pulled her into his arms again. "I sometimes wonder if I measure up."

"To what?"

"To who."

"You're not serious," she chided him. "I love you." He was silent. "I see," she continued, "I also loved Jack and if he had lived we would never have met and married."

"But we did." Dusty ran his lips over her forehead.

"So, does that mean there are more people that we can love than just one?"

He kissed her temple. "I think there are special people for certain times. I don't think I would have noticed you twenty years ago."□

"Why?"

"I was looking for a different kind of relationship, loose
– "

"Women?"

" – loose alliances, variety," he shrugged, "things that I'm not interested in now."

"Why?"

"Because I found you."

She sighed and wrapped herself around him.

Chapter Thirty-Four

The Sunday morning paper had screaming headlines: *Local Nonprofit Under Investigation*. Dusty slammed the paper down on the kitchen table. "It's all our work and he's taking the credit."

"Yes, dear." Lynn got out a skillet to make some bacon and eggs.

"Don't 'yes dear' me," he sputtered as he put water in the coffee pot. "You know we did the work. And most of the evidence we found at the PFM office solidified the AG's case."

"But it was just what the AG needed for Rothman to admit to usury and point the finger at his boys for the murder rap," Lynn reminded him. "So your murder is solved. What do you want – banner headlines proclaiming your success?"

He looked at his watch, looked at his wife then walked over to the stove and took her in his arms. "I think I want someone to congratulate me on another murder solved."

"Since I'm the only one here who knows that you solved a murder," she said, "what did you have in mind?"

"I was thinking we should take advantage of all this time we have alone." He nuzzled her neck.

"What's for breakfast?" asked Will as he pushed through the door. "I came to get the low down on this story." He waived the morning paper at them. Lynn turned back to the frying pan making certain her clothing was still in place as Dusty went back to making coffee.

"Don't you have a home?" the detective growled.

"I want the real story." Will got himself a dish and scooped eggs out of the pan and bacon off the warming tray. "Not this drivel you spew for the paper. Bah! A spokesman for the police department says ... right ... you never say anything that's worth printing." By this time Will had put his plate on the table and was standing beside Dusty waiting for the coffee.

Lynn divided the rest of the eggs between herself and Dusty. Carrying two plates to the table she said, "Dusty, bring my coffee before Will starts grilling you."

They finally settled for breakfast as Piper and her son, Jeff, barged into the kitchen.

"Don't start until I get my coffee," ordered Piper. She fussed around the kitchen, as Lynn jumped up to scramble some eggs for Jeff. When the women finally got back to the table, Lynn noticed a large dish of pastry. "Wow. Did you make that?"

"I stopped at the bakery. That's why Will got here first," replied Piper. As they all sat at the table ready to eat and listen, Jim and Marianna pushed through the kitchen door.

"I want the real story," declared Jim. "What did that stupid Nevada Utley have to do with this?"

Marianna placed her hand on Lynn's shoulder as the younger woman began to rise. "We'll take care of ourselves." She handed Jim two coffee cups as Jeff made room at the table while protecting his breakfast. He had seen how much these old people eat.

Piper looked around the kitchen. "I thought Tim would be here this morning." Eyes darted around the table and everyone looked at Jeff, always leery of talking about behavior not appropriate for teens.

The youngster, misunderstanding the looks, thought he was to speak, so he said, "He's at Janet's. I talked to him outside the bakery while Mom was inside."

Another dish of food appeared as Marianna announced, "Muffins from the bakery. Umberto said you had already picked up some Danish." Finally they were all at the table ready to eat and listen.

And Dusty didn't disappoint them!

~ ~ ~

Tim stopped at Lynn's on his way back to Norfolk. "I'll see you in two weeks," he told Lynn. "You take care of my girl. Thel's going to be staying at the house for awhile."

"Then what?' asked Lynn.

Tim shrugged. "One day at a time. We have to see how Bergy recovers. But I'd like Janet to come back here when I go to sea. She can have the baby here and Thel and Bergy could live at the house and help her."

Lynn grinned. "That's a great idea. Does everyone agree?" They were standing on the porch as the dog sniffed Tim's shoes.

"What's a great idea?" asked Dusty as he came out of the house and ruffled the dog's ears.

"Tim says Janet will come back to River Bend when he goes to sea and Thel and Bergy will stay at the house and help her."

Dusty shook Tim's hand. "Sounds like a plan. If you and Bergy agree, the women will fall in line."

Lynn gave her husband a squinty-eyed look.

"I'm sure he meant," Tim hastened to explain, "that

some women need more encouragement than others to find sensible solutions."

Lynn laughed and hugged her brother-in-law. "Drive safely and we'll see you at the wedding."

~ ~ ~

What a Sunday! The family had barged in on breakfast, Tim stopped by before he took off for Norfolk. And here it was almost Sunday evening and Lynn hadn't done anything productive. She heard the dog yip and then footsteps on the back porch.

"Glenda!" Lynn gasped in surprise. "Is something wrong?"

"I just had a fight with Bri and I don't want to go back to Piper's until I calm down." She plopped on a kitchen chair. "This getting old is for the birds."

Lynn gave her a quick hug. "Do you want to talk about it?"□

"I could use a glass of wine."

"It must be serious," teased Lynn. She got the wine, some glasses and some leftover breakfast pastry to snack on. "Okay, spill your guts. My lips are sealed."

Glenda gave her a half smile. "My kids were so doting. They make me feel about a hundred years old."

"They love you."

"Piper always thinks I should be resting and taking it easy. Will always wants to drive me someplace." Glenda slammed her hand on the table. "I can drive. I'm not as helpless as my children try to make me believe."

Lynn sipped her wine and waited for Glenda to finish her oration.

"My children love me, but if they don't fuss over me and

treat me as they do their children, they worry that I won't know they care." Glenda paused, "Maybe it's good that we're having this talk. I need to hear myself say these things instead of always being angry at Piper and Will's concern for me."

"Maybe the talks between adult children and aging parents need a third party, almost like a mediation. Someone who can keep the discussion on track. I thought Dad –"

"He tried, but Bri is still concerned about our privacy."

"So all of you can't talk to one another?"

Glenda smiled. "The discussions always deteriorate into the kids complaining that we don't trust them. And Bri getting angry because he feels helpless."

"Are your children really suggesting horrible solutions?" asked Lynn.

"No, they're just trying to make my decisions for me."

"Are you sure? Or are they trying to help you frame a decision that works for all of you?" Lynn sipped her wine and waited for Glenda to think about her answer.

"What do you mean?"

Lynn thought for a moment. "Look what happened. You and Bri want to be independent, so independent that you endangered yourselves. You wouldn't ask Will for money. You frightened Piper out of her mind. So much anxiety could have been prevented if you had all talked."

"We survived," pouted Glenda.

"Tell me this," asked Lynn, "Are you honest with your kids? When they ask how you are, do you tell them, not everything, but at least, that you take care of yourself, that you're following doctor's orders, eating right, taking your meds. Or are you evasive, you don't want them to know some health secret, you want your privacy? And then one day they get a call that you're dead and they never had a clue."

"They want us to move where we'll be safe."

"And you're angry that they care?" Lynn gave her a hard stare.

Glenda blushed. "When you ask me that way I can understand Piper's concern. But I don't feel old."

"You don't act old. But being safe isn't a concession to old age," Lynn argued. "I just think you have to consider how your independence could play out with your family. Think about how much control you could lose with an injury or illness and how much they would have to alter their lives to care for you, because you already know how much they love you."

"You're saying I should surrender to old age and death to keep Piper's life simple." Glenda didn't like the direction this conversation was taking.

"No, I'm suggesting that you and Bri should think about organizing your life while you're healthy so that you have control even in sickness or injury. Out of necessity your kids will do what they feel they must, but if you have organized you life along your terms, they'll probably follow your lead."

"So you think we should move into an apartment?"

"No, I think you should consider all your options, discuss things with your kids and then make a choice. Just don't act so tough that your kids are finally forced to act on your behalf because you and Bri never told them what you wanted. It's not surrendering, it's being realistic."

"How'd you get so smart?" Glenda asked.

Lynn shook her head sadly. "It took Bergy's health crisis and a dead man in your barn for me to understand."

"I came here to rant about my situation and you've given me a lot to think about in return." Glenda sipped her wine. "I think I should go home and talk to Piper and Will."

Chapter Thirty-Five

Lynn walked down to the coffee shop, escaping from the noise of the workmen in her office. As she neared the door, Vicki from the Council on Aging barged out almost knocking Lynn over.

"Lynn, I can't tell you how energizing your idea was," Vicki bubbled. "It fired up my board and has them ready to work. And when Danny spoke to them during the retreat, they were ready to elect him king."

"I think kings are born, but I get the idea." Lynn laughed.

"And he brought pastry from his uncle's bakery. Does he always do that?"

"He does always seem to have a little extra to offer. I look forward to hearing your board's plans." Lynn smiled at Vicki as she dashed toward her car with several coffees and a bag of rolls.

Walking into the busy coffee shop Lynn spied her sister-in-law, Salley, in a quiet corner whispering with Bertram Luft the director of James County Hunger Alliance and, as she watched, they were joined by Audrey Decker from Exceptional Children. Lynn made a beeline for the trio. "What's up?"

Bertram jumped, almost spilling his coffee. "That's a guilty response," said Lynn as she prepared for an interrogation.

"Calm down," said Salley, "put away your conspiracy

paranoia. We were just plotting how we should approach you."

"I can't tell you anything more about that case," Lynn confessed. "Most of it was in the paper on Sunday."

Audrey adjusted her beautiful blouse and stunning jewelry, sipped her coffee and said, "We think our clients need the kind of services we thought Joseph would offer."

"But they were crooks," argued Lynn.

"So we have a plan," announced Bertram and beat a riff on the table. "But ..."

"You need money," finished Lynn. They all hung their heads. Busted.

"It's a great plan," said Audrey.

"I'm listening," said Lynn.

"We've talked with those friends of Joseph's in Kentucky," explained Salley. "They're devastated by his murder and want to help us, you know, his friends. They have programs for single mothers who are leaving bad relationship..."

"... and programs to help young families manage their money from month to month," said Bertram. "At the food pantry we get a lot of families who need food near the end of the month because they don't budget well."

"Or don't earn enough to get to the end of the month," offered Audrey.

"That, too," admitted Bertram.

"My clients need the same kind of services plus ideas on how to plan for their aging developmentally delayed children. Parents are always concerned about not out living their children. Who will look after them? Will there be enough money?" Audrey looked at her audience. They all nodded.

"You need more than money." Lynn rained on their parade. "You need someone who knows all these things and can organize a functioning program."

"We have someone," exclaimed Bertram, his dazzling grin lighting up the room. "One of my volunteers is a retired banker from Charlotte. When he heard what we were trying to do, he said he had been looking for a challenge."

Salley added, "I've lined up some other volunteers to work with my clients. And Joseph's friends from Kentucky are willing to help as consultants to our efforts."

"So we just need your money," concluded Audrey.

Lynn hung her head. Busted.

~ ~ ~

After a busy day Lynn thought she needed a treat, so she walked into the bakery for a ... oh, she wasn't certain, anything sweet with calories would be good. Maybe a chocolate chip cannoli. While she thought, Umberto, the baker, slipped a cannoli on top of the display case. "Here you go. I'll put it on Dusty's tab."

"He has a tab?"

Umberto shrugged. "Sometimes he likes to bring folks in to chat."

"Chat?"

"You know he doesn't want to scare them just get some information." The baker shrugged again and turned his attention to the next customer. Lynn scooped up her cannoli and pulled a carton of milk from the cooler. She decided to sit at the high table and watch the street traffic. Her father walked by and she thumped on the window. Jim waved and changed direction, joining her in the bakery.

"A cannoli?" He kissed her on the cheek and waved to Umberto. A cannoli materialized in front of him.

"What are you doing out?" Lynn asked.

"I could ask you the same thing," replied Jim as he licked powdered sugar off his fingers.

"I'm treating myself."

"This whole town should be treating you." He smiled at his daughter as he threw an arm around her.

"What did I do?"

"That early elder safety response thing," he replied between bites. "Everyone's excited."

"Everyone?"□

"I was just at a meeting with the bank board and Jerry Clayton was telling everyone about the Council on Aging retreat and their plans."

"Jerry?"

"Evidently he's the incoming chairman of Vicki's board."

Lynn grinned. She liked Jerry. He did a lot of good community work. "Vicki's lucky to have him."

"He and all the Council on Aging board are happy with you and your ideas. Jerry says it's brought the board together and helped them define a mission and a great work plan to serve the elderly in James County." Jim sipped some of her milk.

"I just suggested the idea to her and Dusty gave Danny permission to work with them."

"You're just like your mother," he said, "you don't take credit for anything but you keep this place moving in the right direction."

"She did that?"

"The Little Theater, the genealogical and historic

society, the woman's shelter." Jim ticked items off his fingers. "She was behind a lot of things. I even think she had something to do with the beginnings of hospice care. She left that idea for her friends to finish after she died." They were both silent and Jim held Lynn's hand.

"I do keep running into folks who tell me stories about Mother. I just didn't know she was that involved." Lynn toyed with the crumbs of her cannoli.

"She did what you do, just threw out ideas, like gasoline on a flame, then stepped back to watch it happen." He finished his cannoli. "You do the same thing. Always for the good. Always without fanfare." He stood and kissed her cheek. "And I'm always proud of you."

"Thanks, Dad."

Umberto came to the table to wipe it down. "He's right. You and Helene, best thing ever to happen in this town." Umberto kissed her cheek and carried away the empty milk carton.

Lynn thanked Umberto and walked to her car, thinking about life and her mother. Helene would always be young and never face the challenges of old age. Lynn would be delighted to have a life where Helene was still alive, where they worked side by side as they aged – someone to talk with, to share with, not someone just to be remembered.

Chapter Thirty-Six

Sunday evening Will and Piper came into the kitchen shouting for Lynn. "I'm in the basement," she called. They heard her climbing the stairs and waited as she ran breathless into the kitchen. "What's wrong?" She was covered in dirt and cobwebs.

"We have something to tell you. Where's Dusty?" Then they heard Dusty clumping up the basement stairs. He was dirtier than Lynn.

"What's wrong?" Dusty asked as he went to the kitchen sink to wash his hands.

"We're going to be your neighbors," Will said slapping Dusty on the back. "We bought the Brewer place. I can just feel all the love in this neighborhood." The Brewer's home was across the street from Lynn's place.

"The Brewer's are moving?" asked Lynn. "I hardly see them any more."

"I guess they've been thinking about it for awhile. Since their son died, they felt they had no need for a big house. And it seems they've been having the same sort of discussions about aging as the rest of us and they realized that they had to make their own decisions and make them while they were still healthy." Will blew out his breath, as everyone thought about the summer the Brewers lost their only child.

"What will they do?" asked Lynn wiping her face and hands as Dusty passed out some beers.

Piper snapped her cap and took a gulp. "They're going to the same place Annie lives. They're getting one of the cottages and will live independently until they do need care."

Lynn was trying to follow how moving to the Brewer's house, across the street, solved Piper's problem with her parents. "Are your parents moving to The Heights with you?"

"No, they'll move into our old house. We thought about Will's old condo, but we're renting it right now to one of my teachers." Piper looked out the window for a moment, then with sad eyes continued, "When they can't live alone, they'll move in with us. The Brewer house has a lovely room with attached bathroom on the main floor, so no stairs. I think Simon uses it as an office."

"What about the farm?" asked Dusty, "I think my brothers would like to rent the land for some crops."

"That's a great idea," Piper replied. "I couldn't face selling the place right now. I promised Daddy he could have a garden out there next year." They sat sipping their beers, each one deep in thought.

Will finally broke the silence. "Get cleaned up," he ordered. "I'm buying dinner at Frank's. We're celebrating family – the closer the better." He slapped Dusty on the back again.

~ ~ ~

At Frank's Tavern the gang caught an interview on the big screen TV with the AG recapping weeks of investigations and court appearances. He bragged – again – about bringing down the nonprofit scam artists. Dusty was so aggravated with the AG that he complained all evening. And continued his displeasure as he and Lynn climbed the stairs to bed. "It's been two weeks and he's still taking credit. Can you believe his nerve? If I see one more interview, I'll puke."

"Yes, dear," Lynn tried not to laugh as he continued.

"He brags about this three state sting and then he throws in my, MY murder and claims credit for that, too."

"You solved Joseph's murder ..."

"Yes, I did. But does he give me credit?"

"Who? Joseph or the AG?" Lynn grinned at him. Dusty scowled and tossed his shirt on the bedroom floor.

"He expects me to vote for him when he runs for governor." Brush, rinse, spit, floss, rinse, spit. "I can tell you right now. He better not ask me to donate to any campaign." Soap. Wash. Rinse. "I've told my staff that they better not get involved in any campaigns for this guy." He slipped on a clean T-shirt.

Lynn have carried on with her own night rituals of washing off make-up and making certain all the random clothing got stuffed into a hamper. She gave Dusty a hug. "I think you should be glad the AG is taking all the credit. You know how you hate publicity. And you know that he will always tread lightly around you because he knows that he took credit that was yours. I think you aren't considering the political pluses if he becomes governor. You'll have a friend in the statehouse."

"Spoken like a politician's daughter." Dusty gave her a kiss. "Thank you for listening. I just had to vent." Lynn raised her eyebrows. "All right, so I vented to Will, Piper and everyone at Frank's. But I feel better."

She laughed. "Just think, with Will moving across the street, you'll always have another set of ears to listen to your problems."

"He has his own problems, he's married to Piper." Dusty scowled, "That's enough of a problem for anyone."

Climbing into bed, she said, "When Will moves across the street, you and he can do all those family things like help each other rake leaves and paint and mow."

"I have family." Dusty turned in bed and took her into his arms. "Before you remind me that we're the only family Will has, I'll say it sounds like a great idea."

"Really?" Lynn settled into his arms and traced his earlobe with her nose.

"He's grown on me."

"What about Piper?"

"She's still scary." Dusty kissed Lynn's neck. "You should hear some of the younger patrolmen talk about her when they were at her elementary school. She's a legend, and scary."

"I'll protect you," whispered Lynn then she moved her lips from his ear to his mouth.

Epilogue

On a glorious Saturday morning the recreation room at the nursing home had been decorated with white flowers on pedestals outlining the space for the ceremony. Folding chairs were aligned along the floor to create an aisle. As guests arrived, Bertram Luft played softly at his keyboard. The chubby cheeked minister stood between the flower pedestals and waited with Tim as Bergy and Janet came down the aisle. Bergy was guided down the aisle in his wheelchair by his nurse, Mutt.

As Tim stepped forward to receive his bride, Janet bowed to kiss her father.

Lynn and Mars served as the witnesses to the marriage. The investment club members had the event organized. As soon as the chaplain pronounced them man and wife, Bertram sent his keyboard into exalted celebration. Tim and Janet dashed down the short aisle to cheers and applause. Within seconds the room was transformed into a delightful reception with food and punch appearing as if by magic.

Bergy, wheeled around the room by Mutt, thanked everyone for being present. Thel, too excited, opted to sit and let the guests find her.

Lynn enjoyed the lovely ceremony. She had never seen Tim so happy, and Janet, who often looked so vague, had a genuine smile. But Bergy topped the charts in enthusiasm. No one was happier at this marriage. His daughter married someone who scored a ten in every one of his criteria. In his wheelchair he spun around the room like an intoxicated dervish

Marianna found her stepdaughter in a corner and asked, "Wedding memories?"

Lynn smiled and gave her a quick kiss on the cheek. "You still rank as one of the most beautiful brides." It had only been five months since Marianna's marriage to Jim.

Marianna scanned the celebrants. "I don't think any family member at my wedding was as happy as Bergy or Thel."

"I agree," said Lynn. "It's a great outcome after some really challenging family care issues."

"Now you're getting philosophical," teased her stepmother.

"I'm just looking back over the last month. I've dealt personally and professionally with aging issues and I've learned some sad lessons. Elder suicide rates, scams perpetrated on the elderly, long term care cost and availability," Lynn blew out her breath, "It got very personal with Glenda and Bergy. But we all survived."

Marianna had tears in her eyes. "Getting old is scary, but we'll all manage. Now let's go celebrate with Tim and Janet."

Both women looked out into the gathering and laughed as they watched the photographer try to corral the happy family – Bergy in his wheelchair, Thel who had to give Tim one more hug, and Janet who looked overwhelmed. That's when Tim caught Lynn's eye and gave her a devilish wink. This was a great day!

Thank you for reading.
Please review this book. Reviews help others find
Absolutely Amazing eBooks and inspire us to keep
providing these marvelous tales.

If you would like to be put on our email list to receive
updates on new releases, contests, and promotions, please
go to AbsolutelyAmazingEbooks.com and sign up.

About the Author

Renee Kumor has lived in North Carolina for almost forty years. The setting for the River Bend Chronicles series reflects her early life in Ohio and her later years in western North Carolina. She was a stay-at-home mom for several years developing a personal ethic of community service. Through the years as her children aged, she became active in the political and non-profit life of the community. She began writing a political opinion column for the local newspaper, but retired from writing when she announced her candidacy for local political office. After eight years as a county commissioner, she returned to non-profit service and began writing a monthly column for the newspaper on non-profit board service and management issues. Renee has been married to her husband for forty-eight years. They have four children and four grandchildren.

Next in the Series

Look for the next installment in Renee Kumor's mesmerizing River Bend Chronicles – *Deadly Politics* – available soon at www.AbsolutelyAmazingEbooks.com and your favorite online booksellers.

October finishes up with a great Halloween but by Thanksgiving life in River Bend has turned as bitter as the weather. A detective has been shot, three children are found abandoned and one local politician is killed in a deadly car bombing. The usual family holiday cheer is dampened as Dusty works to protect three small children from child traffickers while hunting a bomber. Detective Teniquia La Mont struggles with the aftermath of a bullet wound that has taken away her ability to have children. Lynn witnesses the death of a local county commissioner in a car bombing and has difficulty with flashbacks and nightmares. Through it all Lynn and her friends try to rebuild a family and a home for Polly Carmichael, a teenager made an orphan when her mother is murdered in the car bombing.

ABSOLUTELY AMAZING eBOOKS

AbsolutelyAmazingEbooks.com

or AA-eBooks.com